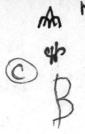

LAST STAGE TO LONESOME

Carter Malone is returning to Lonesome when a thunderstorm forces the stage to stop in Ferry Town. Then, when Bart Merrill rides into town, a gunfight erupts leaving seven men dead, including Marshal McKinney, who, before dying, entrusts Carter to continue the journey and deliver his mysterious prisoner to Lonesome. But there are gunslingers along the trail ready to free the prisoner and an old adversary from his troubled past turns up — can he ever hope to reach Lonesome?

SCOTT CONNOR

◆

LAST STAGE
TO LONESOME

Complete and Unabridged

LINFORD
Leicester

First published in Great Britain in 2008 by
Robert Hale Limited
London

First Linford Edition
published 2009
by arrangement with
Robert Hale Limited
London

The moral right of the author has been asserted

British Library CIP Data

Connor, Scott.
  Last stage to Lonesome - -
  (Linford western library)
  1. Western stories.
  2. Large type books.
  I. Title II. Series
  823.9'2–dc22

  ISBN 978–1–84782–658–9

Published by
F. A. Thorpe (Publishing)
Anstey, Leicestershire

Set by Words & Graphics Ltd.
Anstey, Leicestershire
Printed and bound in Great Britain by
T. J. International Ltd., Padstow, Cornwall

This book is printed on acid-free paper

PROLOGUE

The players were getting ready for the showdown when Sheriff David Blake entered the back room of the Maverick saloon.

Usher Pullman was sitting opposite the door and he raised a finger, delivering a silent order to the two men who were guarding him. Usually Spike Talbot and Bart Merrill were close by, but tonight they were out of town. Their replacements were just as flint-eyed and dour.

The guards pushed themselves away from the wall. One cracked his knuckles while the other fixed Blake with his stern gaze.

Blake didn't recognize the other two men, but they had their backs to him and were more intent on the game than on his arrival. He paced across the room to stand at the table.

1

'You came,' Usher said, smiling like a predatory cat.

'Your message intrigued me,' Blake said.

Usher glanced back at his guards, conveying a silent message that made them relax. Then he placed his cards on the table face down and leaned back with his hands entangled behind his head.

'This one did, but the others didn't,' he mused. 'But then again, every man has his price.'

Blake considered the game. They were playing five-card draw. Around $500 was in the pot. One man had thrown his cards in. The other man had only a few dollars left in his pile, clearly having decided to risk everything on this hand. This was a foolish strategy bearing in mind the huge pile of dollars sitting before Usher and the presence of his guards behind him.

Blake reached for the pack of undealt cards and placed it before Usher.

'Cut,' he said. 'Then deal me five cards.'

Usher did as asked, his eyebrows rising with a question that Blake didn't feel inclined to answer just yet.

'Hey!' the other player whined. 'You can't deal him in now.'

'Silence!' Usher snapped.

'But I'm playing this — '

The man didn't get to finish his complaint when one of the guards paced up to the table, grabbed his collar and yanked him up. He marched him to the door and threw him outside. Blake could still hear him complaining when the door closed, but a brief scuffle sounded followed by a pained shriek. Then the guard returned.

The other player decided that now might be a good time to have an appointment elsewhere. Nobody paid his hurried departure any attention.

Usher pushed the dealt cards to Blake. In response Blake slipped a hand into his jacket and withdrew a sealed envelope, which he threw on to the pot. Then he gestured for Usher to reveal his hand first. Usher presented two jacks then sat back.

Blake lifted up the edges of his cards to see that he'd received two kings. He considered Usher.

'You win,' he said, then withdrew his hand, leaving the cards still face down.

Usher narrowed his eyes, suggesting he knew Blake had lied.

'I understand. Perhaps we should play again and see if a larger pot is more to your liking.'

'Only after you've taken your winnings from this hand.' Blake pushed the envelope towards him.

Usher reached for the envelope. He slit it open, drew out the folded sheets of paper within and began reading. His right eye twitched. The papers fell from his hand. Then he raised that hand.

Blake didn't know the meaning behind all of Usher's gestures to his

4

guards, but this one was clear enough. So without warning he drew his gun and blasted lead through one guard's chest before he could draw, throwing him back into the wall, then swung round to the second one. This man had enough time to drag his gun from its holster, but not enough to fire. A low shot to the guts bent him double. The gun fell from his slack fingers as Blake planted a second bullet in him.

Then he was on Usher. He hoisted him up from his chair and thrust his gun up under his chin, buckling the skin.

'Go on. Kill me,' Usher grunted. 'Spike and Bart will be back soon and they'll make you pay for every bullet you put in me.'

'They'll fail, but you're right that soon someone will risk coming through that door. They could find your dead body and hear my explanation of how you gave me no choice but to kill you, but I don't work like that. After everything you've done to Lonesome, I've decided to do this the proper way.'

Blake pushed Usher away, tumbling him on to his back, then reached down for the papers and threw them on his chest.

Usher glared up at him, still arrogant and unconcerned despite his predicament and his undignified posture.

'You've made a big mistake, Sheriff, serving an arrest warrant on me in my town. You should have taken the bribes like everyone else has. There was a thousand on the table and that could have been just a first instalment for the right lawman.'

'But I am the right lawman.' Blake dragged Usher to his feet and walked him to the door. 'You may think you've sewn up Lonesome, but I will make those charges stick and I will see you get the justice you deserve.'

'You'll never find anyone to stand up in court and speak up against me.'

'There's me for one.'

Usher laughed. 'Like I said, nobody

will stand up in court and speak up against me.'

Blake heard the implied threat, but didn't retort as he led Usher out into the saloon to begin the new era of justice in Lonesome.

1

Carter Malone reckoned the hanging man couldn't have been dead for long. Blood glistened on his lips and the flies had yet to find a home. The body swayed back and forth in the driving rain, its weight dragging an ominous creak from the bough of the dead oak. The contorted face stared unseeingly at the passengers in the stage, frozen for ever in the last hideous throes of a painful death.

'Move on, driver,' Carter shouted, leaning out of the window to brave the rain. 'None of us needs to see this.'

'Sure don't,' Major Pilgrim Kelley and Marshal McKinney intoned together, while the marshal's prisoner looked past the lawman to consider the body with shock widening his eyes. The prisoner had rarely reacted to anything, but Carter presumed this sight had reminded him of the fate that probably awaited him.

The stage's other traveller, Annie White, kept her head buried in her hands as she had done since the driver had stopped their journey beside the corpse, presumably out of curiosity.

'Ain't here to admire him,' the driver, Vance Rogers, shouted from the seat ahead. 'We can't go on. A landslide's blocked our way.'

Carter peered into the teeming rain but the gloom that had accompanied the prolonged thunderstorm was so oppressive he couldn't see what had troubled Vance.

'It might have done, but that don't change the fact you need to move on and get it out of sight. We've got a distressed lady back here.'

This plea had the desired effect when Vance urged the horses to move off the trail. As the stage trundled round in a wide circle taking the swaying man out of view, Carter leaned over to ensure Annie was fine now that they were moving again. She provided a faint smile that suggested that even if she wasn't happy she was at least composed enough to put a brave face on her discomfort.

'Wonder what that man did to get himself strung up beside the trail?' Kelley asked, looking out of the other window to consider the hanging man now that he'd come back into view, although thankfully he was thirty yards away this time.

'Good question, Major,' McKinney said. 'Must have been a crime that affected the folk around here real bad. Displaying him there for everyone to see looks like a warning to me.'

'Who to?'

As Vance drew the stage to a halt a hundred yards past the body, McKinney glanced at Annie.

'Let's hope we don't find out,' McKinney said in a low voice.

Presently, Vance's drenched face peered at the passengers through the window.

'As we can't go forward,' he reported,

'I'll have to use an alternative route. I know several but they're all long and treacherous, and they won't get us to Lonesome until late tonight. I'd hate to risk using them in this weather unless anyone's got a real urgent reason to get to town tonight.'

The five occupants of the stage had been travelling from Leavenworth bound for Lonesome for four days. Today was their last scheduled day of travel and they had been on time until they'd encountered this landslide.

Everyone had caught the emphasis in Vance's tone as to what they should decide and so, with much shaking of heads, Annie and Major Kelley murmured that their business wasn't urgent enough to risk taking this other route. In an unconscious gesture Carter reached into his pocket to finger the silver watch, then shook his head.

'My business can wait too,' he said.

All eyes turned to McKinney. He had been quiet for most of the journey, aside from telling them not to speak to or worry about his prisoner — he hadn't deemed it necessary to reveal his name — so nobody had enquired further as to his business. But if anyone had a desperate need to get to town tonight, it'd probably be him.

'No,' he said, shaking his head, 'like Carter, my business can wait.' He darted a significant glance at his prisoner, who grunted a surly and unintelligible response.

'Then what will we do instead?' Annie asked.

'We'll have to stop somewhere for the night.' Vance said, peering up at the thunderous clouds, 'or until this weather clears. Ferry Town is a few miles back.'

'And is that place suitable?'

Vance didn't reply other than to lick his lips as if he were debating whether to speak his mind, then thought better of it and leaned to the side to spit on the ground.

'I guess,' he said, drawing his hat down into the wind to cover his eyes as he headed back to the seat, 'out here we ain't got a choice.'

When the stage set off, everyone exchanged predictable grumbles about their bad luck in suffering this unforeseen delay, along with some debate about what the town they would have to stay in would be like, before quietness returned.

Fifteen minutes later they trundled into Ferry Town. It was as unpromising as they'd feared, consisting of a handful of rudely constructed buildings set about a short main drag. That drag ended at the river, a ferry-and-winch system for travellers to cross the water showing why this rough town had sprung up here. In the terrible weather nobody would be foolish enough to use the ferry and so it was unmanned. Nobody was out of doors and only one building had a light on, the batwings suggesting it was a saloon.

The stage came to a halt before this building and Vance shouted down for the passengers to get inside quickly. Carter was the first to alight. He jumped down into a sea of mud that encased him up to the knees. With the oozing filth filling his boots and rooting him to the spot, he looked back into the stage and curled his lip with a disgusted expression to tell the others they should be more careful.

Annie and Kelley used more care when they traipsed out into the rain. While they picked a route between the rare islands of drier earth to reach the saloon, Carter took his time, not wanting the mud to drag off his boots. So by the time he'd reached drier ground, McKinney was escorting his prisoner out of the stage.

Marshal McKinney was a careful lawman who used the same procedure, whenever they stopped, that gave his prisoner no chance to run or overcome him. Carter had taken it upon himself to keep an unobtrusive eye on this man in case he ever managed to overpower the lawman, but he need not have worried. The prisoner was as eager as everyone else to get out of the rain quickly and so he and the lawman beat Carter into the saloon.

Inside Carter flopped down on to the nearest chair and started to clean his boots. He noted that aside from the stage passengers, there were no other customers, so the saloon owner was bristling with good cheer at the unexpected bonus of the stage riding into town.

'What can I get for you gentlemen, and lady?' he asked after introducing himself as Walter Pike.

'Rooms for the night,' Kelley said as outside Vance moved the stage, presumably to a stable.

Walter's eyes widened with surprise, suggesting nobody had ever asked to stop here before. Then he got his wits about him and hurried to the door behind the bar.

'Louis,' he shouted into a side room, rubbing his hands with barely suppressed glee, 'get your butt out here. We got customers.'

Presently a morose individual shuffled

in with his eyes downcast and showing none of the eagerness Walter had displayed. Walter explained the situation to him, but this did nothing to cheer him.

'We ain't got no rooms,' he said.

'I know that, but the stage is stopping here tonight.' Walter jerked his head up to confirm that this was the case, receiving several unenthusiastic nods. 'We can put them all up in here.'

'All?' Annie asked before Louis could respond.

'Yeah,' Walter said with a leering lick of his lips, before his previous cheerful manner returned. 'But don't you go worrying your pretty little head. Louis will take care of you, won't you, Louis?'

Louis merely shrugged, but a shove towards the door set him in motion.

'That man needs discipline,' Kelley said. 'If he'd been in my squadron I'd have kept him on report until he got himself a backbone.'

'Obliged for the idea.' Walter sighed. 'But to be honest I'd have kicked him out of town already if it were easy to hire decent help these days.'

'That mean you've had trouble here recently?' Marshal McKinney asked.

Carter couldn't help but notice that Walter glanced at McKinney's star before replying.

'Nothing we couldn't handle,' Walter said cautiously.

McKinney considered him for long moments before he provided the obvious retort.

'We saw the hanging man.'

Walter bit his lip, gulping. His lips moved as he appeared silently to rehearse an answer, but before he could utter it Louis returned laden down with blankets.

'Get those blankets set up for our good customers,' he ordered, gesturing to the back of the saloon, clearly taking the distraction to avoid giving an answer. He issued Louis with numerous unnecessary instructions for how he should lay them out and when Louis didn't respond immediately he gave him a kick to the butt that sent him sprawling to his knees.

Louis glared up at Walter with anger burning in his eyes before he got himself under control. Then he did as ordered and busied himself with setting out the blankets for everyone at the back of the saloon. In accordance with Annie's request he placed one blanket on its own in the corner, then began stretching out a rope between two hooks to create a modesty screen for her.

'So,' McKinney said when he managed to catch Walter's eye again, 'as you were saying. Who was that hanging man?'

Louis uttered a strangulated screech and dropped the rope. Walter shot him a glance, then drew back a foot with an implied threat of kicking him again if he didn't hurry up with his task. Louis quickly set about replacing the rope, but when he again fumbled it, Carter stopped cleaning his boots and headed over to help him string it up.

'He was nobody,' Walter said.

'What did he do?' McKinney persisted.

'He pushed his luck just once too often.' Walter chuckled. 'He won't do it again.'

McKinney nodded. 'Be interested in hearing that story later. We ain't exactly got much of anything else to do tonight other than listen to the major's tales of his exploits in the Plains Cavalry.'

As Kelley harrumphed at this mild criticism of the endless tedious stories he'd regaled them with over the last few days, Walter's face reddened.

'Unless you didn't get the hint,' he said, 'I ain't interested in talking about him. He's dead, strung up, and rotting. That's all I care about.'

Walter turned his back on him and headed to the door, where he looked out at the rain. Louis cast a narrowed-eyed glare at his back as he and Carter folded a blanket over the rope.

'I wasn't interested as a lawman,' McKinney said. 'I was worried for our safety.'

Walter muttered something to himself then turned from the door, his anger gone from his eyes and his jovial saloon-owner persona reappearing.

'Then don't worry. You're all be safe with me tonight in Ferry Town. Now, with the arrangements sorted out for the night, would anyone care for a drink?'

When he received several positive responses, he returned to the bar rubbing his hands. While he busied himself with finding glasses and mugs, in the corner of the saloon Louis smiled at Carter now that they'd finished hanging the blanket.

'Obliged for your help,' he said. He moved to return to the bar to help Walter, but Carter had seen the significant glances Walter had given to Louis and he'd noticed Louis's distress.

'Who was the dead man?' he asked in a low voice.

Despite speaking so softly that nobody but Louis would have heard the question, Louis gulped, his gaze darting

21

from Carter to Walter then back again with unconcealed concern.

'You're a stranger here,' he whispered, 'so know this: it doesn't pay to ask questions like that.'

'The truth doesn't worry me. Who was he?'

Louis looked at Walter, his jaw set firm, implying he was suppressing a strong emotion and making Carter think he wouldn't reply. But when Walter ducked down below the bar he jerked forward and whispered in Carter's ear.

'The hanging man was my brother,' he said. 'And if anyone finds out I've told you that, we'll be the next ones they hang.'

* * *

'What in tarnation is that?' Buckley Sharpe asked.

Max Parker broke off from fishing. He put a hand to his brow to shield his eyes from the rain that pattered on their heads through the inadequate cover of a cluster of oaks. For long moments he looked at the moiling river.

'It looks like a raft,' Max said.

Buckley narrowed his eyes, watching the object drift downriver towards them. It was around 200 yards away and did appear to be a raft, albeit a small one. Then the object hit an eddy and swirled round, letting Buckley see it properly and confirm it was a large crate strapped to several boards. The crate was listing badly with one side of the boards sticking up in the air and so submerging half of the crate. This probably meant the contents were heavy and brought up an intriguing possibility that Buckley was the first to voice.

'There's got to be something in that crate,' he said, 'and it could be valuable.'

Anticipation gleamed in Max's eyes. The heavy rain had swelled the river and the approaching crate could easily have broken loose, perhaps from Ferry Town ten miles upriver where freight often travelled across the river on the ferry.

'Only one way to find out,' Max said. 'Let's snag it.'

Buckley uttered a hoot of support before he joined Max in organizing what would be a tricky and possibly dangerous manoeuvre.

Buckley hurried into the trees and returned with a fifteen-foot length of deadfall. Quickly he snapped off the extraneous twigs to leave the end branches shaped as a two-pronged fork.

While Max removed a rope from his pack and set about making a lasso, Buckley risked wading out into the water. He tentatively edged forward. At each pace he felt the riverbed beneath a questing foot before he trusted putting his whole weight down to ensure he could keep his footing and avoid getting into trouble in the swollen river.

Luckily the bed fell away with a shallow gradient, but even so he stopped wading in when the water reached his hips. Max fed the branch out to him and then he waited, the water swirling around and against him, making him have to fight to keep himself upright.

The crate closed on them, but Buckley's estimate of its trajectory was that it'd pass around ten yards out from him and so several yards further than the reach of his branch. As he didn't dare go any deeper his hopes rested on Max, who had now positioned himself upriver on a rock. When the crate was almost at its closest point to him, he hurled his lasso, but it closed on air ten feet short of the crate, then flopped down into the water.

'Get closer,' Buckley urged, slapping the water in frustration.

So Max yanked the rope back, then jumped down off his rock and into the river. He waited until the crate was level with him, then hurled the lasso. This time he threw it too hard and the noose splayed out beyond the crate, but the rope did flop down on top of it.

Buckley shouted words of encouragement, but he knew that snagging the crate would need speed, agility, and luck. Hand over hand, Max hauled in, scraping the rope over the crate as it headed away from him and towards Buckley. When the noose tipped out of the water to lie on the crate, Max yanked the rope. The noose closed up on the end of a raised plank.

With Buckley whistling in delight, Max drew the rope in. The crate swung round towards land, but the noose was also straining at the very end of the plank. Slowly the crate drifted towards the riverside for another yard, then another, but then the rope tore loose and swirled up into the air.

Max cried out in frustrated anguish, but Buckley didn't join him. He saw that Max's brief tugging on the crate had made its course veer three yards nearer to him. He risked another pace out into the river, feeling the cold water surge above his waist, shoved the branch out to the limit of his reach, and thrust it before the crate.

The crate glided into the pronged end of the branch with as much serenity as it could do in the raging river. It held. The power of the rushing water thrust against Buckley's arms and he had to take steady paces downriver to avoid the force tipping him over.

'Drag it in,' Max shouted behind him.

'Stop telling me what to do,' Buckley shouted back, 'and get in here and help me.'

He took another step backwards and this let the crate slip a foot along the branch, angling it in closer to him. Encouraged he backed away again and this helped the crate break off one of the prongs then embark on a diagonal route towards dry land.

'You're doing it,' Max shouted. 'Just a few more feet.'

'I know.' Buckley took another step backwards. 'I've just got to — '

He didn't get to complete his comment. His foot slipped. The next he knew he was tumbling backwards without control of his body and splashing into the water. He waved his arms, all thoughts of his rescue mission forgotten as he fought to reach the surface. He emerged coughing and blowing in an explosion of water to find he was facing away from the riverside and that there was no sign of his branch or the crate. He started to turn, but his foot again slipped and this time drove him underwater head first.

He dragged himself back to a standing position, drenched and cold and no longer caring about the crate. He just wanted to get to dry land. He waded to the shallower water and, as the water cleared from his ears with a pop, he heard laughter. He turned to see Max chortling at his predicament.

'Quit laughing,' Buckley grumbled. 'We lost the crate.'

'We didn't,' Max said, pointing.

Buckley let out a sigh of relief as he stomped on to dry land. While he'd been floundering, Max had rescued the crate and it now sat on the side of the river.

'Let's hope it was worth it,' he said.

Max nodded then wedged a knife into the top of the crate. With some ease he levered off the topmost planks to reveal the crate's contents. Both men stood in awed silence for several seconds, their eyes wide and agog.

'Well,' Max murmured, 'I guess that means it sure was worth it.'

'Yeah, but who owns all this stuff? Where did it . . . ?'

Max slapped Buckley on the back, silencing him.

'I reckon a better question is — what are we going to spend it on?'

They weren't able to agree on that, but they did agree to dance a jig around the crate and before long, their merry capering drove all thoughts of how wet and cold they were from their minds.

2

Carter Malone sat at a table on his own nursing his coffee.

As he had done whenever they'd settled up for the night, he withdrew the silver watch from his pocket and rested it on his lap. He fingered the inscription, pondering on whether this unexpected delay had given him more time to prepare for an uncomfortable meeting he'd postponed for several years, or more time to let his doubts assail him again.

As always happened when he looked at the watch, the image of another man holding this watch in another time and place came to him . . .

'You can do it,' the man had said, holding the watch up.

'Not with that,' Carter had said, his hand straying uncomfortably close to his holster. 'This is too much.'

'Do it!'

'Sure,' Carter muttered before a bolt of anger tensed his jaw. His hand whirled to his gun. A moment later the man lay wounded, holed through the guts.

'She'll hate you for that for ever,' the man said, clutching his stomach, thick blood oozing through his clawed fingers.

That comment had been enough for Carter to plant another bullet in him.

Then he went to him, prised the watch from his dead fingers, and wiped the flecks of blood from the silver watch. Then he thrust it in his pocket and spent the next five years in hell.

'Just another day,' he murmured to himself, shaking away the memory, 'and all this will finally end.'

He slipped the watch back in his pocket before anyone noticed him looking at it and returned to looking around the saloon.

When everyone had a drink before them, including the returned Vance,

Walter let Louis sidle back into the side room behind the bar. Then he headed to the door to look out over the batwings at the rain. His frequent lifting of his heels to peer outside suggested he was waiting for someone.

Presently Walter turned his collar up, then slipped out through the door and paced down the road towards the river. Carter took the opportunity to go to the bar. His insistent tapping on the wood encouraged Louis to slouch back into the saloon room. He considered Carter's full mug.

'You want something else?' he asked.

'Only some answers.'

Louis shook his head. 'You don't need to hear them. Just spend the night here then move on to Lonesome tomorrow.'

'I choose whether or not I ask questions.' Carter offered a smile. 'But I guess if you won't answer them I can't help you.'

The offer of help made Louis's eyes brighten and he leaned over the bar to look out of the window, confirming that Walter was walking towards the river.

'It's good to hear someone is interested in my problems, but it really is too late to do anything.'

'About what, exactly?' Carter waited for an answer. When Louis didn't reply he leaned on the bar to join him in a conspiratorial huddle. 'Just tell me why your brother got hung, and do it quickly. Walter won't stay out in the rain for long.'

Louis murmured to himself before he replied, suggesting he was still reluctant to talk. But when he did speak, he ran through his story in a hurried manner as if a dam had broken.

'This morning Bart Merrill and Spike Talbot rode into town. They had a package they wanted taking across the river. I looked after their horses while my brother Phillip went across with them. The ferry was almost at the other side when this argument started. I couldn't hear what it was about but it ended when Phillip threw their package into the water. By the time Spike and Bart got back here they weren't in no mood for talking. They took him out to High Point and strung him up.'

Carter gave Louis's back a consoling pat.

'What did you do?'

'Ain't proud of myself,' Louis murmured with downcast eyes. 'But I couldn't see that there was anything I could do.'

'And who are Bart and Spike?'

'Two mean critters who work for Usher Pullman.' Louis raised his eyebrows as if that revelation answered all the questions Carter could ask.

'I ain't been around these parts in . . . in a while.'

Louis blew out his cheeks as he pondered what to say next.

'For the last four years Usher has had Lonesome under his thumb. Anybody who stood up to him ended up dead — until Sheriff David Blake came along. He got together a case and arrested him. His trial's in two days and so Bart and Spike are trying to destroy that case, paying friendly visits to the witnesses who'd got up the courage to talk, if you know what I mean.'

Carter nodded. 'So you're hoping that trial convicts Usher and that then Sheriff Blake will move on to Spike and Bart and get your brother some justice?'

'That sums up the extent of my hopes.' Louis stood back from the bar. 'Now, thank you for asking but take my advice. Stay out this business when it ain't got nothing to do with you.'

Having got his story off his chest, Louis relaxed somewhat and even whistled to himself as he headed into the side room.

Presently Walter returned to the saloon and set himself before the stove to warm and dry, so Carter left the bar to sit with McKinney.

'You hear any of that?' he asked.

'Nope,' Marshal McKinney said, 'but the look in Louis's eyes told me his hard-luck story. That hanging man was innocent. He got hung anyhow. Louis ain't happy.'

'I guess that covers it, but I'd have thought a lawman might have something more to say.'

'Nope.' McKinney nodded towards his prisoner. 'I've got a duty to discharge, and Louis's woes have nothing to do with me.'

'You can't leave everything to Sheriff Blake. He's mighty busy.'

McKinney narrowed his eyes. 'What did Louis tell you about him?'

'He only mentioned this week's trial of Usher Pullman and about how these varmints Bart Merrill and Spike Talbot are intimidating anyone who's prepared to testify against him.'

This comment made McKinney sit up straight. Even his prisoner flinched with surprise then looked at McKinney to gauge his reaction.

'I guess that was likely to happen,' McKinney murmured, his low tone suggesting he was talking aloud to himself. 'What else did he say?'

'Not much, but if you want to hear more, I can distract Walter. He keeps going to the door and — '

'He does, doesn't he?' McKinney said, with sudden urgency in his tone. 'It's almost as if he's waiting for someone.'

'And why is that so bad for you?'

McKinney opened his mouth to reply, but Carter didn't get to receive an answer before the distant sounds of hoofbeats silenced the lawman. Over by the stove Walter heard them a moment later and hurried to the door.

McKinney raised himself to look through the window, confirming that a line of riders was coming into town, then sat back down. He shot a significant glance at his prisoner, then drew his hat down low and leaned back in his chair. Carter matched his posture. Annie, Major Kelley, and the driver Vance were sitting at another table, but they only looked at the approaching men with mild interest.

Five riders dismounted at the hitching rail, then surged in, barging past the jovial Walter to get out of the rain. They stood in a group stomping their feet and batting their slickers, creating a spreading puddle.

Then two men headed to the bar and demanded whiskey while two others went to the stove and rattled the coffee-pots. The remaining man stood in the centre of the saloon and cast an appraising look at the unexpected customers. His gaze rested on Vance for several seconds then roved over everyone else including the lawman with barely a flicker, but his eyes did squint when he saw the prisoner. He turned to Walter.

'Any news?' he asked.

'Nope,' Walter said. He looked at Louis who had now supplied whiskeys and was refilling the empty coffee-pots with boiling water. 'Ain't that so?'

Although Louis glanced up, acknowledging that Walter had asked him a question, he didn't reply.

'That's bad news,' the newcomer said. 'We found nothing. Spike's gone to Brown's Crossing to work his way back upriver and make sure he don't miss it. We searched nearer but had no luck. Perhaps the damn thing sank.' He cast an irritated glare at Louis's back.

His comment let Carter make the reasonable assumption that this man was the notorious Bart Merrill. Spike Talbot was the other man and he was further downriver searching for the package that had fallen off the ferry during the unfortunate incident that had led to Louis's brother being hanged.

'You heading back to Lonesome, then?' Walter asked.

'Nope. We've still got some light today and I've got a theory that that crate didn't go as far as Spike reckoned it did. We'll warm our bones then Louis will get that ferry out and we'll search the other side of the river.'

At this mention of his name Louis broke off from his studious watching of the coffee-pots, now rattling away on the stove, to look at Bart.

'He'll welcome that,' Walter said, with mocking laughter in his tone.

'Yeah. I reckon he's eager to make amends for Phillip's stupidity. Ain't that so, Louis?'

While Walter glanced at the stage passengers, presumably to gauge their reactions after Bart had started to talk openly about the hanging man, Louis gritted his teeth, then turned his back on the men.

'I asked you a question,' Bart persisted.

Still Louis didn't reply, only his hunched shoulders conveying his emotions. Whether he would continue to bite his lip or retort, Carter couldn't tell. With nobody paying him any attention, Carter stood and moved himself closer to the group.

'I don't reckon he wants to talk to you,' Walter said.

'Yeah,' one of the men at the bar said. 'He's almost as quiet as Phillip is now.'

This taunt made Louis swirl round with his eyes blazing.

40

'What did you say?' he demanded.

'He said your brother sure is quiet these days,' Bart said. He bent his head to the side and lifted himself on to his toes in a mocking mime of a hanging man. 'That trouble you some?'

Louis advanced on Bart, his face bright red and his former reluctance to be confrontational gone. The other men detected his change in mood and the laughter died abruptly as everyone watched him pace towards Bart. Carter cut through the silence.

'I don't reckon you should taunt Louis no more,' he said, keeping his tone light and pleasant.

Bart swirled round, his flaring eyes registering his surprise that someone had intervened.

'What's it to you?' he demanded.

Carter took several seconds to respond, ensuring he irritated Bart some more, before he put on his most pleasant smile.

'Because I want a coffee and you're stopping Louis from serving me.'

For several long seconds Bart considered Carter, then snorted a humourless laugh and beckoned to Louis.

'You heard him,' he said. 'The man wants coffee. Give him coffee.'

Louis stomped to a halt and rocked on his heels, his grinding jaw conveying the debate that was raging in his mind as to whether to face up to Bart or take Carter's offer to cool the situation down. He sighed. Then his shoulders slumped and he plodded back to the stove. He returned with a mug, which he gave to Carter, then started to fill it with coffee, but the short break had let his confidence wilt away and his hand shook. Coffee spouted over the floor.

'Sorry,' he murmured, flinching his hand back.

'Let me help,' Bart said, feigning a jovial manner. He joined Louis and clamped a hand on his wrist then guided the pot in to pour Carter's coffee.

Around him, the other men looked

on with lively interest, clearly anticipating that Bart would drag some fun out of Louis's discomfort. Sure enough when Louis had filled Carter's mug to the brim Louis moved to stop pouring, but Bart tightened his grip and kept his hand tilted, ensuring the coffee brimmed over and spilled out on the floor.

Luckily Carter was holding the mug at an angle so the hot liquid dribbled away from him, avoiding scalding his hand, but Bart made sure Louis kept pouring until the pot was empty. He even shook Louis's hand to drag out the last few drops then considered Carter, his eager gaze defying him to retaliate.

Casually Carter ran his boot through the puddle of coffee on the floor while noting the exact position of the men around him. Then he smiled and drew the mug to his lips to take a slurping sip.

'Obliged for the coffee,' he said pleasantly and backed away a pace.

Bart looked him up and down while he searched for a way to continue this confrontation when Carter was giving him no obvious opportunities for a retort, but Carter pre-empted him by turning away. He walked slowly back towards his chair beside McKinney, who was still appraising everyone silently from beneath a lowered hat.

'Get everybody coffee, Louis,' Bart said. He pointed at each person in turn, keeping his finger on that person while he searched their eyes for their reaction. Vance, Annie and even Major Kelley squirmed uncomfortably on their chairs then relaxed when his finger moved on until it finally swung round to the corner. 'And you can start with . . . the lawman.'

This comment made Carter stop and turn so that he kept both McKinney and Bart in view. Nobody spoke as Louis brought a mug over to the table along with the other coffee-pot. He held out the mug, but Marshal McKinney ignored him and instead stared at Bart.

'Take the mug,' Louis urged.

McKinney didn't reply, so Louis nudged the mug against McKinney's exposed hand. The other hand was beneath the table. McKinney shot him a cold glare that made him draw his hand back before returning his gaze to Bart.

'Listen to Louis,' Bart said, settling his stance. 'Take the mug and let him pour you a coffee.'

McKinney ignored him. Beside him the prisoner shuffled on his chair.

'He doesn't want coffee,' Carter said.

'I wasn't talking to you,' Bart said, then snorted a sneering laugh. 'Everybody gets coffee and the lawman will be the next one Louis serves, and he'll get a full pot just like you did.'

The other men were silent but each had stood straight, waiting to see who would react first. It was the lawman. Without warning hot lead blasted up through the table sending Bart flying backwards with a neat red hole exploding across the forehead.

As McKinney upturned the table to free his hand, Carter dropped his coffee mug. Before it had hit the floor he'd swivelled at the hip to face the two men by the stove. Both men were scrambling for their guns, but before either man had cleared leather, Carter hammered lead at them.

One man rocked backwards into the wall before sliding down it smearing a red snail's trail behind him. The other man swirled round clutching his chest before collapsing over the stove to lie with his head and arms dangling.

The other two men by the bar had enough time to draw their guns but not to get a bead on either of them. McKinney took the left-hand one, knocking him backwards over the bar while Carter took the other, his low shot to the hip bending him double before his second high shot winged him to the floor.

The gunfight had lasted but seconds, leaving behind an acrid smell, the pall of gunsmoke, five dead men, and the echoes of Annie's strangulated screech. McKinney stood.

'Everyone fine?' he asked.

This comment encouraged Major Kelley to comfort Annie while Vance lowered his head. Louis hurried over to join Carter, but Carter stood aghast. He had vowed never to kill again, but the moment the situation had become dangerous he'd reacted instinctively and now curiously he didn't feel guilty. He'd had no choice, he told himself, unlike the previous time . . .

With Carter ignoring him, Louis roamed from body to body confirming the men were all dead. He started to blurt out his thanks, but choked on the words. His eyes watered as his relief got the better of his emotions.

'Good shooting, Carter,' McKinney said, turning to check on the prisoner. 'The first time I saw you I was sure I could rely on you.'

Carter shook off his concern and nodded.

'No trouble, but at least we'd been

warned about Bart . . . ' Carter trailed off, a worrying thought hitting him. He started to swirl round as a rifle shot blasted.

In the doorway behind the bar stood Walter Pike, smoke rising from the barrel of his brandished weapon. Carter took him with a shot to the chest that splayed him backwards through the doorway, then he turned to McKinney. But Walter's sneaky action had hit him in the back and slowly the lawman toppled over the fallen table.

'Anyone else?' Carter shouted to Louis.

'No,' Louis said. 'There's nobody else in town. They're all out looking for that package.'

Carter glanced around the saloon. He noticed movement. After four days of sullen torpor the prisoner had sprung to life. He bounded from his chair, dived to the floor, and in a lithe action grabbed for McKinney's gun. But his grasping fingers didn't reach it as Carter's low shot sent the gun skittering away across the floor. It came to rest beneath the batwings ten feet away from the prisoner and slightly further away from Carter.

'Stay,' Carter said.

'Your threats don't worry me,' the prisoner said, looking at the gun with obvious intent. 'You were fast, but I don't reckon you can reload before I can get to that gun.'

'Try,' Carter said.

For long moment the prisoner considered the gun, his shoulders flexing as he rehearsed the actions he'd need to leap at it, grab it, and turn it on Carter. Then he snorted and rocked back on his heels. He righted his chair and sat on it with a nonchalant expression that said he'd sat because he wanted to, not because Carter had made him.

Carter still took the precaution of reloading and telling Louis to collect the other guns.

With the situation under control, Annie threw off her shock and hurried to McKinney's side with a blanket. She folded it and rested his head on it, but Carter didn't think anyone could help him. McKinney was in a bad way. Thick blood poured from his back wound and his breathing was tortured and shallow.

'We need to get you to help,' Carter said, kneeling beside Annie.

'Too late, too late . . . ' McKinney murmured, his eyes glazing as he delivered a wheezing low breath.

Carter reckoned McKinney had breathed his last, but the marshal dragged in another screeching breath, then beckoned him in closer with a weak waft of the hand.

'What is it?' Carter asked.

'Get him, get him,' McKinney murmured, flicking his eyes towards the prisoner, 'get him to Sheriff Blake.'

'Why? What's he done? What — ?'

'No time for questions.' With a supreme teeth-gritting effort McKinney shot up a hand to grab Carter's jacket. He dragged himself up to look him in the eyes. 'Just promise me you'll get him to Blake. Everything depends on it.'

'I promise,' Carter said, but whether or not McKinney had heard him he didn't know as the lawman's grip then opened and he fell back to lie on the floor, lifeless.

3

Marshal McKinney lay in a corner of the saloon with a blanket drawn over his head. Carter and Louis had dragged the other bodies behind the bar.

Solemnly the survivors of the gun-fight gathered in the centre of the saloon room to decide what they did next. Major Kelley, Louis and Vance had claimed guns from the dead men, but Annie had refused the offer. Carter looked at each of them in turn.

'McKinney gave me a duty,' he said, 'and I intend to discharge it. Do you all accept I'll take charge of this situation?'

Carter had only asked out of courtesy, but to his surprise Kelley raised a hand.

'It was only by accident that you were with the lawman when he died,' he proclaimed, 'or he might have laid that duty upon someone else. Undoubtedly you have an ability with weaponry, but do you have the necessary capabilities as regards *command*?'

Carter caught Kelley's emphasis on his final word and saw him raise his heels and puff his chest.

'Perhaps not, but by any chance do you know of someone who has experience of *command*?'

Kelley reacted to Carter's mild sarcasm with a cough then turned on his heel and walked to the door, placing his feet to the floor carefully in a slow march. He looked outside then up at the rain, even reaching out to cup the rainfall. Then he turned briskly on his heel and faced into the saloon. He smiled when he saw that everyone had been watching him.

'I do. And here is what we will do.' Kelley snapped round to face Louis. 'Louis, our only problem in getting our prisoner into Sheriff Blake's care is the possibility that somewhere between here and Lonesome we might run into Bart Merrill's colleague Spike Talbot

— especially if we do that after he has discovered Bart's body. So what is your estimate of Spike's arrival time?'

Although Carter gritted his teeth in irritation as Kelley took control without discussion, he had to admit the crisis appeared to have brought out the best in the retired major. He had barked out his words with swift, military command and Louis was all but standing to attention in response.

'If he's gone downriver to Brown's Crossing,' Louis said, 'and he stays for the night, he won't be back until late in the morning tomorrow.'

Kelley nodded then paced back and forth before the door as he spoke.

'Good. That means we don't have to panic ourselves into acting hastily. So we will stay here tonight, let the bad weather blow itself out, then set off at first light tomorrow to resume our journey to Lonesome, thereby reaching our original destination and fulfilling the lawman's request.'

Kelley looked around. Most people

showed their support by nodding, but the stage driver Vance shook his head.

'Weather's set in,' he said gloomily. 'It might clear by tomorrow, it might not, but either way that landslide ain't going nowhere. Spike should be able to get past it, but not the stage.'

'Then decide on which alternative route you will take.' Kelley pointed at him as if he was aiming a sword. 'That is your task.'

'But that just brings up the other issue,' Carter said. 'We should split up. Someone has to get the prisoner to Sheriff Blake, but there's no need to risk everyone if a gunslinger is out there.'

'Division of our forces is not a legitimate strategy,' Kelley said with a clipped tone. 'That matter is not open to discussion.'

Carter shook his head, but on hearing Annie and then Louis murmur their approval of Kelley's stance, he didn't raise any objections. Kelley then turned his gaze on the prisoner.

'So,' he said, 'what did you do for Marshal McKinney to take you to Lonesome?'

The prisoner didn't react other than to continue sitting, staring ahead sullenly, but then again he wasn't used to being spoken to. Only a prolonged silence and Kelley's piercing glare made him flinch, then look up. Kelley repeated his question.

'Nothing,' the prisoner said, shrugging.

'Much as I thought. Don't talk, then.'

'I could talk,' the prisoner said, with a sneering glance at them all, 'but I don't reckon the likes of you will want to listen to me.'

'And you're right about that. Your duty is to be taken to Lonesome, nothing more. Meeting over.' Kelley clicked his heels, delivered a curt nod, then beckoned for everyone to disband.

With Kelley having outlined their plan of action, for the next few hours they remained quiet, apart from the formalities of serving coffee and finding something to eat in Walter's side room. As darkness replaced the gloom of the afternoon and the rain slowed from a torrential downpour, Carter detected a gradual rising in spirits.

Later they busied themselves with settling down. They spread out across the saloon, each person curling up under the blankets Louis had laid out earlier. Kelley allocated Carter the duty of keeping the first watch along with that of guarding the prisoner. So he stood by the door in a position where he could both watch the prisoner and look outside.

'You planning on giving me trouble?' he asked the prisoner, 'or do I have to chain you to the bar?'

'Chain me if you want,' the prisoner said, 'as long as you complete on McKinney's promise.'

This odd comment bemused Carter, but he avoided reacting to it. He stayed looking outside for a while then grunted to himself as if he'd made a decision. He paced over to the prisoner and sat beside him, looking into the saloon room.

'All right,' he said. 'What did that mean?'

'You sure you want to listen to me?' The man nodded towards the sleeping major. 'That strutting fool wasn't interested in hearing what I had to say.'

Carter smiled. 'You know what to say to get me on your side, so if you want to talk, I'll listen, and we can start with your name.'

'Maverick,' the prisoner said without hesitation, 'Maverick Pullman.'

This answer surprised Carter and it took him a few moments to collect his thoughts.

'A relative of Usher Pullman?'

'His brother.'

'So I guess that means Spike Talbot will try to free you tomorrow.'

'That depends on whether he knows I was coming here.'

'He'll know what crime you're going to trial to . . . ' Carter nodded as he started to piece together what was probably happening. 'A trial you'll face standing alongside your brother.'

Maverick chuckled to himself and when that response didn't please him enough he snorted out a prolonged burst of laughter. He wiped his eyes with his bound hands as if he were swiping away tears of mirth then considered Carter, still smiling.

'And that lawman has entrusted me to a gun-toting fool and a pompous retired officer. It'd be easier on everyone if you let me go and let me make my own way to Lonesome.'

'I ain't letting you roam free, trusting you'll turn up at court.'

'But I would. I'm not standing trial *with* Usher Pullman. I'm the key witness *against* him.'

'His brother!' Carter snorted. 'A man in chains, a man who's come from — '

'Leavenworth,' Maverick said, completing the thought. 'I'm a man who's come from Leavenworth, in chains. People go there in chains, not leave. I've spent the last year there, except now

I'm to be the surprise and key witness against my dear brother.'

'Why?'

Maverick sighed and looked into the saloon. He pondered for several seconds before he replied.

'I used to run the saloon in Lonesome, but this lawman with a death wish hauled me in for shooting up a man. Usher said he'd get me out of the jailhouse, but even though he got rid of the lawman, him and those no-good varmints Bart and Spike let me take the blame for everything.'

'Did you shoot up that man?'

Maverick snorted. 'That ain't important. What is important is I got life.'

'And what'll you get if you speak up against him?'

'Life, but it'll be with the satisfaction of knowing Usher won't be on the outside.'

This answer to the question of why Marshal McKinney was taking Maverick to Lonesome sounded strangely plausible and consistent. But the prisoner had also overheard everything that everyone had said since they'd arrived in Ferry Town and it was likely he'd concocted a believable story from the information he'd learnt. Carter glanced at Louis's sleeping form, noting that when he'd seen Maverick he hadn't reacted as if he'd seen him before. He resolved to question him later as to whether he'd been in town last year.

'In that case,' Carter said, standing, 'I know you won't try to escape. But if you make a wrong move, I'll know that story was just a story and I'll know what I have to do.'

Carter cast a significant glance at his holstered gun then headed to the door. For the rest of his watch he didn't speak again with Maverick. He stood in the doorway watching the rain and looking for the glimpse of a star that might herald the cloud cover breaking.

He fingered the watch in his pocket, forcing himself not to dwell on the death he'd meted out recently. Instead, he considered what he'd have to do tomorrow to assist Kelley in getting to Lonesome while avoiding Spike Talbot, a task that had now become harder. Before Maverick's revelation, he had been worried only about Spike coming across them. Now he knew that Spike was probably specifically interested in finding Maverick.

By the time Kelley relieved him, Carter knew what his first action would be.

'Get someone to wake me and Vance at first light,' he said.

'Why?' Kelley demanded.

'We need to check on that landslide.'

'I allocated to Vance, and Vance alone, the role of considering our future route.'

'I know, but I've been around these parts before. I can't remember the layout of the land that well but if we . . . ' Carter trailed off. Kelley was glaring at him, his flexing jaw suggesting he was merely waiting for Carter to finish speaking so that he could disagree with him.

'There's no need for you both to go,' he said, confirming Carter's suspicion.

'Vance has some fixed ideas about the best routes, all taken from the seat of the stage, but we don't have to use the stage. We could . . . ' Carter sighed as Kelley shook his head. 'Stop disagreeing with everything I say. We'll work best together if you trust me and my judgement.'

'We'll work best together if you keep me apprised of everything that is relevant to our mission.' Kelley rubbed his jaw as he pondered. 'So my decision is you alone will go out at first light. You will find out what you can, return, then you and Vance will provide me with your recommendations. I will then decide whose advice to take.'

The two men looked at each for long moments before Carter inclined his head slightly.

'Agreed.'

Kelley snapped his heels together then turned away and took up a position near to the prisoner.

Carter shook his head, snorting quietly to himself at Kelley's need to posture and enforce his command over a task that should take only a few hours tomorrow, then headed off to sleep. He chose a position between Vance and the blanket behind which Annie was sleeping.

He expected to suffer a sleepless and troubled night, but after the exertions of the last few hours sleep came easily and he was surprised when, after what felt like only minutes, Annie shook him awake.

'What the . . . ?' he murmured.

'It'll be first light soon,' she said, then raised a mug. 'I've made coffee.'

He sat, patted his pocket to feel the watch, then glanced at the dozing prisoner.

'I didn't expect you to be on guard.'

'Why not?' she asked.

Carter didn't try to find an appropriate reply and took the offered coffee instead.

'Any trouble?'

'No, and the rain's stopped.'

'That is good news.' He stood, stretched the aches from his bones then drew her aside to the bar. 'We have to get away quickly. I'm leaving to — '

'I know,' she said. 'The major told me what he'd ordered you to do. And I have my own orders. We're all to be ready to leave by the time you return.'

'He sure is efficient.'

'He is, so don't dawdle.' She waggled a reproachful finger and smiled. 'Or he'll put you on report.'

Carter laughed, noting for not the first time on this journey how much he enjoyed seeing her all too infrequent smiles. He gulped several mouthfuls of coffee then bade her goodbye and headed outside, leaving her to rouse the others. He collected one of Bart's horses from the stable.

As he trotted down the main drag, he noted that people were already moving around in the saloon and making their way over to the bar to collect the coffee she'd made. Not wanting to delay their departure for a moment longer than was necessary, he speeded up and sloshed through the mud up to High Point. By the time he reached the hanging man, the first slither of lightness was on the horizon. He slowed when he'd passed the corpse, peering ahead as he looked for the landslide.

Yesterday Vance had stopped the stage beside the body. At that point he had been able to see the blocked trail in the poor light, and so Carter judged that he should meet the blockage within a hundred yards. But he covered that distance with the trail still being rutted and muddy and showing no sign of the problem that had made Vance seek refuge in Ferry Town.

He'd covered another hundred yards before he started to worry and another hundred before he was sure.

With sudden dread making his heart hammer, he drew his horse to a halt on a slight rise. The ever-increasing light level let him see the snaking trail beside

the river stretching ahead for at least another mile.

Along its whole length there was no landslide.

* * *

Buckley Sharpe awoke with a start with his head pressed up against the crate they'd fished out the river yesterday. Max Parker was still asleep and holding the crate tightly as if it might run away.

He and Max had been travelling upriver for several months, hunting, fishing, trading in pelts as they did during the summer months. Their unexpected discovery yesterday had convinced them that they'd been right to come further north than ever before.

It had been long into the night before they'd finished looking through the crate, after which it'd been too late to move on. But most of Buckley's initial elation had worn off long before they'd reached the bottom. Although they'd found several intriguing valuables such

67

as watches and rings on the top of the crate, deeper down there were letters, journals and other items that were of no value, except perhaps to whoever had owned them.

This last thought had been on Buckley's mind when he'd drifted off to sleep and had ensured he didn't have a restful night. Accordingly, with the coming of daylight, Buckley slipped several of those written documents out of the crate, being careful not to wake Max.

The papers had now dried out and so he paged through them, but they contained few clues as to who had owned them and it wasn't even obvious to him what he was reading. Names, places, dates featured heavily along with lengthy statements that made Buckley's eyes glaze.

'Find anything interesting?' Max asked, snapping Buckley out of his torpor.

Buckley turned to watch Max stretch.

'Nope. I've still got no idea what they are.'

'But we know everything we need to know without reading.' Max crawled over to the pile they'd made of the valuables. 'These don't have any confusing writing on them.'

He hefted a handful of rings and grinned, his wide smile suggesting he was calculating the amount of gold and silver he was holding.

'But some of them do.' Buckley joined him and picked up a silver watch. He read the inscription on the back. 'To Samuel, from Frank Doyle.'

'What you getting at?'

'I mean these things once belonged to someone. When we found them they were just valuables without an owner, but now I've seen names, taking them somehow seems . . . well, it somehow seems just plain wrong.'

Irritation flashed in Max's eyes before he provided a weak attempt at a comforting smile.

'But we don't know these people. They are just that — names.'

'If we read through these journals,

perhaps we might put people and places to those names.'

'Then I propose we don't do that.'

Buckley sighed, Max's comment finally helping him to make a decision.

'I know what you're saying and I'm mighty tempted to do just that myself, but I don't reckon we can.'

Max glared at Buckley, but when Buckley returned a resolute stare, his shoulders slumped.

'I guess we can't, but we don't know where this stuff came from. We can't spend forever trying to return it all to its rightful owners, can we?'

'You're right, but we can at least try. We can head up to Ferry Town and perhaps even Lonesome then ask around and see if anyone knows of the people I've read about in these journals.'

'And if we don't find out anything after we've done that?'

Buckley offered a smile. 'Then I guess it'll be our lucky day because we'll both know we tried and that we have no choice but to accept this stuff is ours to keep.'

This comment did make Max laugh for the first time today.

'All right. We'll do it your way and try to find the owners so you get no complaints from your conscience.'

In a happier frame of mind Buckley helped Max reload the crate. But he couldn't help but notice the slow way Max fingered the watch and other valuables before he replaced them.

When the crate was full, Buckley even started to rummage through it to make sure Max had replaced everything they'd removed. Then he saw the irritated glance Max shot his way and decided to trust him. He slammed shut the lid.

'So,' he said, 'Ferry Town or Lonesome?'

4

Carter left his horse in the stable. He'd ridden back to town as fast as he could, then taken a route that avoided passing by the saloon to give him a chance of arriving back unseen.

As he'd feared, contrary to what Annie had suggested during his last conversation with her, the stage was in the stable. She was efficient and appeared to be carrying out Kelley's orders when he'd left. So that implied that Vance now knew that Carter had uncovered his double-dealing.

He hurried out of the stable and looked to the river. A light shone in the saloon, illuminating the grey-shrouded town. He listened for movement inside the saloon to give him a clue as to what was happening, but heard nothing.

Why Vance had lied about the landslide and directed the stage to

Ferry Town he didn't know, but Carter's thoughts revolved around sinister intent. So he carefully made his way down the road, closing on the saloon.

He edged up to the window and risked darting a peek inside. The scene inside was as he'd feared. Vance stood by the bar with his gun drawn and brandished. Nobody else was in view, although from Vance's posture Carter surmised he had lined the passengers up against the wall he couldn't see and was guarding them.

He reckoned he could get in through the front door and overpower him, but if he didn't act quickly enough Vance might kill one of his hostages first. So Carter decided to find a less obvious route into the saloon. He turned on his heel and made his way back towards the stable.

He'd covered only a few paces when a creak sounded behind him.

He continued walking, not wanting to appear concerned in case his assumption was correct. Three barrels were lined up ten feet ahead of him and he resolved to reach them first before he risked turning, but the sound came again and this time he was sure someone was pushing through the batwings. He took another pace then threw himself to the side.

A gunshot tore out. Carter saw the slug send up a fountain of mud to his side. He kept his roll going and came up on his feet. He didn't dare risk wasting time by turning so he threw himself forward another pace then dived for the barrels. Lead tore splinters from a barrel rim before he scrambled to a halt behind cover.

He rolled round to a crouching position and after a moment's thought decided he had no choice but to draw his gun again.

'You wasted your only chance,' he shouted, his taunt aiming to make Vance speak and so reveal his exact location.

'You're wrong,' Vance shouted back. The creak of batwings accompanied his response, suggesting he'd slipped back into the saloon. 'You're out there and I'm in here with plenty of hostages.'

'What you want with them?'

'That ain't none of your business. The only thing you should worry about is that I don't need any of them alive.'

Carter reckoned that that statement confirmed that Vance had taken the stage to Ferry Town under the secret orders of Bart Merrill and Spike Talbot, although it still left one question unanswered.

'So,' Carter shouted, 'you directed us here to keep Maverick Pullman away from Lonesome, but was that so that Spike Talbot could rescue him from Marshal McKinney, or so he could kill him?'

'I'm doing what I was paid to do and I don't ask no questions, but if anyone gives me trouble, I will get rid of that trouble. So come out and join my hostages before I start thinning them out.'

Carter had no doubt Vance would

carry through with his threat. Although giving himself up was something he hated doing, Spike Talbot was several hours away and that gave him a chance to act later. He stood, his gun thrust high in a raised hand and paced out into the open, walking sideways to stand before the saloon door.

'I've given myself up,' he said when Vance swung into view inside. 'Don't shoot anyone.'

Vance peered at him over the batwings. 'Throw your gun to me and I won't.'

Carter shuffled the gun on to the palm of his hand then threw it, but with limited force to ensure it landed his side of the batwings. Then he settled his stance by digging the toe of his boot into the mud.

Vance would have to come outside to get the gun and the only person who would then pay for Carter's reckless action if he failed would be Carter himself. Carter rocked forward ready to launch a clump of mud at Vance when he bent for the gun, but he didn't get the chance.

Vance flinched then turned from the door.

'Stay there!' he ordered.

'No reason for that no more,' Maverick said, pacing into the doorway to eye Vance's brandished gun. 'If you're getting too much trouble, I'll help you keep things under control until Spike gets here.'

'Those weren't my orders.'

'Don't know about those, but then again nobody expected us to get into this situation.' He nudged through the batwings to look down at the gun.

'Stop right there,' Vance said, although his tone was more uncertain than before. 'I've heard about the tale you told Carter about going up against Usher Pullman.'

'You really reckon that was the truth and that I'd speak out against my own brother?'

'I don't know.'

'You don't.' Maverick took a pace to stand over the gun. He considered

Carter then looked down at the weapon. 'But decide now because I'll tell you one thing for sure. You don't ever want to make an enemy of anyone who works with Usher Pullman.'

With Vance watching him Maverick bent for the gun, hefted it in his bound grip then straightened and paced back into the saloon.

'I guess I've got no choice but to trust you,' Vance said, then gestured outside for Carter to follow him in.

Maverick nodded. Then, in a lightning gesture, swung the gun to the side. He shot Vance low in the guts and then a second time, to send him spinning to the floor.

'Except you made the wrong choice and trusted the wrong man.' Maverick stood over Vance as Carter came through the door. When Vance uttered a rattling grunt then rolled over to lie on his back, he turned to him.

'I'll take that gun,' Carter said, holding out a hand.

Maverick glanced down at the gun,

then swung it round in his grip to present it to him.

'Take it, then prove to me I'm not wrong to trust you. Shoot these chains off.'

Carter took the gun then gestured for Maverick to splay his hands as far apart as he could. Maverick did as requested. Slowly Carter raised the gun and sighted the chains, but Maverick's hands shook.

'Keep still,' Carter urged.

'It's hard. You're about to shoot at . . . ' Maverick narrowed his eyes when Carter still didn't fire. 'What you want from me?'

'Ain't decided yet.' Carter lowered the gun. 'But I sure ain't freeing you.'

'Do not double-cross me,' Maverick snapped, his eyes flaring, but Major Kelley provided the most strident complaint.

'What are you're doing, Carter?' he demanded, coming over from the wall. 'Free that man.'

'Free the prisoner?' Carter murmured aghast. 'That's ridiculous.'

'It is not. That man proved himself when it counted and in the military trust is everything.'

'It's the same outside too.'

Kelley considered him then held out a hand for the gun.

'As you can't bring yourself to shoot his chains off, your commanding officer will do it.'

'You will not. It's time you faced the fact that none of us is in the military and we only have to follow your orders if we reckon they're good ones. And I don't judge that someone who let a man like Vance capture him is competent enough to order me to free our prisoner.'

'Vance also fooled you and if you'd have let me allocate to him the duty of visiting the landslide as I'd intended, I'd have uncovered his subterfuge earlier.'

Carter cast his mind back to their conversation last night. As far as he could recall he had suggested that Vance visit the landslide with him, but then again he was getting the feeling that Kelley was the kind of man who never admitted to making a mistake.

'That sure is a ridiculous excuse!'

'It isn't, but speak plainly, Carter. Are you trying to take charge of our mission, because if you are you'll lead us all to disaster. I am thinking of the welfare of everyone in this saloon. You are only concerned about yourself and your gun.'

'I am not!' Carter snapped then looked outside to calm himself. The light level had risen sufficiently to let him see the whole town and High Point beyond. 'But we can't waste time arguing. Vance has led us into a trap and we have to leave quickly. I suggest we keep Maverick chained for now and discuss freeing him later, but either way, we have to leave.'

'And we would have already if you hadn't have wasted time by disobeying my orders.' Kelley turned to face the others before Carter could retort. 'The prisoner stays chained because I believe that to be the best option. Now we need a new driver.'

'I can take Vance's place,' Louis said, then thought for a moment. 'That is in driving the stage and not in leading you into a trap.'

Everyone laughed, lessening the tension slightly.

'Good man,' Kelley said then beckoned for everyone to follow him outside. 'Carter, guard the prisoner. Everyone, move quickly. Spike won't return for a few hours and I intend to make the best use of that time.'

Carter took Maverick's arm, receiving a surly glare and a significant shaking of his chains by way of protest, but he let Carter lead him outside.

'The quickest route,' Carter said, 'is the one Vance was taking us on yesterday now that we know the trail is really clear.'

Louis shook his head. 'That starts out heading towards Brown's Crossing. We could meet Spike coming the other way.'

'Good point, man,' Kelley said, stopping outside the door. 'We need a different route . . . '

Everyone else continued walking then stopped when they saw that Kelley wasn't heading to the stable.

'Come on,' Carter urged, swinging round to face Kelley. 'We have to hurry.'

'Haste is not always the best option to get somewhere quickly.'

'Is that another military strategy?'

'It is and it has served me well.' Kelley turned on his heel and paced to the barrels that Carter had hidden behind earlier. He looked to the river then gestured downriver. 'We will not take your route. We will head across the river on the ferry and ride down to Brown's Crossing on the side where Spike won't be looking for us. Then we will cut back across the river and make our way to Lonesome, coming in from a direction Spike won't expect.'

'That's too far. We'll never make it in time for the trial.'

Kelley looked at Louis with his eyebrows raised, inviting him to talk.

'It'll take half the day to get to Brown's Crossing,' Louis said, 'and the same to get back. The trial's tomorrow, but if we don't rest up for too long overnight, we should arrive in time, just.'

Kelley looked to Carter, keeping his eyebrows raised with what was now a look of triumph.

'Then it's a mighty fine idea,' Carter said, 'except for one thing. Unless somebody swims across, we can't winch ourselves across the water.'

'You're wrong,' Kelley said. He raised a hand, paused to ensure everyone was looking at the hand, then thrust it into the nearest barrel. He rummaged inside then removed two red flags with a flourish and waved them above his head.

Carter was about to ask him what he was doing when he saw a flash of red on the other side of the river. He narrowed his eyes and discerned the shape of two men, with one waving identical flags.

'The other ferry workers are still here,' Carter murmured. He tipped back his hat to scratch his forehead in genuine surprise. 'How did you know?'

Kelley smiled smugly then threw the flags back in the barrel.

'In the military, observation is everything.'

'I thought trust was everything,' Carter murmured. 'But I still reckon we should get to Lonesome by the quickest route.'

'You would never have survived in the military. You always do the unexpected.' Kelley turned on his heel, effectively ending the debate, and headed off to the stable, beckoning with an overhead gesture for everyone to follow him. 'Move on out.'

Carter gritted his teeth in irritation as Kelley's planned route would delay his return to Lonesome by another day, then glanced at Louis.

'I never told him about the flags,' Louis said. 'He must be observant.'

Carter considered their strutting self-proclaimed leader.

'I know exactly what he is.'

From then on they wasted no more time in preparing to leave. Under Kelley's unnecessary directions Louis hitched up the horses and manoeuvred the stage out of the stable. Kelley allocated Maverick the duty of collecting feed and water, possibly to prove a point that he believed him to be trustworthy.

Throughout the journey from Leavenworth nobody had exchanged a word with the prisoner and his sullen demeanour had left none of them in any doubt that the lawman was taking him to receive justice. So Carter found his sudden change in status hard to accept, and the suspicious looks Annie and Louis gave him suggested they did too. But Kelley showed no such qualms and Carter had to accept that Maverick had acted to save everyone's lives when he didn't need to. The only explanation Carter could think of for his actions was that his story of going to Lonesome to testify against his brother was in fact a true one.

That didn't mean he was prepared to shoot off his chains or give him a gun or stop watching him, as he guessed he would do throughout the journey.

Louis drove the stage out of the stable and, with a skill that spoke of the many years he must have worked here, he directed the horses on to the ferry efficiently. Then he encouraged them to roll the stage forward until they bustled against the forward rail.

The stage filled the ferry with only a few feet of leeway, but the gap was wide enough for Louis to secure a rail across the back. With the passengers strewn out on either side of the stage, he waved across the river for the others to start winching when he gave the final signal. Then he walked around the sides of the ferry, making sure they were ready to leave.

Carter stayed out of his way at the front of the ferry while Kelley enjoyed himself barking out orders that Louis didn't need. He looked across the river and ran his gaze away from the men waiting to haul them across then down the riverside, picturing their lengthier route that would keep him from his uncomfortable meeting for another day. His slow turn took in the expanse of water before he looked up to the hills on his side of the river.

Staying on this side still felt like the most sensible route, but nobody else was prepared to back him in disagreeing with Kelley . . .

Movement caught his eye.

Carter flinched, but then decided that as he had been looking at High Point he'd probably glimpsed the hanging man silhouetted against the dawn sky. He made his way round the ferry to join Louis.

'When can we set off?' Carter asked, running his gaze along the hills.

'Another five minutes,' Louis said.

Carter saw the movement again and this time he confirmed it wasn't the hanging man. A line of riders was making its way down from High Point, heading for Ferry Town.

'That ain't good enough,' he said. 'We haven't got five minutes.'

5

'Hurry up, man!' Kelley urged, although there was nothing Louis or any of them could do to get their journey under way.

On the other side of the river the men had now urged their mules to begin circling. The motion was winching the rope, but the rope was still thrashing about as it took up the slack and it had yet to become taut enough to move the ferry.

The riders were now halfway down from High Point and in Carter's estimation were sure to arrive within minutes, and perhaps before the ferry had even left the riverside.

Kelley joined him to watch them until they reached the far end of town, then hurried back down the ferry. He quickly issued everyone with their orders and this time Carter didn't object to them. He positioned Louis at the front of the ferry to keep the horses calm while he placed himself and Annie between the front wheels. He ordered Carter and Maverick to lie down behind the two back wheels in a position nearest to the riverside, then ordered everyone to keep their heads down.

Around the side of the wheel, Carter watched the riders head down towards the river, willing them to slow and willing the ferry to move off. He got his first wish when the riders veered away, then drew to a halt outside the saloon.

There were four men and they all peered forwards in the saddle looking at the ferry. From their position they wouldn't be able to see any of them clearly and so might not immediately realize what was happening. If the story Carter had pieced together was correct, they were only looking for Maverick and the rest of them weren't important.

In apparent confirmation of this view the men looked towards the saloon. One man shouted something through the door, waited for an answer, then darted glances at the other men. Then they rolled out of their saddles and headed into the saloon.

Carter breathed a sigh of relief as their actions bought them another few seconds, but he didn't expect them to take long to piece together what had happened when they found the bodies.

At last the ferry lurched, rocking the stage against the blocks that held it. The rope that connected the ferry to the winch on this side of the river strained until it was taut then started to slide. The ferry glided off at an agonizingly slow speed, but at least they were now moving out into the water. Carter raised himself to see that a gap of a foot had opened up.

He looked at the saloon, imagining what was happening inside: the men leaning on the bar and calling out for Walter and perhaps Vance, then not getting an answer. He felt a surge of irritation that they'd left the bodies in an easy place to find instead of moving them, as they had the horses. Sure enough, after the men had been inside for only a minute, he heard a distant cry of alarm coming from the saloon as presumably someone made the inevitable discovery.

The ferry was now moving smoothly away from the riverside, but the gap was only five yards when a man hurried outside. He looked down to the river then shouted something back into the saloon. Another man poked his head through the door to look towards the ferry, then went back in. Carter couldn't work out why they were so confused as it seemed obvious to him that their quarry was escaping, but he welcomed their confusion.

'Do you recognize them?' he asked Maverick.

'Why should I answer your questions?' Maverick grumbled with a significant glance at his chains.

'To earn my trust.'

'Didn't do me no good before.' Maverick sighed, then softened his tone. 'I don't know them, but luckily they look like the kind of men Spike hires.'

Carter caught the inference. Spike Talbot wasn't with these men and so they were leaderless. They were not fully aware of the situation and because Spike had picked men who blindly followed orders, they were being indecisive as to what they should do next.

'Then,' Kelley called out from the back of the stage, 'we just need to stay down and hope they don't work out what to do.'

The ferry had opened up a gap of twenty yards by the time all the men had emerged from the saloon. They made their way down to the river, but slowly and talking amongst themselves. When they reached the edge of the water they peered out at the ferry.

'You're close enough to pick them off,' Maverick said.

'Hold your fire, Carter,' Kelley said. 'We delay any confrontation for as long as we can.'

Carter nodded then settled down to watch the men recede as the ferry made its slow way across the river.

'What you reckon they're up to, Maverick?' Carter asked when another minute had passed and still they hadn't reacted.

'Don't care what their reasoning is,' Kelley said before Maverick could answer. 'All that matters is they're standing around doing nothing and letting us get away.'

'But now it won't be unseen. They'll eventually work out we're heading down to Brown's Crossing.'

'Perhaps, but we'll have a better chance than if I'd accepted your plan and gone up to High Point.' Kelley poked his head out from under the stage to beckon for Louis to join him as Carter grunted with irritation. 'Can we get back across the river somewhere else?'

'I know of some places,' Louis said, crawling under the stage, 'where the water's shallow enough to attempt a crossing, if we're desperate.'

'We are,' Carter said. He considered the men who were now examining the winch. 'Provided we can get across before they act.'

Louis shook his head. 'As soon as we'd set off it was already too late for them to stop us. Anyone who tries to cut the rope is looking to lose a hand with it playing out all the time.' Louis frowned. 'But they might still have enough time to break the winch and cut us loose.'

So Carter watched the men, hoping they didn't get their wits about them, but when they did react, it was with only a minor action. One man pointed at the ferry and they all bunched up to talk. Carter surmised that they'd spotted Maverick hiding behind a wheel.

He glanced back at Kelley to see if he'd noticed, but Kelley had already drawn his gun and so had Louis. Kelley gestured downwards, signifying they should remain calm. His decision proved to be the right one as out on the riverside the men kept their guns holstered and just watched them while talking amongst themselves.

Not that gunfire would be effective. They were over halfway across the river and Carter judged that any shots they might trade would be mainly wild.

Louis voiced this opinion then crawled out from under the stage to check on the horses. Carter continued to watch the men until he was sure they were too far away to bother shooting at them, then joined Kelley.

'Their behaviour is most surprising,' Kelley said.

'I thought there were no surprises in the military,' Carter said, then crawled out from under the stage before Kelley could retort. He joined Louis at the front.

'Everything fine?' he asked.

Louis nodded towards the approaching riverside, fifty yards ahead.

'Sure. Those men haven't got enough time to destroy the winch now. We will escape, for now.'

'We can hardly call it an escape when they didn't bother trying to stop us.'

Louis snorted a laugh. 'They'll regret that when they have to explain themselves to Spike . . . ' Louis flinched. His mouth fell open in shock. Then he pointed at the approaching riverside. 'I know what's happening.'

Carter joined Louis in peering ahead, looking for what had shocked him. He saw the two men leading the mules in a circle, winching the ferry across the river. Then he saw a third man who appeared to be quietly supervising the activity while leaning back in a chair behind them.

'I don't see it,' he said. 'There's just those three — '

'There should only be two men,' Louis said with a pronounced gulp. 'The man sitting down is Spike Talbot.'

Carter narrowed his eyes to look at him then glanced up and down the riverside. As his eyes become accustomed to the terrain, he saw other men lying down facing the river or positioned at vantage points to look down on them. He winced as he understood the situation.

'Those men didn't let us escape,' he said. 'They just let us head over the river and into Spike's clutches.'

★ ★ ★

Although it was still early, Lonesome was quieter than Buckley Sharpe or Max Parker had expected it to be. But that suited their agreed purpose.

As the crate was heavy they'd removed some valuables, then buried it close to where they'd found it. Then, after some debate as to whether to go to Ferry Town or Lonesome, they'd headed to the larger town. Partly, under Max's suggestion, on the reasoning that they might be able to sell their goods there if they decided they could keep them, and partly, under Buckley's guidance, to see if they could find out who had lost them.

They roamed around town, listening in on conversations. They visited three mercantiles, quietly perusing goods while they sized up whether to ask the storeowners whether they knew of anyone who had lost anything recently. Unfortunately all three men stayed behind their counters eyeing them with distrust and so they didn't ask.

They read notices, a page from a discarded local newspaper and they treated themselves with a visit to the barber. But nobody was keen to talk about town business and neither man felt inclined to risk enquiring about the names they'd read about in the journals. They were familiar with the distrust that townsfolk often held for strangers who asked too many questions and Lonesome was a town that didn't encourage idle chatter.

With even the barber not being talkative, when they left they noticed that everyone they passed looked at them as if they'd ridden into town to raid the town bank. So feeling in an uneasy frame of mind, they slipped into the Maverick saloon to consider their next actions. But if everyone they'd passed so far had considered them as if they represented trouble, it was nothing compared to the cold reception they then received.

The saloon room was half-full and silent. All eyes turned to them and watched every echoing pace they made to the bar and then to a table. The silence continued even when everybody grew bored with looking at them.

'Don't like this town,' Max whispered, speaking for both of them.

A man at the nearest table shot them an aggrieved look as if he'd heard Max's quiet comment.

'Yeah. I've already had enough of this place,' Buckley said in a normal tone. 'We drink up our coffees then move on.'

This comment received a grunt of approval from the nearby table. Then the people around them began to move around and talk, but still using subdued tones and with frequent glances their way.

'Agreed,' Max said. He considered Buckley with his lips pursed. 'And that means we have at least tried to find out.'

Each man looked at the other. Max looked with hope lighting in his eyes, but Buckley could hardly meet that gaze as he felt a pang of conscience. He had been meaning to suggest they should now try Ferry Town. But if they couldn't find an answer there, he had to admit he didn't welcome a potentially endless journey upriver trying to find out whose valuables they'd found.

'We did try,' Buckley said, nodding. 'I guess nobody can blame us if we give up, what with nobody being particularly friendly like.'

'Nobody can blame us,' Max murmured and for emphasis he downed his coffee and slammed the mug on the table.

Buckley matched his action, but when the echoing thuds their empty mugs had made encouraged people to look at them again, Buckley picked them up. While Max headed outside, he took them to the bar.

He tipped his hat to the barkeep, then turned to leave, but a board behind the bar caught his eye. Chalked names were listed down one side and numbers down the other. He considered the names with a thought tapping at his mind. The barkeep noticed his interest.

'You want to bet?' he asked.

Buckley shook his head, although he'd now realized the numbers were betting odds, with the shortest odds at the top.

'Nope. I ain't staying in town.'

He backed away a pace, aiming to leave, but his comment gathered a grunted laugh from several customers at the bar. The barkeep took advantage of the animated activity to move down the bar and stand closer to Buckley.

'Plenty of people aren't bothering to stay in town these days, but that didn't stop them betting.' He smiled. 'You can always come back for your winnings later.'

'On what?'

The barkeep ran his finger down the list of names.

'The Usher Pullman trial,' he said, his tone bemused as if he was stating the obvious.

Buckley almost turned to leave as he had no idea what the barkeep had meant, but he also had a gut feeling that perhaps he ought to find out. He looked again at the names and this time he identified his concern.

'I don't know who Usher Pullman is,' he said, 'I really was just passing through, but that don't mean I ain't intrigued.'

The barkeep pointed at the names one at a time as if he was explaining something painfully obvious to a child.

'Usher's trial is tomorrow. These are the people whom Sheriff Blake's persuaded to testify against him, except we've all got an opinion as to who will have the guts to actually walk into court and accuse him.'

Buckley nodded. 'So the odds of Frank Doyle testifying are two against one, and the next man, Tex Fraser, ain't so likely at three against one?'

'You got it.'

'Interesting, but not enough to waste my money when I don't know these people.' Buckley tipped his hat then headed off to join Max outside.

'What were you talking to the barkeep about?' Max asked.

Buckley took a deep breath before he replied.

'I'm sorry,' he said. 'I learnt something that we'd decided we didn't want to know.'

'Where the crate came from?' Max asked, his low tone sounding disappointed.

'Not exactly.' Buckley patted his pocket. 'You remember the watch?'

'Yeah. Inscribed from Frank Doyle to . . . to Samuel.'

'Well, apparently Frank will be

testifying against someone called Usher Pullman in court this week.'

Max considered this information while making several sighs.

'And?'

'And that means he must live here and we ought to find him and give him back his property.'

'We ought to,' Max said with a pronounced sneer, 'but I just wish you hadn't bothered to ask that barkeep a question.'

To his disappointment, Buckley agreed with him.

6

The riverside was forty yards away and Carter could see the reception that awaited them.

Aside from Spike Talbot, who was still sitting casually in his chair, seven other men had emerged from where they were watching their progress to line up behind the winch, waiting for them to reach the side.

'They just want me,' Maverick said, joining him. 'I'll give myself up. Keep everyone else back and Talbot will leave you all alone.'

'I am not giving you up,' Kelley said, placing a hand on Maverick's shoulder for emphasis. 'Carter made a promise to Marshal McKinney and I intend to see we complete on that promise.'

As Kelley looked around, his glazed eyes showing he was pondering but failing to devise a plan of action, Carter looked at the swollen water rushing by. He judged that that escape route would provide only a different kind of end for them, but Louis intervened to provide his solution.

'I have a plan,' he called over his shoulder as he headed off down the ferry, 'but it'll take too long to explain. Just do what I say and we'll all be going on a little journey.'

For once, possibly because Louis had made the suggestion and not Carter, Kelley accepted this suggestion without question and stood back.

Louis told Annie to stay out of the way behind the stage, then even told Kelley to help him. They got to work and Carter quickly saw what he intended to do. The planks that made up the base of the long ferry were broadly in two halves with a join running down the middle. Louis planned to break those two halves apart and split the ferry in two. Presumably he judged this to be easier than cutting through the ropes.

The join ran down before the front wheels of the stage. So Kelley removed the rigging to free the horses while Louis set about using a sledgehammer to drive spare lengths of wood into the gap between the planks to drive them apart.

In the two minutes or so they had before they reached the riverside, Carter didn't reckon he had any hope of breaking through the seam, and with only one tool available there was nothing anyone could do to help him.

He looked to the riverside, now twenty yards away. Spike was moving behind the winch with his other men to prepare for whatever resistance they were about to face. Carter planned to give them plenty. When Kelley had unhitched the horses he exchanged a glance with him, then they both drew their guns and blasted lead at the winch.

They aimed away from the innocent men who had been forced to help Spike, but their volley of gunfire made these men drop to the ground and crawl away. Without their encouragement the mules mooched to a standstill, thereby stopping the winch from dragging the rope in. But the ferry already had sufficient momentum to overcome the rope's tension and it carried on towards the riverside, slowing, but still appearing as if it would ultimately nudge into its moorings.

Lead winged off the winch, keeping Spike and his men down, but when the first volley ended they risked coming out. Two men ran to the left then threw themselves to the ground while three men risked the same manoeuvre to the right. While presenting as small a target as possible, they fired back.

Kelley and Carter dropped to the deck of the ferry and with slugs whining overhead they crawled towards Louis. He had created gaps between two sets of planks and was working on a third, but with the ferry being around forty planks wide, Carter could see no way in which this plan would work.

He knelt to blast gunfire at the riverside, now just ten yards away, and was rewarded when he heard one man cry out. He saw him roll away, clutching his shoulder. This encouraged the other men to seek cover wherever they could and this at least reduced their gunfire to sporadic bursts.

A huge crack sounded beneath Carter's feet and the ferry lurched, throwing him on his back. Beside him the horses, now free from the stage, panicked and bustled against the forward rail.

Carter raised his head to see that Louis's plan was succeeding, after all. He had broken through only three planks, but he knew which ones held the ferry together and was hoping the tension on the rope that kept them on a straight course would do the rest to tear the ferry apart.

Louis moved to attack the fourth plank, but then stood up straight, dropped the hammer and hurried behind the stage. Clearly he thought he'd done enough. Sure enough, the fourth plank exploded upwards, sending splinters flying, then a fifth and a sixth. Plank after plank tore away, opening a widening gap between the two halves of the ferry.

Carter whooped with delight, but the sound died on his lips as a second crunch sounded and he tumbled to his knees.

The ferry had reached land. The gap closed up with a grinding of timbers, but that also had the effect of breaking the remaining planks that were holding the ferry together. Slowly the half with the stage peeled off then moved away as the current took control of it.

Carter caught Kelley's eye then together they backed away to the gap aiming to jump it before it widened too much. As one they raised their arms and fired blind over the horses at the men on the riverside while keeping hunched to avoid their returned gunfire.

Carter grunted an offer for Kelley to leap over first while he covered him. Kelley and he locked gazes. Kelley's bunched jaw suggested he'd refuse, but then he turned and lightly leapt over the yard gap. He knelt beside the right stage wheel. Carter then aimed to complete his leap, but before he could move Maverick came pounding round the side of the stage, hurried to the edge then jumped over the gap to join him.

As he was chained and armed only with a short plank, Kelley shouted at him to get back. But instead he stood beside the nearest horse then whipped its rump with the plank. The horse reared as he moved on to the next one where he delivered the same treatment.

This proved to be too much for the already frightened horses and they drove themselves against the forward rail, breaking through it. Then they galloped for freedom, not caring about what was in their way.

Talbot's men rolled and dived for

safety to avoid the trampling hoofs. One man made the mistake of getting to his feet and attempting to run, but he was too slow and they drove him to the ground. First one horse then a second ground him into the dirt.

Maverick stayed to watch the success of his manoeuvre then turned and leapt back over the water. He landed on the other side of what was now a two-yard gap and received an enthusiastic pat on the back from Kelley.

Carter took a few paces backwards to prepare for his own leap across the water, but then heard Kelley shout out a warning. Footfalls pounded behind him. He spun round and walked into a pile-driving punch to the chin that threw him backwards. His foot caught on the edge of the ferry and only a trailing hand grabbing hold of the end of the rail stopped him from falling into the moiling water.

Carter teetered, waving his free arm as he fought for balance. He heard a gunshot come from the other half of the ferry, then dragged himself back up to a standing position. He saw that his assailant was Spike Talbot and that he'd crouched to splatter lead at Kelley.

Carter's own gun had fallen from his grip when Spike had hit him and he looked down for it. From the corner of his eye he saw that the gap had opened up to eight feet and that his gun was four feet ahead of him. He made an instant decision and lunged for Spike instead.

He grabbed his free arm as Spike fired at Kelley again, forcing the shot to wing up into the air, then he tried to push him over the rail. Spike staggered back a pace then dug his heels in to stop his backwards motion. He swung himself round until Carter stood between the stage and himself.

'Ignore him, Spike,' Maverick shouted on the other half of the ferry. 'You're after me.'

Spike didn't respond to Maverick's taunt as he dragged his gun arm down. Inch by inch he lowered the gun until with a final lunge he tugged it down to aim the weapon at Carter's chest. From only inches away he would be sure to rip a fatal hole in him, but as Spike's finger tightened on the trigger the two men made eye contact for the first time.

Spike froze, as did Carter, the two men staring at each other from inches apart. This was their first close contact. And yet . . .

Carter had met this man before and from the shocked look in Spike's eyes, Spike had had the same thought.

'You!' Spike murmured, still frozen in surprise.

The moment could have lasted for only seconds, but it felt longer. Carter was the first to break out of his surprise. He swung a fist backhanded and upwards to slam it under Spike's jaw, cracking his head back and throwing him into the rail.

Spike wasted a bullet into the air as he fought for balance with a frantic waving of his arms. Carter didn't give him the time to right himself. He bunched both hands together and hammered them down on Spike's chest with so much force that Spike broke through the rail to tumble backwards into the water.

The force of the blow wheeled Carter forward and he almost followed him into the river. But he grabbed hold of the broken rail and righted himself on the edge. He looked down, seeing Spike flounder, then disappear below the surface. He allowed himself the luxury of remembering for a few moments then turned away to leave him to his fate.

The other men were now heading down on to the ferry, but slowly as they tussled with their own indecision as to whether they should try to help Spike or head for Carter.

Carter didn't waste time waiting to see what they decided. He turned on his heel, scooped up his gun, and ran. The two halves of the ferry were now six yards apart and Carter doubted he'd be able to leap the distance, but he had to try.

He pounded to the edge then launched himself over the water. For a moment as he hurtled through the air he thought he'd make it, but the ferry was swinging away from him all the time and when he came down, his feet sliced into the cold water. Luckily his momentum kept him moving forward and his half-submerged upper arms crashed into the edge of the wood.

The jarring blow and the shock of the coldness tore the air from his lungs. He clung to hold on, desperate to avoid losing his grip and being carried away as Spike had been. But the current was strong and it dragged one hand away. Then the other hand tore loose. He dropped below the surface, water filling his mouth. He clawed his hands about, seeking purchase but finding nothing to grab hold of. He had the impression of sinking down and down . . .

A hand slapped on to his forearm then pulled him up. He half-emerged from the water, coughing and spluttering to see Kelley standing over him.

'Get up, man!' the major demanded as he smacked his other hand down on Carter's back to grab a handful of his jacket.

Carter was breathless and his strength had deserted him. So it was mainly Kelley's tugging that dragged his upper body out of the water.

A slug tore out, ripping splinters from a plank beside him.

This gave Carter all the encouragement he needed and he did the best he could by rocking himself forward. With him now pushing himself up and with Kelley redoubling his efforts, he sprawled out on to the ferry and rolled over on to his side to lie gasping and twitching like a beached fish.

He glanced back at the other half of the ferry as Kelley began peppering lead at the riverside. A combination of his gunfire and the fact that the men didn't want to risk being on a ferry that was now also drifting away meant they were hightailing it back to dry land.

With Kelley's help in holding him up, he staggered around the side of the stage and flopped down to sit leaning back against a wheel. Annie knelt beside him and laid a hand on his arm.

'Fine?' she asked, with more concern than Carter had expected to see in her eyes.

'Sure, I . . . ' Carter forced himself not to dwell on the fact that he'd recognized Spike, but that let a terrible thought hit him. He thrust a hand into his jacket. His finger closed on a cold object within, but he still withdrew the watch slightly to confirm he hadn't lost it during the chaos of the fighting and his fall into the river.

With Annie looking at him quizzically he closed his eyes and gave himself several seconds to regain his breath. Then he tried to stand. He rose for only a few inches before his legs shook and he flopped back down. So when she bade him to stay and take some time to get his strength back, he took her advice.

A few minutes later he felt composed enough to flex each of his limbs. Then he crawled over to join Louis and Kelley, who were peering around the side of the stage.

Louis had cut through the ropes that secured them to the other side of the river. So the freed half of the ferry they were on was turning slowly in the current and taking them away from the men on the riverside. They were already eighty yards away and out of easy gunshot range.

The men appeared to have accepted that fact — and to have given up any hope of rescuing Spike — as they hurried to their horses.

'Obliged to you for taking us on this little journey,' Carter said, patting Louis's back.

'Some men's ideas are to be trusted and supported.' Kelley said.

'That journey will be more like an adventure,' Louis said, his glance at

Kelley acknowledging he'd heard the unnecessary reprimand. 'I don't reckon anybody's ever risked sailing down the river before.'

'Then we'll be the first,' Kelley said. 'How long will it take us to reach Brown's Crossing?'

'And back on foot?' Carter said before Louis could reply. 'Now that Maverick's lost our horses.'

Kelley shook his head. 'He did what he had to do and besides they were lost already, so I applaud his efforts.'

'And mine?' Carter snapped, letting his fatigue and his cold, wet clothing get the better of him. 'Are my ideas good enough to be applauded?'

Kelley swung round to look at Carter, his eyes narrowing as he probably tried to deduce whether or not he was being insubordinate.

'They have been good enough for me to save your life, even though you don't sound grateful that I did.'

'I'm as grateful as you were back in the saloon when I — '

'Stop arguing, you two,' Louis murmured. 'We've got real problems to face long before we reach Brown's Crossing.'

'Such as?' Kelley demanded, turning away from his appraisal of Carter.

'My idea to cut us free might have been a good one at the time, but now we're out here on the river.' Louis pointed at the riverside, passing by just thirty yards to their side. 'That means we'll be open targets for Spike's men all the way to Brown's Crossing.'

* * *

Frank Doyle lived ten miles out of town, towards the river, so Buckley Sharpe and Max Parker had to broadly retrace their steps. Despite the short distance it took them several hours to mooch to the ranch house.

Max didn't keep his irritation quiet and Buckley was disappointed in himself as he also felt let down by how the situation had played out. In the

123

space of a few hours they'd had the good fortune to find a crate stuffed with valuables, then had the misfortune to find out who owned at least one of those items.

Presumably Frank would be able to help them trace other people who had lost items, and so they were probably fated to spend the next few days traipsing around visiting these people, an activity neither man relished.

Max's complaints became more vociferous when they arrived at the ranch house as the prosperous, if slightly ill-maintained, abode and spread suggested that Frank Doyle was not someone who would have suffered financial hardship after having lost a silver watch. Still, they'd set themselves on this course of action and they had to see it through.

A young woman welcomed them into the hall, identifying herself as Frank Doyle's daughter, Victoria. Buckley drew the watch from his pocket and held it out.

'I believe you might have lost this,' he said.

She took the watch, her furrowed brow showing her confusion, then turned it over to read the inscription.

'This is ... was Samuel's,' she murmured, 'but it isn't lost.'

She looked up, smiling hopefully in expectation of receiving an answer they couldn't provide.

'Well, perhaps you didn't know it'd been lost yet. I'm guessing you sent it somewhere but we found it ... ' Buckley trailed off when Victoria shook her head vigorously.

'I don't understand. It's always in Father's study. You should ... ' She sighed. 'Not that I'm not grateful for your honesty in bringing it back, but I never knew it'd gone missing.'

She hefted the watch, still shaking her head and with the uncomfortable moment stretching on, Buckley and Max rocked from foot to foot, neither man knowing what to say or do next. Luckily, the door at the end of the hall opened and an imposing man with a shock of white hair appeared, saving them all from further embarrassment.

'Father,' she said, swirling round, 'you'll never believe what these men have brought us. It's Samuel's watch.'

'Just his?' he murmured, coming over to them.

'Of course I meant that, but I'm surprised. I didn't even know it'd gone missing.' She lowered her voice. 'I wish you'd told me.'

Frank's jaw bunched as he struggled to find an answer. He resolved his problem by patting her shoulder.

'I'm as confused by this as you are, but in the circumstances I think it best if I talk to these men alone.'

Frank took the watch from her and turned on his heel, not giving her a chance to object.

Victoria again thanked them. Then Buckley and Max followed Frank into what turned out to be his study.

Frank went to a desk, located a key, then placed the watch in a drawer but he kept it open. He went to the window and looked outside, lengthening out the silence as he raised his heels several times and patted a hand against the other. Buckley glanced at Max and they both raised their eyebrows, registering their bemusement about how this meeting was going.

'All right,' Frank said at last, 'what do you want from me now?'

The possibility of a reward had been the only thing that had kept Max's complaints in check earlier, but now that Frank had brought the subject up, Buckley found it an embarrassing topic and struggled for words.

'That isn't why we came,' he said after some thought.

'But you promised you'd keep my family out of this.'

'I don't understand,' Buckley murmured.

Frank turned and fixed both men with his steely gaze.

'I realize you two are just messengers, so you can take this message back. I'm not doing anything else. I want that watch, but you can still walk out of here with it because our deal doesn't change.'

Buckley gulped to moisten a throat that had become dry under Frank's fierce gaze then rubbed his jaw while he collected his thoughts. He tried to piece together what he thought Frank had meant and came to an uncomfortable conclusion.

'I reckon there's been a mistake. We found that watch and we're returning it. We don't want anything from you.'

'Found?' Frank murmured, narrowing his eyes as he looked from one man to the other, receiving nods from them both.

'Yeah,' Max said. 'We were fishing in the river and we found it in a crate. We asked around and, well, here we are.'

Frank left the window and flopped down into a chair.

'Then I'm sorry,' he murmured, rubbing his brow, 'I'm truly sorry.'

'There's no need to be,' Buckley said. 'I guess you sent it somewhere and it got lost.'

Frank nodded, accepting this explanation even though his previous troubled comments suggested it didn't explain how the watch had happened to come into their keeping.

'Then I'm sorry again. It appears I have misjudged you. Perhaps I can make amends with a meal, and I'm sure there's something more I can do to reward your honesty.'

'I'm sure there is,' Max said, a little too quickly, but Frank didn't react other than to lock the watch away then bid them to await his return.

When Frank had left the room Buckley and Max looked at each other and shook their heads, their pursed lips and significant looks acknowledging that they would discuss what they thought was happening here later. Buckley heard Frank talking down the hall and presently the front door slammed shut.

Through the window Buckley saw a rider trot through the ranch gates, the rider's trim form possibly being a woman's, presumably Victoria. Then he turned to the door to meet the returning Frank, who this time had composed himself and smiled warmly. With his hands placed on their shoulders he directed them into the dining-room.

The next two hours drove the concern from Buckley's mind as Frank foisted a huge meal on them, followed by liquor, along with promises of the reward he'd give them for their honesty. Buckley gently probed as to the circumstances that had led to Frank's property going missing, apparently without his daughter knowing, but Frank always changed the subject and frequently murmured again as to how sorry he was.

But Buckley was certain about one thing. He hadn't liked the idea of taking property they didn't own, but if they were to receive the promised reward, the task of taking the remaining valuables to the other people who had lost them would satisfy them both. They might even get several small but honestly earned rewards and his conscience would be clear.

Buckley was trying to steer the conversation round to mentioning the names of other people he'd seen in the journals when he heard hoofbeats patter as riders approached outside.

'That'll be Victoria returning,' Frank said, sitting up straight.

Buckley heard the front door clatter open then several sets of footfalls sounded coming down the hall.

'Then maybe after we've spoken with her again,' Buckley said, 'we can be on our way.'

'I believe you can,' Frank said, his tone low. 'But I am sorry.'

'You keep saying you're sorry, but there's no need to apologize. You've done nothing wrong.'

'I haven't,' Frank said, his tone becoming graver and his eyes drifting downwards, 'but then again, neither of you have, and so for what is about to happen. I am genuinely sorry.'

131

Two sets of footfalls stomped to a halt outside the door, both too heavy to be Victoria's. Then the door swung open. Frank's words and the potentially ominous arrival of visitors made a twinge of concern ripple in Buckley's guts, but Max must have been more attuned to the situation. He jumped to his feet, knocking over his chair, then ran for the window.

Buckley also stood, torn between following him and staying in the hope that his concern was misplaced. As it turned out, the man who came through the door put his mind at rest. He wore a star and lurking behind him was another man, who also had the authoritative look of a lawman.

'Ah, Deputy Ford,' Frank said, nodding towards the fleeing Max, 'I kept them for as long as I could.'

Although this was an odd thing to say, Buckley called to Max.

'It's all right,' he shouted. 'Don't run.'

Max was oblivious to his demand. He

threw open the shutters and swung a leg outside. He glanced back at Buckley, his eyes wide and beseeching him to follow, then vaulted outside. Ford did a double take, then barked a quick order to the other man in the hall. Footfalls receded down the hall as the man hurried away to cut Max off.

Ford glanced at Buckley then faced Frank.

'Obliged to you for calling me,' he said.

'I didn't want there to be any more misunderstandings,' Frank said.

Ford nodded then paced round to consider Buckley as from outside the sounds of a struggle filtered through to the study.

'You won't get any trouble from me,' Buckley said. 'I'll tell you everything that's happened and to be honest it'll save us having to work it all out for ourselves.'

'I'll save you the trouble of explaining,' Ford said. 'You found a crate. You kept it and tried to sell the items you found in there to Frank.'

'That wasn't the way it was,' Buckley murmured, flashing a hopeful look at the stern-faced Frank, who didn't meet his gaze.

'Then I'll just have to question you until I do find out the way it was.' Ford paced up to him and grabbed Buckley's arm.

Buckley didn't resist, but Ford still swung him round, yanked his arm up his back, then pushed him into the wall, blasting all the air from his chest.

Ford frisked him, finding the knife he used to gut fish, a discovery that received a triumphant grunt as if this was further evidence of his guilt. Then he kept his arm yanked high up his back as he dragged him away from the wall and marched him into the hall.

Buckley called to Frank to speak up for him, but he didn't reply. When he reached the front door he even called out to Victoria to back up his story, but again heard nothing.

Ford kept up a brisk pace as he

kicked open the door and marched him outside, but then he stopped and grunted with irritation. Buckley soon saw the reason. Two riders were heading away from the ranch, throwing up dust in their wake.

Buckley allowed himself a brief moment of pleasure. Max was riding away and with a gap of one hundred yards on his pursuer, he stood a good chance of escaping.

'Enjoy seeing that?' Ford muttered in his ear, his breath hot on his neck.

'Sure,' Buckley said. 'We're innocent, and no innocent man should get arrested.'

'You ain't innocent.' Ford snorted a laugh and yanked Buckley's arm a few inches higher, forcing him up on to tiptoes to avoid his arm being wrenched away from the shoulder. 'But if your partner's gone and run, that means you'll get to enjoy all my questioning on your own.'

7

'Who's Victoria?' Annie asked.

'What do you mean?' Carter replied, playing for time after her question had taken him by surprise.

'I saw the inscription on your watch: to Victoria, with Frank Doyle written underneath.'

The ferry was now drifting along, having settled with the back of the stage aiming downriver. They had had the luck to drift out to a point where they were a third of the way across the river, giving them some distance between themselves and the banks. This also meant they were closer to the other bank and so perhaps were also sitting targets for the men who had let them leave Ferry Town and who might also be keeping pace with them. With this in mind they were mainly keeping on one side of the ferry to use the stage as cover from the near riverbank.

'When did you see it?' he asked, staring over the rail at the riverside.

'I'd seen you holding it from time to time, but when the major dragged you out of the water and you were resting. I looked at it.' She sighed when Carter bunched his jaw in irritation. 'I'm sorry to have pried.'

Carter shook himself to free a surge of water from his clothes.

'I don't mind, but the watch ain't important.'

She considered him for several moments. 'I thought it might be. You appear to have more on your mind than just our current predicament.'

He took a deep breath. 'In that you're right, but why should that worry you?'

She looked at him with narrowed eyes, her mouth opening to provide an answer, but then she closed it, her slight shrug suggesting she'd decided not to provide her original retort.

'Because I also saw you and Spike Talbot look at each other in an odd way, and . . . ' She looked away.

'Don't let any of this worry you, and get back into the stage. The first we might know of any trouble could be gunfire.'

'I really am sorry I pried.' She turned away and climbed into the stage to return to sitting with the prisoner and Major Kelley.

Carter watched her go then resumed his patrol of the ferry.

'When do you think they'll try something?' Carter asked Louis when he stopped beside him.

'Not sure.' Louis pointed downriver. 'But the river closes up around the next bend and the trees thin out. My guess is it could be there.'

'Then I hope Kelley's ready for a gunfight.'

'It doesn't matter so much whether he is. I reckon we all feel safe having you with us.'

'Obliged for your confidence in me, but that don't mean I'm happy being stuck out here on the water.' Carter looked ahead at the approaching bend then at the Lonesome side of the river.

'Are you blaming me for us being out here?'

'Nope. You did the only thing you could do to keep us alive.'

Louis sighed. 'Then don't go blaming Kelley either. He wasn't to know Spike Talbot would be waiting for us on the other side.'

'I can when he took control of us without asking and when his decision turned out badly. If we'd stuck with my plan I could have seen off those men who rode into Ferry Town. Now we'd have horses, be halfway to town and Spike's men would never catch up with us.'

'Maybe, but he made his decision based on what we knew then, and to me it felt like a good one at the time.'

Carter might have been prepared to concede that point if anyone but the pompous major had made that decision, but standing here with unseen assailants waiting to pick them off, he wasn't feeling charitable.

His mood hadn't brightened when the terrain beyond the next bend swung into view and confirmed Louis had been right. The riverbanks closed in to more than halve the river width and this forced the water to swirl and eddy. Worse, boulders poked out from the foaming water at regular intervals.

'Good decision or bad,' Carter said, 'and gunfire or not, those boulders are bad news. If we drift into one of those, we're all ending up in the water.'

Louis nodded then looked around the ferry. Quickly he grabbed hold of the topmost side rail and started to prise away. Carter didn't ask for a reason for his action and helped. After two minutes of struggling they had two long poles lying beside the stage.

Carter looked up to see that the first of the protruding rocks was level with them, although thankfully far enough away not to cause a problem. They had also made enough noise to alert Kelley and he leaned out the stage to give them their orders.

'You will use those poles,' he said, while gesturing, 'to steer us away from those boulders and keep us on a straight course.'

Louis caught Carter's eye and winked. 'Now why didn't I think of doing that?'

Carter laughed. 'Because you're not in charge.'

'Yeah. I reckon — ' Louis didn't get to complete his comment when a burst of gunfire blasted from the riverbank.

Carter only heard the reports and didn't see or hear where any of the lead landed, but it was worrying enough for Kelley to poke his head out from the stage.

'I can't see where it's coming from yet,' he said, 'but I'll cover you. Stand your ground, men.'

'Pity I ain't in charge,' Louis grumbled. 'Being in that stage feels like a good idea right now.'

More reports sounded from the riverbank, but although Carter ran his gaze along the trees that covered the banks, he couldn't see where the shooters were. But he judged they were some distance away as the shots were so wild. That probably meant their assailants were ahead and had taken up positions around the tightest cluster of boulders, some one hundred yards ahead, choosing the point where they would be at their most vulnerable.

Carter considered those obstacles and saw that the first craggy lump that would be in their way was thirty yards ahead. So he and Louis dragged the poles along the base of the ferry and stuck them out over the side, waiting to deflect them away from a collision. By the time the poles were in position, they'd halved the distance to the rock and Carter judged that if Louis's idea failed, the middle of the ferry would hit it.

'Wait until the last moment,' Louis urged, as another burst of gunfire sounded, this time louder but still no more accurate, 'before we decide whether it'll be easier to direct us to the left or the right.'

'Sure,' Carter said. He stared at the boulder and counted down the yards until the ends of the poles reached it. The poles were ten yards away when he detected they were going more towards the right and when that gap shortened to five yards he was sure.

'Right,' Louis said in confirmation, moving his pole a few feet to the side to get the angle right to deflect them. Then he kicked the other end until it was secure against the blocks that stopped the stage from rolling. Louis looked at Carter with his eyebrows raised, silently asking him whether he understood what to do.

'Understood,' Carter said. He flexed his arms preparing to follow Louis in jamming the pole in at the correct angle, but his motion let him look towards the left and to the riverside on which there were apparently no shooters.

He made a sudden decision and took a long pace to the left then jammed his pole out at an oblique angle to Louis's pole. Louis shot him a glance but Carter grabbed the other pole then placed it beside his own.

'What the . . . ?' Louis murmured, but Carter ignored him.

A moment later both poles collided with the boulder and drove back against the blocks before the stage wheel. They flexed then skittered across the base of the ferry until they knocked against the ferry's corner post where they held firm between the ferry and the rock.

Then slowly the ferry pivoted to the side, the poles working as Louis had planned and steering them away from the boulder, albeit on a different side from the one Louis had intended.

Within seconds the ends of the poles scraped away from the boulder then whipped back along the base of the ferry as the motion released their tension. But their brief contact had veered the ferry around ten yards to the left.

Carter looked at Louis, hoping he'd

see the reasoning behind his action without explanation. The two men were looking at each other when a slug punched into the base of the ferry two feet from Louis's foot and provided its own answer.

'Another boulder coming up,' Carter said, pointing ahead.

Louis swung round to look at the next protruding lump of rock, twenty yards on.

'And we steer to the left again, I suppose,' he said, 'and away from the gunfire?'

'Sure!' Carter didn't add the remainder of the explanation for his plan because he didn't know how Louis would react.

They completed the next manoeuvre proficiently after which the obstacles arrived quickly and the gunfire from the side grew in volume, even if none of it was as accurate as the shot that had narrowly missed Louis's foot.

After they'd steered around another four obstacles, always taking a route that took them to the left, they'd moved to within twenty yards of the Lonesome side of the river.

'We've got a problem,' Louis shouted over the roaring of the river. 'We're getting away from the gunfire, but we're getting too close to the other side.'

Carter placed his pole in position ready to deflect them to the left then looked at Louis.

'And the problem?'

'Kelley said to steer a straight course.'

'He did, and the one we're on is straight.' Carter smiled. 'Straight to the riverside.'

Louis shook his head. 'That ain't what he meant.'

Carter held out a hand for Louis to give him his pole. Louis bunched his jaw implying he wouldn't hand it over, but then he nodded and placed it beside Carter's. Again the poles hit the boulder and expertly steered the ferry away, and this time they ended up only ten yards from the side. It was close enough to swim, Carter decided, except another boulder was coming up and one more manoeuvre should be enough to push them out on to dry land.

He placed his pole in position, but then a hand slammed down on his shoulder.

'What in tarnation are you doing, man?' Kelley demanded behind him.

'I don't have to explain myself to you,' Carter murmured, shaking off the hand. He took the other pole from Louis and placed it beside his own.

'But we're already too near to the side. Move us out into the river.'

Carter judged they would reach the boulder in about twenty seconds. He glanced over his shoulder.

'And risk getting closer to that gunfire?'

'There are people on this side too who are after us.'

'Not so many,' Carter murmured. 'And I don't see them.'

They were almost on the boulder. He kicked his pole a foot to the side to get it to lie at the perfect angle, but then Kelley lunged for the pole. His grasping fingers brushed the wood before Carter tugged him away. Kelley retaliated by throwing Carter's hand off him, then knelt to grab the pole.

They were only feet away from the boulder and Carter launched himself at Kelley. He grabbed him around the shoulders and tumbled him away from the poles before he could move them. They rolled over each other, heading towards the edge of the ferry. When they came to a scrambling halt, the poles collided with the boulder.

The ferry lurched then pivoted round. Now powerless to affect their motion both men looked up to see the ferry slice through the water. Then, with a grinding of timbers, the ferry beached itself on the riverbank. The front of the ferry ploughed into the muddy side, scraping a long furrow before it came to a halt, mired deeply in the earth and foliage.

'You fool,' Kelley murmured, peering

down at him. 'Do you know what you've done with your gross insubordination?'

'You can't — ' Carter didn't get to complete the rest of his complaint when Kelley raised himself and swung a fist at him.

The blow came from close to and hit Carter's chin without much force, but it was enough to annoy him and with a great roar he threw Kelley away. Kelley rolled before coming to a halt on the edge of the ferry. Slowly, he got to his feet.

Carter heard movement behind him as presumably Annie emerged from the stage but he was beyond caring how this situation looked. He advanced on Kelley with a fist raised then launched a scything mow of a punch at Kelley's face, but with a skill and strength that belied his age, Kelley raised a forearm and deflected the blow. Then, with his other hand, he drove a short-armed jab into Carter's stomach that had him folding over and staggering away.

Kelley must have known exactly where to hit him because all strength fled from his limbs and he had to fight to regain his breath. Long moments passed before his senses returned and he was surprised to find himself kneeling. Kelley was standing over him. He took another moment to regain his breath then rocked back on his heels and stood, stepping backwards in the process.

'So,' Carter said, 'you did learn to fight in the military. Now I'll teach you a proper lesson.'

A part of his mind told him he shouldn't waste time on this squabble, but Kelley had annoyed him just once too often. He paced to the side to circle round Kelley, keeping his eyes locked on him as he awaited the first sign that he would make a move for him.

'Carter!' Annie shouted from behind him. 'Stop this.'

Carter ignored her, but Kelley then looked over Carter's shoulder and flinched. He advanced a pace and that was enough of an opening for Carter to move. He swung back his arm and launched a fist into Kelley's stomach. It connected with more force than Kelley had used and it made Kelley stagger back a pace then fall to one knee, but he didn't appear to be in the same incapacitated state as Carter had been.

Carter advanced on him, ready to hit him again, but Kelley raised a hand.

'Wait!' he said, then pointed.

Carter stayed his planned blow then swirled around to see that Annie was also pointing and looking over the side of the ferry. Louis was making his way off the ferry and, amidst the trees, Maverick was running away, having taken advantage of the distraction.

'Damn,' Carter murmured, sense finally defeating his sudden burst of anger. He reached down to give Kelley a hand, but Kelley shook his head.

'Just go after him, man.'

This time Carter did as ordered. He ran to the edge of the ferry and leapt on to dry land. His momentum made him spring forward and a foot caught in a root. He went tumbling to his knees in the soft earth.

He stayed on all fours, gathering his breath, then jumped to his feet and resumed chasing the prisoner. He was twenty yards behind Louis and Louis was the same distance behind Maverick, but after his exertions and his fight with Kelley Carter ran slowly and they widened the gap on him.

He slowed to a halt, irritated with himself for having squandered his energy on a pointless fight with Kelley. He looked around, considering the lie of the land to see if he could take another route and head Maverick off as, with a casual gesture, he patted his pocket, but the hand landed flat.

With his heart beating faster he rummaged in the pocket, but his first fears were in fact correct.

He'd lost the watch.

★　★　★

Buckley rolled twice before he slammed into the back wall of the jail cell.

He lay curled in a ball while Deputy Ford locked the cell door, then got to his feet. A single cot was in the bunk and he sat on it.

His cell was in a row of four with two unoccupied ones between himself and the only other prisoner. This man was considering him, but Buckley didn't feel like talking and instead watched Ford potter around the jailhouse.

As far as he could tell, Max had escaped. He was pleased about that, even if that did mean Ford would probably follow through with his threat to rough him up, although Buckley hoped he'd said that purely to scare him into revealing more details of his exploits. In that Buckley had no concerns as he had done nothing wrong and so surely before long the truth about his story would become apparent to even the most sceptical of men.

'What's your name?' The question came from the other prisoner and

Buckley saw no reason not to answer.

'Buckley,' he said turning to him, 'Buckley Sharpe.'

Even before he received a response, Buckley had worked out who his new companion was.

'And in case you don't know, I'm Usher Pullman.'

From the brief conversation he'd had in the saloon, Buckley had gathered that this man was a notorious outlaw who had controlled Lonesome, but he didn't look like trouble to Buckley. He was smartly dressed and relaxed as if he was in a hotel room rather than a cell behind the courtroom.

'Your trial's tomorrow, is it?' Buckley asked, after struggling to find anything to say.

'I believe that formality is then. And why did our deputy feel a need to bring you here?'

Buckley knew the name on the top of the list of potential witnesses against this man was Frank Doyle. But after Frank's recent actions, he found a need to share his annoyance with someone who presumably also felt aggrieved about Frank.

'Frank Doyle reckons I stole from him.'

'And did you?'

'Does it matter? The law took his side.'

'Perhaps I could have a word with Ford later.' Usher smiled.

'Perhaps,' Buckley murmured, then to effectively end a conversation that was making him feel uncomfortable despite the friendly comments he lay on his back on the cot and contemplated the ceiling.

Time passed slowly in the cell letting Buckley repeatedly run through the events of the last few hours, trying to understand them. He'd gathered that Frank hadn't believed their story and that they'd been victims of mistaken identity, but what exactly he thought them guilty of doing, he didn't know.

The rectangle of light cast by the afternoon sun through the grill in the back wall had drifted a few feet closer to him when he heard voices in the office outside. Deputy Ford was questioning a new arrival and, from the frequent mentioning of his name and Max's along with the lawman's irritated tone, he gathered that the man who'd pursued Max hadn't found him.

When Ford paced over to the cell to consider him, Buckley sat up.

'What you looking so pleased about?' Ford muttered, peering at him through the bars.

'Just hoping you've checked out my story and I can go free.'

'You ain't going nowhere.' Ford grunted an order to the other man to stay by the main door then opened the cell door. He paced inside to stand over Buckley. 'And that means we can start at the beginning again.'

'What can I say? We found this watch. We returned it to Frank Doyle. There ain't no more to it than that.'

Ford snorted at the unlikelihood of this being true, then lunged down and grabbed Buckley's collar. He hoisted him to his feet then dragged him higher so that Buckley had to stand on tiptoes. Then he walked him over to the back wall and threw him against it. He placed his face up close to Buckley's.

'You picked the wrong day to steal and the wrong people to steal from.'

Over in the other cell Usher coughed, his slight noise grabbing Ford's attention.

'What did he say he stole off Frank Doyle?' he asked.

'This watch.'

Usher raised his eyebrows. 'Then is it necessary to treat him so roughly?'

'It sure is, because it leaves a whole lot of questions unanswered.'

Ford released his grip slightly, letting Buckley slide down the wall and get his footing. Ford turned towards Usher, but then swung back and hammered a bunched fist deep into Buckley's guts making him double over in pain. He retched and that sent another bolt of pain lancing through his stomach. He staggered forward a pace and retched again, but before he could vomit, hands slapped down on his back and grabbed his jacket. Then Ford ran him forward and threw him into the bars.

Buckley managed to swing himself to the side so that a shoulder and not his head collided with the bars but he still hit them with a jarring thud, then slid down to the floor where he lay. Without control of his body he vomited, the dinner he'd enjoyed with Frank spouting out on to the cell floor. Spasm after spasm racked his body.

He was aware that Ford and Usher were talking, but he couldn't hear what they were saying over the sounds of his own retching. At last the spasms stopped, but he had no respite when Ford grabbed his hair and yanked his head up.

'Finished?' he asked, mockingly.

'I . . . I don't know what you want me to say.'

'Where I can find your associate would be a start.'

'I don't know. He — ' Buckley didn't get to finish his answer as a slap to the cheek rocked his head to the side.

'Who did you steal that watch off?'

'We didn't — ' Another slap to the cheek rocked his head to the side, but this time Buckley persisted with trying to answer. 'We didn't. We just found it. We'd returned it to Frank when you arrested us.'

Ford swung his hand back ready to hit Buckley again and Buckley closed his eyes, but the blow didn't come. He opened his eyes to see the hand held suspended. Ford was nodding approvingly.

'Now I'm starting to see what might have happened here. Carry on.'

'We found this crate filled with stuff in the river and — ' The hand bunched into a fist then crashed into Buckley's nose. Pain exploded across Buckley's face as he fell on his back.

'You never said you stole more than that watch!' Ford shouted, but Buckley was beyond caring. Blood was pouring down his face and the pain was so severe he was finding it hard to breathe. Even when Ford yanked him up and shouted his question in his face, Buckley still lolled.

Then Ford released his grip and Buckley fell to the floor. He lay and gingerly felt his nose, deciding it wasn't broken. As the pain subsided, he heard two people talking close by and at first he presumed they were Ford and Usher Pullman.

'Frank reckoned he stole it,' Ford said.

'But that doesn't seem likely,' the other man said, his voice being deeper than Usher's was.

'Perhaps not.'

'Then beating him isn't the answer.'

'He lied and I was just trying to get an honest answer, bearing in mind how important this is.'

'You should still have waited for me to return.'

This comment made Buckley open his eyes and look up. Another man with a star was in his cell — Sheriff David Blake, he presumed.

'I'm sorry,' Ford said, 'but at least I found out he knows where the crate is.'

Blake gripped Ford's shoulders while grinning in delight, then hunkered down beside Buckley.

'You all right, son?' he asked.

'I guess,' Buckley murmured, 'but I'm innocent. I didn't steal nothing and I was just trying to do what was right. I was . . .'

Blake raised a hand, silencing Buckley's babbling.

'I understand. Deputy Ford can get a little zealous in his pursuit of the truth sometimes, but this is important.' Blake looked over towards Usher Pullman then raised his voice. 'It's essential I have that crate. Where is it?'

'I can take you to it,' Buckley murmured in relief.

Blake slapped Buckley on the back then hoisted him to his feet.

'I'll take him,' Deputy Ford said.

'No,' Blake said. 'You stay here. I

don't want him getting questioned again.'

Ford blocked Blake's path, his flared eyes suggesting he was about to argue, but then he sighed and stood to the side.

'You're the boss,' he said without conviction.

'I am, and never forget again that I never tolerate mistreatment of my prisoners. Even the likes of Usher Pullman.' Carted softened his expression. 'But you did good in bringing this one in. It's changed everything.'

Blake escorted Buckley out of the cell then released him to walk on his own. He said nothing more as they headed to the main door. Outside Blake passed Buckley a kerchief for his nose, then directed him to mount up.

After his beating Buckley was still stunned but he did as he'd been told. When he was sitting up in the saddle and moving, the fresh air and the feeling that his ordeal was at an end enlivened his senses.

'I'm no outlaw,' he said when they reached the edge of town. He removed the kerchief to see there wasn't any fresh blood.

'I gathered that,' Blake said lightly. 'Just tell me what happened.'

So Buckley did. Deputy Ford might have been a nightmare of a lawman, but he judged that this man was different and he enjoyed unburdening himself of his woeful tale. He left nothing out, including how he and Max had almost kept the valuables they'd found. Although Blake grunted at this revelation, Buckley reckoned the truth was the only way he could end this situation and move on.

'And so we buried the crate near to where we found it,' Buckley said, finishing off the part of his tale that he understood.

He took a deep breath. The next part would be difficult to explain as he didn't know why Frank hadn't believed him or why Ford had reacted so violently, but Blake wasn't interested in what happened next.

'And you'll take me to this crate with no tricks?' he said.

'Sure,' Buckley said. 'Like I said, we're no outlaws.'

'I'm pleased to hear it, because this sure is important.'

'Why? I've gathered there's a trial tomorrow. Is it connected to that?'

Blake snorted. 'Connected? It is the trial. Every scrap of evidence, every witness statement, every journal I ever kept of Usher's activities is in that crate.'

'And someone stole them?'

'*Someone* did. Two nights ago they broke into the sheriff's office and bundled it away. I'm guessing Frank's watch and those other valuables you found are effectively being held for ransom. But without those journals it'll be hard to prove the case against Usher. Now what Deputy Ford did to you wasn't something I support, but I hope you can see why he showed so much zeal. That crate is vital to Lonesome's well-being.'

Buckley rubbed his ribs ruefully, trying to convince himself that his painful bruises were for the best.

For the next hour they rode on towards the river without speaking other than to discuss the occasional change of direction. Their route took them past Frank Doyle's ranch house and Buckley couldn't help but look at it and sneer, but after they'd passed it a worrying thought hit him.

As far as he knew, Max had escaped from his pursuer. The last Buckley had seen of him Max had been galloping away on a course parallel to the river, but that was many hours ago. After escaping he would have faced the decision of what he did next and one possibility was that he could have returned to the crate.

Buckley didn't like to speculate on what he'd do then. Although bearing in mind Max's lack of enthusiasm for their actions today, it was possible he'd taken the crate's contents for himself then hightailed it away from town, leaving

Buckley to face the consequences alone.

He kept those thoughts to himself, but they still ensured that when they entered the forest bordering the river he was pensive with a grim sense of foreboding overcoming him.

That foreboding increased when he smelt smoke. He glanced at Sheriff Blake to see that he was sniffing while looking around.

'How much further?' Blake asked.

Buckley listened to the roaring of the river gushing by ahead.

'Around a hundred yards.'

'Did you light a camp-fire?'

'We did, but that was last night and we smothered it. It shouldn't be still smoking. It must be someone else's.'

'Such as your friend Max's?'

Buckley admitted this was the case and although that meant Max would either still be here or close by, that possibility did nothing to cheer him. When he saw the first slices of the river through the trees, he also saw tendrils of smoke spreading out through the trees in a thin layer. Later the smell of cooked meat mingled with the smoke.

After another fifty yards, the smoke had grown denser and was swirling around them. They looked around for its source. Blake was the first to spot something. He raised a hand to point out the direction, then flinched back in the saddle and swung round to Buckley. 'Stay here,' he said. He dismounted and headed towards a clump of trees.

Buckley dismounted and watched him head off, assuming he'd seen Max and wanted to approach him alone. Then he saw that he was only partly correct. He stared aghast at the sight that had alerted the lawman then moved on to follow him, moving his feet forward in a stunned and shocked state. Blake glanced back when he heard Buckley following him and shook his head, but still he advanced.

Then Buckley's mind caught up with what his eyes were seeing and he fell to his knees to retch on the ground. After his beating in the cell he had nothing left to bring up, but he dry-retched several times before he could control himself. Then he staggered to his feet and in a dreamlike state joined the lawman.

'Is it him?' Blake asked.

Buckley stared up at the body, still unsure, but there was no mistaking the face, despite everything.

'Yeah,' he croaked. 'That's Max.'

Blake edged closer to the dangling body to investigate further. Max had been suspended from a tree over the hole in which they'd buried the crate this morning. Whoever had killed him had started a fire in the hole and roasted Max, presumably while still alive.

Blake peered into the hole then kicked the burnt debris aside.

'And it's worse,' he said, kneeling to finger the ashes. 'They've burnt my journals too.'

'Then why do that to him?'

'I guess they forced him to talk

before he died to find out if there was anything more to find.'

'And is there?'

'No. All the evidence was in that crate.' Blake rocked back on his heels, shaking his head. 'With it destroyed it'll be nearly impossible to prove Usher Pullman's guilt.'

'There's still you. You can speak up.'

'I'll have to hope that's enough.' Blake offered a thin smile. 'But everything else is going wrong. A key witness was supposed to be on the stage yesterday, but the stage never arrived. I guess they headed that off too.'

'And who are *they*?'

'It's a long story.' Blake blew out his cheeks then pointed up at the body. 'Come on. Let's cut him down.'

Blake moved towards the tree but then stumbled backwards, a gunshot sounding a moment later. Buckley saw the neat red hole exploding in the centre of Blake's chest before he hit the ground.

He bent to help him, but then a

second shot tore into Blake's sprawled form, making him jerk backwards, although from Blake's minimal reaction Buckley presumed the lawman had been killed instantly.

Buckley looked around for the shooter until he saw a man emerge through the trees from the direction of the river. He was huge and strode purposefully towards him. But he kept his gun lowered.

One glance at Max's dangling body convinced Buckley that if this man wasn't going to kill him, then it sure wasn't good news.

8

'Get up, Carter,' Kelley demanded, standing over him. 'We're moving out.'

'You can wait,' Carter grumbled while looking at the earth between his feet then crawling on for another shuffled foot.

Five minutes earlier Louis had caught the fleeing prisoner and dragged him back to the beached ferry, but Carter had little interest in his success, not when the watch was missing. He assumed it'd fallen from his pocket when he'd leapt off the ferry. But although he'd found where he'd landed, there were so many roots and so much muddy earth that the small item could easily have sunk from view and so remain unseen even if his fingers were inches away from it.

'We can't,' Kelley said. 'After you violated my orders and beached us here we must leave now.'

'Then go! I'll catch up with you.'

'Splitting up our forces is not an option.'

'Quit the military strategy. I'll make my own decisions.'

Kelley considered him, shaking his head and muttering to himself, but with Carter not looking up, he turned on his heel and joined the others.

'We have a situation,' he announced. 'I don't have the authority to order an insubordinate man to act and I'm not risking another unseemly scene. So for the good of the outfit, someone must make him see sense.'

Carter wasn't surprised when Annie came over. By now he had searched for five feet around the point where he'd landed when he'd jumped off the ferry and he was considering the uncomfortable thought that maybe he'd lost it earlier. He tried to think back to the last time he was sure he had it, but couldn't drag up an image of that time, so he looked up and provided an attempt at a disarming smile.

'I know how important that watch is to you,' she said then knelt and peered around at the surrounding ground. 'I'll stay and help you find it, no matter what Kelley orders me to do.'

'There's no need for you to stay. I'll join you later.'

'I'm not leaving you,' she said with a stern tone that confirmed she was determined to counter any objection he might raise.

Carter stood and looked down at her as she painstakingly inched forward examining every bit of the ground before her. He wondered whether she was persuading him to move on with a clever tactic. Nothing anyone said would make him leave the watch behind, but he didn't want to risk her life if she aimed to stay.

'Don't waste your time with me. You saw the way I attacked Kelley.'

'As you know you did wrong, there's hope for you. The moment we've found the watch, I'm sure you'll apologize.'

Carter wasn't sure about that, but he was sure about one thing.

'We're leaving,' he said.

She looked up, her eyes bright. 'You're leaving because of me?'

He gulped. '*All* of you, and anyhow this stage ain't going nowhere. Unless someone finds it and moves it on soon, I can easily find this spot again later when I know you're all safe.'

Although every pace away took a concentrated effort, he headed over to Major Kelley and Louis. Annie stayed on her knees for a few moments then stood, batted the dirt from her skirt and followed. As she joined him, her knitted brow and fixed smile provided an unfathomable expression, being a mixture of triumph for having proved something and irritation at having failed to achieve something else.

But Carter was too preoccupied to spend time working out what was worrying her. For the last five years that watch and what it represented had been on his mind. Now, within a few miles of his destination, he had lost it and he couldn't shake the feeling he wouldn't see it again.

Admittedly for his purpose he didn't actually need it, but he'd convinced himself that this sign of good faith might go a small way towards alleviating the suffering he'd caused.

'We will now follow my orders without further question,' Kelley announced. 'As Carter has seen fit to strand us here rather than letting us go to Brown's Crossing where we could find horses and reinforcements, we must move on immediately.'

Carter glared at Kelley, but gritted his teeth to avoid retorting. They set off, walking away from the river towards Lonesome.

Kelley stayed at the back with Louis leading. As Louis had recaptured Maverick, Kelley ordered him to guard the prisoner, leaving Annie and Carter to walk in single file in the middle.

Under Louis's directions, they maintained a steady pace, picking a route where the trees were sparse. Kelley gave them permission not to try to disguise their passage as he figured that Spike's men wouldn't slow themselves by venturing into the forest.

After an hour Carter reckoned they'd covered over two miles. If his hazy recollection of the terrain was correct, that meant they would soon emerge from the trees.

Kelley instructed them to rest briefly, during which time nobody spoke, but the rest let Carter bring his brooding as to why Kelley had annoyed him so much to a conclusion. The closeness to completing his journey was making him edgy, he decided. Worse, the bizarre fact that he had met Spike Talbot before and what that meant was making his forthcoming encounter with Frank Doyle even more uncertain.

He also decided that his desire to reach the riverside had more to do with getting that encounter over with quickly than whether it was best for the group. So, having accepted that he'd acted selfishly, he resolved to avoid squabbling with Kelley again, although he doubted he could bring himself to apologize.

When they resumed their journey Annie walked beside him and Carter felt relaxed enough to offer her a smile.

'You're still not reconciled to leaving that watch behind,' she said, 'are you?'

'It's hard,' Carter said, accepting his smile was perhaps not as wide and pleasant as he'd hoped. 'I've had it for some time.'

She didn't respond for several minutes.

'We must hope that Frank Doyle will understand,' she said, after giving the matter some thought, lowering her voice she added, 'He'll know you to be a good man and that you tried.'

'I'm sure he will.'

'Then why are you looking so depressed?'

'I could ask you the same question?'

She laughed. 'You're not very good at changing the subject.'

'Perhaps I'm not, but I do know I annoyed you with something I said back by the river, except I don't know what it was.'

'If you don't know, there's no point me telling you, is there?'

'And I sure don't know what that means.'

'And *that* is the problem.' She speeded to hurry on ahead, leaving Carter trailing in her wake and feeling even more confused.

He hurried after her. 'Wait!'

She ignored him and kept her gaze set forward forcing him to jump over deadfall and fight past dangling branches to draw alongside her. He kept looking at her until she looked at him.

'We need to keep moving,' she said, 'so save your breath.'

'I'm worried about you.' He took a deep breath then placed a hand on her arm to slow her down. 'You seem mighty concerned about me having lost that watch, as if that's important to you.'

'It's not the watch.' She looked at

178

him with her eyebrows raised as if that answered his question before continuing. 'If it's important to you, it is to me. I was interested in your business because as we're both going to Lonesome, it . . . it might help me to understand what kind of man you are.'

'And why . . . ?' Carter blew out his cheeks and tipped back his hat as he finally worked out what she meant, or at least what he thought she meant. 'Believe me. You don't want to know me better.'

'And what does that mean?' she demanded, stomping to a halt and slamming her hands on her hips.

'It means you're a woman any man would be proud to . . . to have on his arm, but it doesn't work the other way round.'

She cocked her head to one side. 'I've spent four days travelling with you and I've seen you're a decent and brave man. Your argument with Kelley didn't show you at your best, but I can understand how he annoyed you, so I can't see how you can judge yourself not to be a good man.'

'You don't know me and what I'm capable of.'

'And that watch shows up your bad side, is that what's on your mind?'

He sighed as she got uncomfortably close to the truth. He touched her arm to signify Louis was getting ahead of them and they needed to move on.

'Come on,' he said.

She didn't move immediately then followed, shaking her head.

'You really are terrible at changing the subject,' she said.

They didn't speak again as they settled down to following Louis through the trees. But Carter detected that this time it was a companionable silence after their somewhat uncomfortable conversation had clarified some matters, even if it had confused him about others.

Fifteen minutes of tramping through the undergrowth later Carter saw a lightening in the canopy ahead and after another ten minutes they reached the tree line. Kelley called for them to rest.

Open plains stretched ahead. Carter didn't recognize the place where they'd emerged, so he was unsure how long it'd take them to reach Lonesome, but when they'd got their breath back, Louis relayed the bad news.

He pointed. 'Lonesome is twenty miles that way.'

'Twenty?' Annie murmured, giving a significant look at her frayed boots that were already showing they hadn't been designed for walking for any great distance.

'I'm afraid so,' Louis said. 'But if we're lucky we might meet someone who can take us there.'

Carter snorted. 'I reckon meeting someone will be bad luck.'

Louis acknowledged this view with a rueful smile.

'I don't agree,' Kelley said, Carter's comment encouraging him to talk for the first time since they'd left the stage. 'We will set off on a straight course just as soon as we're rested.'

Carter sighed, steeling himself for what would probably be another fruitless argument with Kelley, but Annie spoke up first.

'We could wait here until dark,' she said, making her view known for the first time, although her steady rubbing of her feet suggested she was more tired than supporting Carter.

'If anyone has picked up our trail they'll catch up with us,' Kelley said, 'and then we'll face an attack in the dark. We might even be late for the trial.'

'Or miss Lonesome in the dark,' Louis said.

The debate meandered on, but Carter didn't join in as the realization had dawned on him of what they had to do next. The problem of how he would fulfil both of his duties today was something he hadn't been able to reconcile, until now.

He ran his gaze across the plains, looking for landmarks and although he couldn't see any, he knew the general direction of Frank Doyle's ranch house. He waited until everyone had had their say and Kelley was about to make what would probably be another disastrous decision. Then he stood up.

'Major Kelley,' he said, 'I have another option for you to consider. It's one that'll let us rest and get you to Lonesome safely.'

'I am not interested in your plan.' Kelley said, sneering. 'I have already decided.'

Annie looked at Carter with her eyes narrowed and her head cocked to one side, perhaps because she'd noticed his carefully chosen words. She spoke up before Kelley could present his decision.

'Will you consider my suggestion, Major Kelley?' she asked.

'Of course,' Kelley said, turning to her.

'We can go to a ranch near here.' She pointed, vaguely outlining the direction they could take. 'One owned by a man called Frank Doyle.'

* ★ ★ ★

Buckley hurtled through the trees, unmindful of the branches slashing his face and not caring where his feet landed. He stumbled frequently, but quickly got to his feet and carried on. All that mattered was getting away from Sheriff Blake's killer and avoiding the same fate as had befallen Max.

He maintained a frantic meandering course but one that was broadly parallel with the water and heading downriver. When he reached a clearer stretch of ground, he looked back. He didn't see any sign of a pursuer, but he didn't take any chances and ran on into the trees again.

Presently he saw a black object looming ahead, large and incongruous in the forest. He was minded to keep on running past it, thinking anything he came across out here would probably be bad news, but when he was level with the object, he saw that it was a stagecoach.

This was such a bizarre sight standing beside the river in the depths of the forest that he temporarily forgot his terrible situation and slowed to look at it. He hadn't been mistaken. The stage was on what appeared to be a raft and had washed up on the side of river.

'Odd things sure are washing up here these days,' Buckley murmured to himself. Then he remembered the last conversation he'd had with Sheriff Blake about him waiting for someone to arrive on the stage. That thought made him veer away and hurry down to the river.

He paced out on to the wooden raft then swirled round to look over his shoulder, realizing he'd probably made a fatal mistake. The man who had killed the lawman could be close; standing here he was clearly visible.

He made an instant decision to hide in the stage. He ran around the side of the stage to put himself out of view from the forest, then moved to climb up inside.

A flash of silver caught his eye and stopped him.

He looked down. Trapped beneath the back wheel of the stage was a silver watch. It appeared to be identical to the one he'd returned to Frank Doyle. Bemused now, Buckley reached down for the watch and turned it over. There was an inscription and again it was Frank Doyle's, this time dedicating the watch to Victoria, his daughter.

'What the . . . ?' Buckley murmured, straightening up. His neck pushed backwards into the cold end of a gun barrel. He flinched away from it but a hand clamped over his mouth and dragged him back.

'Buckley Sharpe again,' a familiar voice grunted in his ear before removing the hand. 'Now what are you doing here?'

'I was hiding. This man killed Max and then Sheriff Blake and he's after me. He could be here any minute.'

'Now that's an unlikely story.' Ford jabbed the gun barrel into his temple. 'I reckon the truth is you killed them after they uncovered your secret plan.'

Instead of directing Buckley into the stage, he pushed him forward and around it. With the gun pressing against his temple, Buckley didn't reckon he had any choice but to obey. When they reached the other side, he saw movement through the trees.

'I know you don't trust me,' he said, trying to convey the urgency of the situation by speaking quickly, 'but you have to now. That man is coming here and he's a brutal killer.'

'Can't see no reason why I should believe you after all the lies you've told.'

The movement had now resolved itself into the form of the man who had killed Sheriff Blake and presumably Max. He was walking down to the river, a gun drawn but held low.

'Do something,' Buckley urged, 'while there's still time.'

'Do what exactly? That man is Spike Talbot and he don't take kindly to anyone who stands in his way.'

The man, Spike, was now ten yards away and his angry gaze had picked out Buckley.

'You're a lawman. You have to try. You can't let him take me.'

Ford chuckled. 'I've got good news for you there and some that ain't quite so good. The good news is — I am a lawman and a lawman has to save you. The trouble is, I ain't a lawman like Sheriff Blake and if Spike wants to tear you apart and eat you alive, I'll just sit down and watch.'

Spike stomped to a halt. He stood before the stage, looking Buckley up and down. His cold, cruel gaze made Buckley's bowels churn with the terrible memory of Max's fate and the certainty that Ford wasn't joking.

'Who is he?' Spike muttered.

'Just some idiot who got in the way,' Ford said. 'You want him or should I throw him in the river?'

'Ain't got time to waste.' Spike wrung out an end of his jacket, spilling water on the ground. 'I've spent too much time in that river already. Get rid of him. Then we've got one last loose end to tie up.'

'The stage?'

'Sure.'

Ford nodded then ground the gun more tightly against Buckley's temple, his hand flexing as he prepared to fire.

'Wait!' Buckley screeched.

'Why?' Ford murmured.

Buckley could think of nothing to say that would persuade Ford not to kill him, but as he shifted his stance, he felt the cold weight in his left hand and the germ of an idea came to him. But the few seconds that had passed since Ford's question weighed heavily on him and Spike's eyes were narrowing with anger.

'He ain't got nothing,' Spike grunted, 'but maybe we do have enough time to have some fun first.'

Spike advanced on him, as Buckley forced his mind to connect facts he felt sure he ought to be able to understand. Everything he'd learnt recently whirled through his mind: the evidence to convict Usher Pullman, the stage carrying a key witness, Spike and Deputy Ford being in league to help Usher, two watches with Frank Doyle's inscription, Max's terrible death . . .

'I know how you can tie up that last loose end,' he said.

'You?' Ford snorted. 'You weren't convincing as a thief and you sure ain't convincing as someone who knows how to help us.'

'But I am. I read those journals in the crate. I know what's going on here as much as anyone does.'

Spike snorted. 'Now that's another good reason to kill you.'

'It ain't!' Buckley blurted. 'I'm more useful to you alive. I could work for Usher too and I can start now.'

'Say your piece,' Ford muttered in his ear, 'then I'll stand aside and let Spike slice you up.'

Buckley took a deep breath and clutched the watch tightly.

'You're after someone who was on

this stage,' he said, 'and I know where he's gone.'

Ford and Spike looked at each other.

'You,' Spike said, 'have just bought yourself a few more hours before we have to kill you.'

9

It'd been five years since Carter had left
Frank Doyle's ranch house and aside
from being in a more run-down state
than he remembered, it hadn't changed
much. Not that his recollection of that
time was strong, seeing as how he'd left
in the middle of the night, at a gallop,
and with Frank's ranch hands in
pursuit.

Everyone was quiet with even Kelley
being content to let Louis direct them
without unnecessary comment, although
it was probable he was as tired as everyone else was. But when they approached
the ranch gates, Carter felt a need to
break the silence and talk to Annie for
what would probably be the last time.

'How did you know Frank was a
rancher?' he said.

'I lived in Lonesome as a child. I
remember Frank Doyle, vaguely. My

cousin still lives here. In fact that's why I've come. To make a fresh start with her.' She raised her eyebrows. 'And will I find out soon why you've come to Lonesome?'

Carter could think of nothing to say to that other than to nod. They walked through the ranch gates without anyone noticing them, then made their way to the door. Carter looked at the windows. When he saw someone move inside, he stopped.

'You'll be safe here,' he said, turning to the others, 'but I'll go in first. Do nothing to interfere no matter what happens then.'

'You will not order us,' Kelley said. 'I will decide — '

'Enough!' Carter roared, filling that one word with all his pent-up rage. The sound echoed off the surrounding buildings and contained sufficient venom to make Kelley take a step backwards.

Behind him he heard the ranch door open and so he turned away from his current problem to face up to the questions he'd avoided for the last five years.

Victoria Doyle stood in the doorway, looking at the arrivals with her eyebrows raised in an enquiring manner, but that interest died when her gaze fell on Carter. She stared at him, her blank expression registering the fact that for several moments she was unable to work out who he was. Not that Carter could blame her. Nobody would expect him to return.

Then she registered the truth and she staggered backwards a pace, a hand coming up to her neck. She backed away another pace to stumble into the door then, as if that jolt had helped to break her out of her shocked state, she ran off into the house calling out for her father.

'That woman appeared to recognize you,' Kelley said.

'She sure did,' Louis said. 'Do you usually have that effect on women?'

Carter moved round to look at them, his narrow-eyed stare conveying that it wasn't appropriate to find this situation amusing.

'Louis, Kelley, Annie,' he said, 'with Frank Doyle's help you can head to Lonesome with Maverick. But I won't be taking part in that final leg of your journey. I did something terrible here five years ago and no matter how the man who comes through that door reacts, take no part in this.'

'We will,' Annie said with determination.

Carter took a long step to the side to position himself away from her, then removed his gun from its holster. He held it at arm's length, dangling on a finger, and waited.

He didn't have to wait long. Frank Doyle's voice echoed inside the building interspersed with Victoria's. He couldn't hear what they were saying but knew what they were discussing. Moments later Frank stormed into the doorway. His gaze centred in on Carter.

'Victoria,' he said, darting back from the door, 'get my rifle. Then stay away.'

Retreating footfalls sounded as Annie swung round to look at Carter.

'What's happening?' she demanded, concern contorting her face.

'Speak,' Kelley said when Carter didn't reply. 'You must keep me informed of all developments.'

'I already have,' Carter said. 'You will be safe here. Go to Lonesome. Do nothing to help me. There is nothing more to say.'

Annie hurried over to stand before him.

'But that man sounds as if he plans to shoot you,' she said.

'He sure does.'

Annie shot a glance at Kelley, who again demanded that Carter explain himself, then another at Louis, who merely shrugged. She even looked at Maverick, although he just looked at Carter with the hint of a smile on his lips.

She stomped a foot in irritation, turned on her heel and ran towards the house.

'Stop,' Carter shouted, but he was already too late. She barrelled through the doorway just as Frank Doyle emerged.

As expected, Frank held a rifle. He quickly swung it towards Carter then flinched away as Annie ran into him and pushed him backwards. She moved to tear the rifle from his grip, forcing Frank to swing it away from her. Then they both disappeared into the building.

'This is just plain wrong,' Carter muttered, shooting the others an aggrieved look that demanded they stay back. Then he ran to the house.

He holstered his gun as he hurried inside, to be greeted with the sight of Annie still lunging for the rifle while Frank repeatedly backed away from her and tried to yank it away from her grasp. Victoria was further down the hall and she was the first to see Carter arrive.

'Watch out, Pa!' she shouted. 'It's Carter.'

Frank grunted with rage and barged

Annie away, but as she fell backwards she clawed out a hand and grabbed his left arm. This stopped her from falling and almost dragged Frank down on top of her.

'Get away,' Frank snapped, struggling to extricate himself from her determined grip.

'There's no need to panic,' Carter said, raising his arms. 'I'm here to give myself up.'

'More lies,' Frank muttered as he wrested his arm free and shoved Annie to the floor. As she fell to land on her back, he took a long step to the side, raised the rifle, and sighted Carter.

With a calm settling of his stance, Carter looked at Frank as he had promised he would do if his return were to go as badly as he'd expected it to. The calm moment lasted for only brief seconds before Annie did the only thing she could do. She slid herself along the floor and grabbed Frank's leg. Frank tried to tear his leg away and his motion made the rifle waver away from its steady aim. As he again struggled to aim at Carter, Kelley came through the door.

'I am Major Pilgrim Kelley,' he said with his usual imperious tone, 'and you will not shoot that man.'

Although Carter expected his colleague's unwelcome intervention to make Frank even more determined to kill him quickly, he was surprised to see Frank twitch, then raise the rifle high.

'You brought him here?' he said.

Annie caught his change in tone to a more conciliatory one and released his leg.

'He didn't,' she said as she stood up. 'Carter came here of his own volition.'

Frank sneered but continued to look at Kelley.

'Is that true?' Frank asked.

As Kelley nodded, Carter recalled that as a younger man Frank had ridden with the cavalry and perhaps some deference to military authority had remained with him. Not that he particularly liked the idea of having his life saved by Kelley, again.

Frank then swung round to look at Carter and the anger that had burned in his eyes had faded, a tired and perhaps sad sheen replacing it.

'Why?'

Victoria had asked the question but Frank nodded as if that one word summed up everything he wanted to say.

Carter had prepared several speeches over the years to cover all the possible outcomes when he returned, but he settled for stating the truth.

'I've come to apologize,' he said, 'and to receive justice.'

'I don't want your apology,' Frank said, 'but I will see you get justice.'

Frank started to turn away but Carter coughed.

'There's one more thing. I did have Victoria's watch, but I lost it earlier today. I know where it is and you should get it back soon.'

'We lost that five years ago. We can never have it back.' Frank turned to Kelley. 'Thank you for helping to get him here. Please stay and enjoy my hospitality. Victoria will tend to your needs shortly, but you will have to guard him. I cannot bear to be in his company.'

With that comment he headed over to Victoria, put an arm around her shoulders and led her away down the hall. A door slammed some distance away.

While Annie and Kelley looked at Carter, clearly hoping he would explain what had happened, Louis led Maverick inside.

Nobody spoke and after the uncomfortable silence had dragged on for several minutes Victoria returned and bustled them through to a room where they could sit and relax. She promised to return soon with food and drink. She didn't meet Carter's eye, but she did look at Maverick and especially his chains with surprise. Then she hurried away, presumably to tell Frank that the situation was more complicated than he knew.

After the tense incident none of them sat close to Carter, even when they ate their meal.

What passed for darkness in midsummer had fallen by the time everyone felt rejuvenated although that only encouraged them to become restless. Louis was the first to voice his concern after which everyone but Carter debated what they should do next. Kelley decided he would seek out Frank, leaving Louis in charge of Maverick.

When Kelley had left the room, Annie sat beside Carter. At last she asked the question he'd expected someone to ask him for the last two hours.

'Why did Frank try to kill you?'

'I shot and killed Samuel Doyle, his son,' Carter said. 'There's nothing more to it than that.'

Her only reaction was a steady shaking of the head.

'You're a good man. I can't believe you're the cold-blooded killer Frank appears to think you are and that you're claiming to be.'

'Then I guess there is more to it than that, but anything else I could say will sound like excuses and I didn't come here to make those.'

'Then tell me what happened and if it sounds like an excuse I'll tell you so before you explain it to Frank.'

Carter didn't respond immediately. He had always intended that the only person he would talk to would be Frank. But her offer made sense, especially as Frank didn't appear to want to hear what he'd come to say.

He leaned forward in the chair and hunched over to look at his hands to avoid looking at her as he spoke.

'Five years ago I stopped in Lonesome looking for work. Frank employed me for a month and I got friendly with Samuel . . . and with Victoria, but in different ways.'

'I can imagine,' she said, her tone being more terse than after his revelation that he'd killed Frank's son. 'I saw the way she looked at you.'

Carter hadn't seen that. 'She was

good for me, but Samuel wasn't. He was getting involved in things he shouldn't. He'd stolen various things and needed to convert them into money, but with everyone knowing him he couldn't do it, so he asked me to help.'

Carter sighed and the pause let Annie speak.

'You refused?'

'Nope. Like I told you, I've done things I ain't proud of. I was eager to earn money, no matter where it came from. I found people who'd give me dollars for his stolen goods.'

'I find this hard to believe.'

From the corner of his eye Carter noted she was looking at him with disgust curling her lip and her disapproval made him squirm on his chair.

'I'm just telling you the truth. I didn't intend our dealings to last long as I was to move on, but I hadn't planned on getting real friendly with Victoria. At the end of the month I had a problem.'

'And you moved on and left her?'

'It'd been better for everyone if I had, but I stayed and got a job in town. I resolved to do things the right way from then on, but Samuel had other ideas. He'd got himself involved with ... with this other man and they'd concocted a plan that moved on from petty theft to intimidation. Samuel wanted my help.' Carter glanced at her to see if she'd worked out who this other man was, but she was still staring at him agog in surprise at his revelations. 'I only met that man once, but I now know he was Spike Talbot.'

'I believe you.'

'I refused Samuel's offer. So he blackmailed me, saying if I didn't help him he'd tell Victoria what I'd done. I couldn't risk that, so I agreed to meet him. I tried to explain that I wanted to move on. He refused. We argued. We fought. I killed him.'

She narrowed her eyes, shaking her head.

'It sounds as if you had an honest motive.'

'You're being too fair. I didn't. I was angry. You saw how I have a temper. I couldn't let him . . . I've been over this in my mind many times, but I can't get away from the fact it wasn't an accident. I intended to kill him to stop him talking to Victoria.'

'And the watch?'

'He'd stolen that to sell, so I took it and everything else he had to make it look like a robbery if anyone found the body. Then I bundled his body into the river and went back with my business. I even joined in the search for him.'

She gulped. 'That's terrible.'

'I know. I tried to comfort Victoria through a distressing time, but every time I looked at her I remembered what I'd done and I couldn't live with that. After a week I told her we couldn't be together and I'd decided to move on.'

'At least you had the decency to do that.'

'She didn't think so. She was distraught. I babbled a story and accidentally revealed more than I

206

should have. She worked out I was lying and accused me of being behind his disappearance. I panicked and ran, with Frank and every ranch hand in pursuit.'

'And then?'

'Then I tried to forget what I'd done, but I couldn't. So I finally decided I had to come back and face the truth, even if part of that truth is that Samuel wasn't the saint his father reckons he was.' He shrugged. 'I guess now I'm here I realize that most of what's gone wrong in Lonesome started from the moment he associated himself with Spike Talbot.'

'Then I'm glad we talked about this first because that's the part Frank won't want to hear.'

'But I have,' a voice said from the hall outside. The door swung open to reveal Frank with Victoria standing behind him. Kelley was loitering further down the corridor.

'I didn't mean you to hear that,' Carter said, turning to the door. 'I came to tell you the truth.'

'And is that the truth?' Frank asked. 'That it was all my fault for the way I raised Samuel and that forced you to kill him?'

'I didn't say that. You haven't heard the full truth. I did so many things wrong and I intend to face justice in Lonesome's court just as soon as Usher Pullman's trial is over.'

The mention of Usher Pullman made Frank grunt with anger. He slapped the door then paced into the room to stand over Carter.

'Stand up!' he demanded.

Even after Frank had calmed down earlier Carter had expected him to have a need to vent his anger before the law arrested him and so he stood and faced him.

'I've done that,' he said, spreading his hands to show he wouldn't resist whatever Frank did. 'What now?'

'Hit me.' Frank pointed at his chin and even thrust it forward. 'Then keep on hitting me until I feel something.'

Carter shot a glance over Frank's

shoulder at Victoria in the doorway, but she looked down and wouldn't meet his eye.

'You will feel something when Sheriff Blake throws me in a cell.'

'I don't care about that. I want to feel something now. Hit me.'

'I'd never do that. I've wronged you and I won't add to your pain.'

'Hit me.' Frank pushed Carter and when that didn't move him, he pushed him harder, this time forcing him to take a step backwards. 'Hit me. Go on. Hit me.'

Frank kept on demanding that Carter hit him, all the time pushing him backwards. Carter didn't know why Frank's rage was boiling out of him in such a bizarre manner, but he kept on taking a step backwards and kept on refusing to take up the offer.

Frank's demands became more adamant, his face darkening by the moment. Tears brimmed then flowed in a way that suggested either he would get angry enough to hurt Carter or collapse and bawl like a baby.

Eventually Carter backed away into a wall and could go no further. He looked around the watching people, imploring someone with his concerned gaze to intervene, but Frank's disturbing behaviour had turned everyone to stone. Frank pushed Carter back against the wall and then a second time.

When Frank pushed him a third time, Kelley entered the room. He surveyed the scene, coughed, then when that failed to get a reaction coughed again. Then he paced across the room and placed a hand on Frank's shoulder.

'Man . . . Frank,' he said, 'I believe — '

Kelley didn't get to complete what sounded as though it would be a military-style request for him to stand down before Frank swung round and delivered a fierce blow to Kelley's cheek, of the kind that Carter had expected to receive. Kelley wheeled backwards.

In any other circumstances Carter might have enjoyed seeing Kelley getting hit, but he stumbled into Annie. Her foot became entangled in a chair leg and she went tumbling over the chair to land sprawled and undignified.

'Hit me!' Frank shouted again, turning back to Carter. 'Do it!'

A sudden burst of anger overcame Carter and this time he obliged. He delivered a blow that was more of a slap than a punch. The sound of flesh slapping against flesh echoed in the room.

Frank went down like a felled tree. He landed on his side then slapped his hands over his face and bawled, all dignity gone. By degrees he curled up in a ball. Carter bent to see if he could help, but Victoria stepped up and shook a warning finger at him.

'You've done enough damage to our family already,' she said with no hint in her aggrieved tone of the warmth they had once shared. 'Leave him.'

'But I don't understand. I returned to make things better, not to destroy him.'

Frank looked up at them through his entangled fingers and gathered control of himself for a few moments.

'I've destroyed myself,' he said between bursts of crying. Then he gave up trying to keep control and resumed crying.

Victoria bent over him and tried to calm him, but could do nothing to stem the hysterics. Annie picked herself up and joined her. The two women stared at each over Frank's sprawled form and Carter thought Victoria would also rebuff her, but she nodded, accepting her help, and they fussed over him.

Embarrassed by Frank's demise, Carter joined Kelley.

'You fine?' he asked.

'Yes,' Kelley said, straightening his jacket, 'but that performance is most . . . '

'Unmilitary?'

'It is.'

Carter considered Frank and the women trying to calm him. As he could see nothing he could do to help he changed the subject to a less controversial matter.

'When you were with Frank earlier,' he said, 'did you discuss what you'll do next?'

'We will stay here tonight and leave at first light tomorrow. You are to stay here until Sheriff Blake can deal with you.' Kelley glanced at Frank. 'Or at least that is what I thought our arrangements were before he broke down.'

'That sounds — '

'Come and see this,' Louis said, from by the window. 'I think our plans are about to change.'

Carter joined him at the window to see a stage was trundling through the gates. Carter took a moment to confirm that it was in fact their stage, surprisingly having been reclaimed from the riverside.

But this wasn't as shocking a sight as the fact that the stage was on fire, flames rippling into the night sky from the windows, and the driver was heading straight for the house.

10

Carter was the first to reach the front door with Kelley trailing in his wake. Outside the stage was heading for the house, but the driver was pulling back on the reins, slowing the horses.

Carter also noted that ropes crisscrossed his chest, possibly binding him to the seat, and that the fire was burning only in the back of the stage.

Behind the stage in the darkness he saw other forms milling about beyond the gates, their forms thrown into relief by the burning stage. One man lay sprawled on the ground in the open gateway as if he'd hurriedly jumped from the stage. This sighting convinced Carter that the driver was trying to avoid ploughing the stage into the house.

'Cover me,' he shouted to Kelley then set off before the major could respond.

The driver yanked the reins, making the horses rear then veer away. With much rattling and screeching from the protesting wheels he drew the burning stage to a halt outside the door.

'Get back inside,' the driver shouted. 'They're out there.'

Carter didn't need to ask who 'they' were. He carried on running up to the stage and leapt up on to the seat to join the driver. The man was young and wide-eyed with fear as he babbled an explanation of his situation in which Carter learned he was Buckley Sharpe. Bruises and cuts covered his face and Carter confirmed his original impression that he had been tied into the seat.

From the doorway Kelley fired at the gate. This encouraged whoever was out there to return a volley of gunfire, pinning him down. The stage was still burning with flames rippling out of the windows, but after Kelley risked darting out to fire again, Annie and Victoria hurried out with buckets of water.

The horses and stage partially covered them so they weren't being completely reckless and by the time they'd thrown their water through the windows, Carter had untied Buckley and helped him down to the ground.

'No more water,' Carter shouted at the women. He wrapped an arm around Buckley's shoulders to support his weight and helped him to the door.

'It's still burning,' Annie shouted over her shoulder while following Victoria through the door.

'Then let it burn,' Carter said as he dragged Buckley in after them.

Kelley stayed in the doorway to fire one last time, then slammed the door shut. He hurried off to the study, presumably to keep watch on the situation from the window.

'It's a pity to let it burn,' Annie said with mock indignation in her tone. 'I've become quite attached to that stage.'

Carter smiled at her attempt at good humour in the desperate circumstances. Then he signified that she should follow

Kelley while he helped Buckley get down the hall. When they arrived in the study the situation was much as he'd left it.

Victoria had returned to comforting her father, who was now sitting propped against the wall and rocking back and forth. Louis was guarding the prisoner. Kelley was standing by the window, looking outside.

As soon as Carter had deposited Buckley in a chair Kelley ordered him to take over the task of keeping lookout so he could question the new arrival. Carter looked out through the window to see the fire was now dying out and by its low glow and the moonlight he couldn't see any sign of anyone approaching the ranch house.

While he ran his gaze back and forth along the fence, in a low voice the young man provided his story. It clarified the reasons for many of the events of which they had seen only a small part, including the terrible news that Spike Talbot was still alive. All the time Buckley looked at the floor as if his actions in those events had ashamed him.

'And so,' he said, finishing his tale, 'Deputy Ford and Spike Talbot captured me by the stage and they . . . they decided to tie me into it and forced me to come here.'

'Why?' Kelley asked.

Buckley gulped then darted his gaze around the room until it centred on Maverick. He asked him for his name. The prisoner glanced at Kelley, presumably to confirm he was allowed to talk.

'I'm Maverick Pullman,' he said.

'In that case,' Buckley said, 'I have a message from Spike. He only wants you. If you give yourself up, he won't attack the house and the others can go free.'

'Then I give myself up,' Maverick said.

'You won't,' Carter said before anyone else could speak. 'No matter what anyone says, we still haven't proved whether Spike wants to silence you or to free you. You'll stay here with us.'

'Carter's opinion is irrelevant,' Kelley said. 'He is now also effectively a prisoner and has no say in the matter. But I do believe Spike is aiming to silence you, so I will not hand you over. Sheriff McKinney gave me a sworn duty and I will complete it.'

Carter sighed, deciding it wasn't worth the effort involved in correcting his statement about the lawman giving him the prisoner.

'I know Spike,' Maverick said. 'Everything Buckley said is right. He will kill you all if you don't let me go.'

Nobody responded to this comment although from the determined set of everyone's jaws, Carter gathered nobody was prepared to give up at this stage. Only Victoria and Frank failed to react to this conversation as if it didn't concern them. Kelley brought them into the debate by heading over to them.

'How many ranch hands do you have

to help us defend the house?' he asked Victoria.

She glanced at her father to check he wouldn't reply before answering.

'None any more. They all left last week after we had some . . . some trouble.'

Her cryptic comment made Frank snuffle and mumble to himself. Victoria laid a comforting hand on his shoulder.

'So the forces in this room are all we have,' Kelley said, turning to Buckley. 'How many are we facing?'

'There was Deputy Ford and Spike Talbot,' Buckley said. 'Then they joined up with another six men, I think.'

'Then we're outnumbered and I must consider our options.'

Carter looked around at the group that consisted of three able men, two women, a broken man, a prisoner, and a young, frightened man.

'We may not be in a good state,' he said, 'but we have the benefit of the house as cover. All we need to do is — '

'Is to do nothing,' Kelley said. He

paced across the room to the window then paced back, ensuring he had everyone's attention. 'Our first duty is to keep everyone safe. Spike only wants to keep Maverick from testifying tomorrow. Therefore he will keep us pinned down here and will not attack while he has the situation under control. So we need do nothing but stay calm and wait him out.'

'And then what?' Carter asked. 'We have to leave sometime.'

Kelley clicked his heels. 'Often the best strategy is not to do what your adversary expects you to do.'

With that comment Kelley turned his back on Carter, effectively ending the argument, but Buckley then stood.

'But Spike doesn't expect you to fight,' he said, his eyes remaining downcast. 'And I can see why. Look at us — a prisoner, two women, that crying man . . . ' Buckley flinched as if a sudden thought had come to him, then turned to look at Frank. 'Is he Frank Doyle?'

'He is.'

'Then I might have something to cheer him up.'

Buckley went over to Frank and stood over him. Frank didn't look up, but Buckley rummaged in his pocket and withdrew a silver watch.

Carter murmured to himself. When Annie shot him a glance he nodded, confirming it looked like the one he'd lost.

Buckley didn't notice their interest and held the watch out. When Frank ignored him, Victoria took it from him, glanced at the inscription, then placed it in Frank's hand while whispering comforting words in his ear.

For long moments Frank stared ahead, seemingly beyond caring about any attempts to jar him out of his withdrawn state, but then he looked down at the watch. For long moments he stared at it. He blinked. His hand shook. Then he gripped the watch tightly and held it to his chest.

'It ends now,' he murmured, his low

voice perhaps not addressing anyone but himself. 'I have turned a blind eye to Usher Pullman and ignored his activities for too long, but no longer.'

He stood and without further comment headed to the door and into the hall. Everyone looked at everyone else, bemused by his sudden apparent recovery. The only two people to follow him were Victoria and Carter, but they reached the door together. Both of them stepped back a pace to avoid the other. Carter couldn't meet Victoria's eye and they stood uncomfortably waiting for the other to make a move first. Then Carter heard footfalls receding down the hall and realized what Frank was about to do.

He slipped out into the hall to see Frank throw open the front door, then stand framed in the doorway with his shoulders hunched and a rifle dangling from a hand before pacing from view.

Carter broke into a run, drawing his gun as he pounded down the hall. He heard Victoria come out into the hall then shout back into the study for help, but by the time people followed her, Carter was running through the door.

Ahead Frank was striding purposefully past the still smouldering stage towards the gates. Carter cautiously waited for a moment to let his eyes grow accustomed to the dark and to try to work out where Spike was. Frank was showing no such caution.

'Spike,' he roared, still advancing, 'get out here now. We end this.'

He received no response. So he thrust his rifle high and fired into the air.

'The next shot is for you,' he shouted, 'if you don't come here.'

He continued to advance while Carter stayed beside the horses, looking out for movement. Frank had reached the gates when he first saw someone move beyond the fence, fifty yards away.

'Stay there,' the man ordered. Carter recognized Spike's voice.

'I ain't doing nothing you say no

more,' Frank said.

'We had a deal,' Spike said, 'no harm to your family if you kept quiet. Those people in — '

'That deal never existed because you'd already broken it. You got Samuel killed five years ago when you dragged him into your dealings.'

Frank swung the rifle towards the fence and fired. He kept walking and firing, but only managed two more shots before gunfire blasted at him. Carter also fired in the same direction as Frank had as the lead peppered Frank's chest, sending him tumbling to the ground.

Carter broke into a run, halving the distance to him in seconds but he was already too late. Frank raised his head, swung the rifle round and fired one last time. Then he flopped down to bury his head in the dirt. A slug whistled past Carter's side as on the run he fired again at the people beyond the fence. This time he hit a target, seeing a man stand up straight then go tumbling backwards.

Behind him he heard others coming out of the house. Covering gunfire thundered, this at least giving Spike's men more targets at which to aim. He skidded to a halt beside Frank and looked up. He discerned the shapes of around six men crouched at regular intervals behind the fence. He searched for Spike's larger form, then had his problem resolved when Spike loomed up behind the fence. Spike placed a steadying arm on the fence and aimed at him.

Carter had but a moment to react but it was long enough as he swung his gun around and planted a bullet in him. He didn't see where it landed but did see Spike flying backwards to disappear from view in the gloom and this had the doubly rewarding benefit of making the other shadowy forms back away.

Taking advantage of their confusion Carter grabbed Frank's shoulders and dragged him backwards. He'd nearly reached the stage when Louis joined him and helped him carry Frank to the house.

Kelley had also emerged and with him providing covering fire they reached the ranch house without further trouble, but the moment he stepped into the light inside Carter saw that Frank was beyond help. At least three spreading blooms marred his chest.

Victoria sobbed and held Frank against her chest then lowered him until his head rested on her lap. She pleaded with him to recover, but when Frank cracked open an eye, he sought out Carter.

'Did I get him?' he asked.

'You shot Spike,' Carter said. 'I saw him go down.'

Frank nodded. 'Then I got my justice for Samuel.'

Carter nodded and backed away. It was possible that if Frank thought he'd killed the man who had been behind his son's fall from grace he might forgive Carter before he died. But Carter hadn't returned for that and besides, he wasn't certain Spike was in fact dead.

He joined Kelley and the others and they retired to a respectful distance away. Using only gestures, Kelley ordered Louis to keep lookout and for the others to prepare for whatever might come.

But the anticipated attack didn't arrive and presently Victoria laid her father out on the floor, then stood and made her way over to join Carter.

'You tried to save his life,' she said with her head lowered.

'I tried,' Carter said.

She took a deep breath then met his eye for the first time.

'Father knew about the trouble Samuel was in and from what I've just learned, Spike Talbot was behind that.'

'He had a role.'

'Then this is over.'

Carter gulped to moisten his dry throat. 'I never came here for forgiveness.'

'Nobody is offering any, but my father's last words were that the matter ends here. I can do nothing but accept your story. Now it's up to you to live with what you did.'

She turned and headed back down the hall.

'I'm sorry,' Carter said, 'for everything.'

She stopped for a moment then carried on to sit with Frank. Annie joined her, leaving the others to debate what they should do now.

'If Spike is dead,' Louis said from beside the window in the study, 'we stand a chance of getting out of here.'

'We might,' Carter said, forcing himself to think about their current predicament to avoid brooding about what had just happened. 'But from what Buckley's told us of Deputy Ford, it still won't be easy.'

Everyone looked to Kelley to see what he'd suggest, but surprisingly the newcomer spoke up first.

'I reckon Frank ain't the only one,' Buckley said with a determined slap of a fist against his thigh, 'who needs to start fighting.'

Buckley raised the reins then cracked them, sending the horses off. Covering gunfire rang out from behind and he guessed plenty would come from beyond the gates, but it was too late to worry about that.

He had acted like a coward in directing Spike Talbot to Frank Doyle's house, but now he had a chance to make amends and he wouldn't fail, no matter what the men out there did.

At first he steered the stage on towards the ranch house. Then he turned it in a tight corner until the gates were ahead of him. Then he surged on towards them. First light was illuminating the terrain beyond the gates, not brightly enough for him to see what he was facing, but that difficulty would work both ways.

When he'd trundled through the gates the first burst of gunfire blasted up at the stage from the side of the fence. It peppered along the top of the rail and Buckley felt at least one slug thud into the seat beside his feet.

Retorts blasted from the back of the stage, broadly aiming along the fence. That had the desired effect when the gunfire from Spike's men petered out.

Cheered now, Buckley built up to full speed forcing the horses to strain onwards as he embarked on the agreed course to Lonesome.

His joy at the lack of return fire was short-lived. After no more than 200 yards he glanced back to see that a line of riders was now galloping after the stage, intent on cutting them off long before they reached their destination.

Buckley remembered the route he and Max had taken to get to the ranch yesterday. Sure enough, after a mile he saw the fork in the trail ahead. A rutted and well-travelled trail headed towards Lonesome and a less used trail veered off to run parallel to the river. The rutted trail would be hard to navigate at speed and he raised in the seat to look back and see how much of a lead he had.

The horses were one hundred yards away and closing. He turned back to face the fork, then at the last moment tore the reins to the side to veer the horses away to take the less-travelled route, avoiding the direct trail to Lonesome. He speeded, getting the horses to strain onwards and when he again looked back the confusion he'd hoped to sow had born fruit.

The pursuers had stopped at the fork, staring ahead at the receding stage as they presumably debated why they'd gone this way. Buckley's heart raced as he awaited that decision and it came soon enough when they surged on to follow him.

'As you should,' Buckley murmured to himself then concentrated on getting as far as he could before they ran him down.

Gunfire from the stage did its best to slow the pursuers as lead peppered from the right side then the left, and that forced the trailing riders to spread out.

Buckley looked back to see that his hope of Spike's demise was misplaced. He was still directing the pursuers, although the stiff way he rode confirmed he'd been wounded, but his ingenuity hadn't been affected. He split his men into two and they swung out to flank the stage, drawing level with them around fifty yards out. Then, in a co-ordinated move, they charged in using a pincer movement.

Buckley whooped with delight when a well-directed shot from the back of the stage made one man fly backwards from his saddle. Then a second man reined back clutching a bloodied shoulder. But that was the extent of their successes before the riders drew level with the stage. The horses kept pace with them and the riders laid down such a barrage of fire that they subdued the inadequate defence.

One man made the reckless move of swerving in then leapt from his horse on to the seat. He almost didn't make it but a trailing hand grabbed hold of the side. Then he yanked himself up to sprawl over the seat, rolling to a halt beside Buckley.

Buckley thrust the reins into his left hand and with his right delivered a swinging uppercut to the man's chin. It landed with only minimal force but the man's precarious position meant it was strong enough to tumble him from the seat.

As the man disappeared from view, Buckley lunged to again take the reins in both hands, but then a solid blow punched him in the base of the back. He just had time to feel warmth flooding down inside his clothes along with a gut-churning numbness when a second solid punch of lead hit him in the side. He tumbled over on to the seat to lie sprawled, the reins falling from his grip.

He tried to force himself to sit but couldn't make himself move. Sprawled on his side he looked up to see the lightening morning clouds and even a solitary bird swooping high above. Even with all the shouting and thundering hoofs and gunfire around him, in his disorientated state the bird held his attention. He watched it close slowly, a part of his mind telling him that the bird's slow movement meant the horses were now drawing to a halt.

Finally with a lurch the stage halted.

He heard gunfire from behind, then the stage doors clattered open and another shot sounded followed by an aggrieved shout of disgust.

Buckley let himself smile. Then hands slapped down on his chest and dragged him from the stage. He couldn't gather the strength to protest as the person tugging him deposited him before the open and swaying stage door.

The body of a solitary man, Louis, lay sprawled and still in the doorway, multiple bullet wounds holing his chest.

'What's this?' a voice demanded.

Buckley summoned up the strength to move his head towards the speaker and see that Spike Talbot had spoken. Deputy Ford was at his shoulder. Both men were glowering, anger darkening their faces.

'It's for Max Parker and for Samuel Doyle and for Louis's brother Phillip and for all the others you've destroyed, that's what it is,' Buckley said. He grinned, pleased beyond reason that his reckless and suicidal plan had worked well enough for him to have one last measure of revenge.

'Duped,' Spike roared, then kicked Buckley in the ribs.

Buckley heard a crack, but felt no pain in his numb state, but the blow did roll him over to lie beneath Louis's body.

A gunshot sounded kicking into his side and nudging him forward a few inches. Footfalls receded away from him. Then all he could do was listen to Spike and Ford argue about how they'd been led away on a decoy mission and whose fault it was.

Presently horses galloped away, leaving Buckley alone. He managed to raise a hand to touch Louis's head, but the man didn't stir.

'It worked,' Buckley murmured, accepting that these would probably be his last words and that it was all up to Carter and Kelley now. 'We got 'em.'

★ ★ ★

Carter and Kelley sat together on the front row of the packed courtroom, waiting for the proceedings to start. Victoria and Annie had come with them to Lonesome, but thankfully they'd agreed to take refuge in the hotel and not risk venturing into what could prove to be a dangerous situation.

Kelley had warned the stewards to expect trouble, although as some of that trouble would come from a sworn-in deputy, Carter was unsure how seriously that warning had been taken.

On time, the judge called the court to order, Usher Pullman was led in, and he began the preliminaries.

Kelley leaned over to Carter.

'I guess we got Maverick to the law after all, Carter,' he said.

'With Buckley's and Louis's help,' Carter said, 'I guess we did, Major Kelley.'

'And you? I trust I don't need to hand you over to the law?'

'If Victoria ever asks me to, I will hand myself over. I reckon that's the right thing to do.'

Kelley considered him then nodded. 'I believe so.'

With that being the extent either man was prepared to discuss the arguments that had festered between them for the last day, they then returned to awaiting developments.

They didn't have to wait long.

The first witness was Maverick. In chains he stood in the witness stand and cast his gaze across the rows of watching people until it centred on Kelley and Carter. He looked at each man in turn, a slight smile on his lips. Then he took the first question.

'Let's hope,' Carter whispered to

238

Kelley, 'that what he has to say makes it worth everyone's efforts.'

'And sacrifices.' Kelley smiled. 'But I trust this man and I'm sure you'll see you were wrong not to trust him too.'

Carter didn't reply as he waited to hear what Maverick would say. Across the courtroom, Maverick listened to the lawyer's question, glanced again at Kelley and Carter, then spoke up.

'I will reveal the truth,' he said, smiling. 'All the allegations against Usher Pullman are lies. He is an innocent man.'

11

For a long and infuriating thirty minutes Carter watched Maverick systematically rebut every allegation made against Usher Pullman. He even knew details of his activities since he'd gone to prison, and was able to cast doubt on Usher's supposed crimes during that time.

Kelley muttered to himself as the litany of denials continued, then leaned over to Carter.

'Perhaps you were right,' he said. 'That man is not to be trusted.'

'It was almost worth getting double-crossed to hear you admit I was right.' Carter sighed. 'But good men died to get this man to court.'

'They did, but I don't understand. I know how men think and he shouldn't be doing this.' Kelley hunched his shoulders. 'Things can't get any worse.'

Beyond the court door raised voices sounded, followed by someone falling against the door. Then the door swung open.

'I think they're just about to,' Carter said as he saw Deputy Ford head inside.

The corrupt lawman glared around the courthouse until his gaze fell on Maverick in the stand. Ford had been divested of his gun but he still raised a hand as if it held a weapon and pointed an accusing finger at Maverick.

'Everything that man says is a lie,' he shouted, his voice echoing through the court. 'He has a grudge against Usher and is wasting this court's time.'

The judge banged his gavel, demanding quiet, but didn't receive it as Deputy Ford continued to accuse Maverick of lying.

Carter snorted to himself then stood to face him. His loud clear laugh rang out in the court, only this unexpected sound making Ford's demands peter out. Quietness returned to the court except for Carter's continued snorts of laughter. Only when the judge turned his attention to him did Carter fall silent, then look at Ford over the seated people around him.

'You've made a stupid mistake, Ford,' he said, 'one anyone can see through. Maverick testified as to Usher's innocence. He didn't come here to destroy his brother but to clear his name, after all.'

Ford stared at Carter then at Maverick, who gave a slight nod and a smile. He rubbed at his forehead, shaking his head.

'But that means . . . ' He darted his gaze to the other door behind the judge.

Carter turned to look at the door. Then he set off a moment before the door swung open to reveal Spike Talbot. Dried blood encrusted his left shoulder, his left arm dangled uselessly, but in his right hand he clutched a gun, which he swung round to aim at the witness stand.

Maverick dived to the floor, ducking out of view as Spike's shot tore splinters from the stand. Spike took a long pace forward and fired again, but his determination to silence Maverick from his presumed testimony against Usher gave Carter the time he needed. He threw himself forward, bundling into Spike, and grabbed his arm. Then he ran him backwards and slammed his gun hand against the wall.

Behind him, cries of alarm sounded and the stewards called for everyone to evacuate the courthouse. Carter heard a stampede of feet moving away from him as he and Spike again locked gazes as they had done the day before. This time Spike wasn't surprised to see him and thrust his head forwards, aiming to headbutt him.

Carter jerked himself to the side avoiding the full force of the blow, but it still smashed into his cheek and sent him tumbling backwards, releasing his grip of Spike's arm. He landed on his knees and stared down at the floor, his senses whirling, then pushed himself up to see that Kelley had come to help him and was struggling with Spike.

As Carter got to his feet he looked round the courtroom. The stewards were manoeuvring Usher away to the main door behind the outpouring of people, but Ford was standing in their way, still looking bemused as to how events had worked out.

As Usher passed him he shouted abuse at Ford for being a fool. Ford responded by confronting him. Further away the chained Maverick had been left free and he was making his way over to join the argument.

Carter tore his gaze away from them and turned to help Kelley, who was now trying to wrest the gun from Spike. Using both hands Kelley slammed Spike's arm against the wall, but Spike managed to keep his grip of the gun, then swung his free hand backhanded into Kelley's face and sent him reeling.

Then he swung the gun round and aimed it down at Kelley's sprawling form, but before he could fire Carter lunged forward. He slapped Spike's hand upwards, directing the shot over Kelley's head then kept his movement going as he piled into him. He hit him full in the side and wrapped his arms around Spike's chest as he drove forward. He must have connected with Spike's wounded shoulder because Spike cried out in pain and with him being off-balance, Carter tipped him over.

The two men fell heavily and entangled with Carter landing on top and the gun lying trapped between them. Carter made to grab the gun again but the pressure of their tightly pressed bodies squeezed out a shot. Hot fire burnt across his chest.

He froze, waiting to suffer the result of a potentially fatal shot, but a spasm racked Spike's chest before he collapsed to lie flat.

Gingerly Carter levered himself off Spike and saw the deep self-inflicted wound in his chest then looked down at himself to see that aside from the smoke rising from his jacket he had emerged unscathed.

He battered away the residual embers as he confirmed that Spike was dead, then turned to look down at Kelley.

'You saved my life,' Kelley said.

'Then that makes us about even.' Carter smiled. 'I guess neither of us wants to be in the position of owing the other.'

'Perhaps not . . . ' Kelley looked into the courtroom where the stewards had almost cleared the room. But they weren't in control of the situation.

Deputy Ford was lying on his back, having been knocked down, and Maverick and Usher were free and heading for the open back door. Carter reckoned they must know the court would be surrounded and that it was unlikely they would be able to escape. Sure enough, Maverick caught Usher's attention, then dragged him down behind the witness stand.

Carter helped Kelley to his feet, then

pointed at Ford.

'You keep that one under control.' Carter picked up Spike's gun. 'I'll get Maverick and Usher.'

Kelley looked at Carter for just long enough to make sure Carter realized he was showing no surprise in taking his order, then hurried over to Ford. Carter took his time in walking to the stand, not wanting to inflame the situation. He reached it just as he saw Kelley step up behind Ford and place a restraining armlock around his neck. Then he looked over the stand.

His mouth fell open in shock. Maverick was kneeling on Usher's chest, his hands clutched tightly around his neck. Usher's face had suffused to blackness, his tongue lolling.

Maverick looked up. 'I ain't taking my hands off him.'

'I don't reckon it'll help now,' Carter murmured, hurrying round the stand. 'He looks dead already.'

He moved to tear Maverick's hands

away, but Maverick hunched his shoulders and resisted, putting all his strength into closing his hands around his brother's neck.

'Ain't taking no chances,' Maverick spat out while squeezing. 'This one can wriggle out of anything. Except this.'

Carter gave up on trying to prise Maverick's hands away and aimed the gun he'd taken off Spike at Maverick's chest.

'Release him,' he demanded.

Maverick kept squeezing for several more seconds. Then he opened his hands with a crisp snap. He rolled back on his heels as Usher lolled away, lifeless.

'I have, for all the good it'll do him.'

'Why?'

'I never lied to you. I came back to make sure my dear brother got what he deserved, except there's no way I'd let a court deliver that justice.'

'I understand.' Carter felt for Usher's pulse, but found nothing.

'And now,' Maverick said, breathing a

contented sigh, 'you can let me return to the care of the court so it can carry on delivering its justice to me.'

'Justice is an odd thing, as I've learnt recently.' Carter hefted the gun then did what he'd refused to do yesterday and shot through Maverick's chains. 'Perhaps it's time I admitted I should have trusted you.'

'Obliged.' Maverick spread his hands and smiled, enjoying the simple joy of unfettered movement for the first time in a while, then pointed. 'And the gun?'

'I don't trust you that much.' Carter nodded towards the open back door of the court. 'I've given you a chance to run. If you're real lucky, you might even stay free for a while.'

'If I'm real lucky, I'll get to die,' Maverick said, standing.

'Either way, what happens next is up to you, as it always should be.'

12

The stage sat alone on the plains.

Carter approached it at a steady pace. Annie and Major Kelley had insisted on accompanying him, but they were all silent as they waited to see what they assumed, and dreaded, they would find.

Carter held his breath as he hurried round the stage's restless horses. When he saw the men lying sprawled beside the stage door he knew that his worst fears would be realized. He told Annie to stay back. Then he and Kelley jumped down from their horses to investigate.

They soon confirmed that Louis and Buckley were dead. Multiple bullet wounds had riddled both men's bodies.

Carter knelt down beside Louis and patted the dead man's shoulder. He might have been fooling himself into believing this terrible discovery wasn't that bad, but in his opinion neither man had a pained look and he could almost imagine they were smiling.

He helped Kelley wrap both men in blankets. Then they moved to drape the bodies over the horses, but Carter stopped and looked at the stage. It had been badly burnt and damaged, but it was still intact.

'I reckon I'll take them into town in the stage,' he said.

'Why?' Kelley asked.

'It'll be more dignified that way and besides, Annie ain't the only one who's become attached to it.' He patted the open door. 'It sure has served us well these last few days.'

Kelley agreed with this sentiment and so they placed the bodies inside.

When they'd finished Annie came over. She didn't look inside, but she did lower her head. This encouraged Carter and Kelley to join her in a silent and sombre tribute.

Then they set off back to Lonesome

with Carter in the driver's seat and with Annie and Kelley riding along flanking the stage.

'What will you do now?' he called out to her after they'd ridden along in silence for a mile.

'I'll stay with my cousin as I'd planned to do before,' she said, looking ahead. 'And you?'

'Now that Usher Pullman and the rest are no more, I reckon Lonesome might be a mighty fine place to settle down.'

'You thought that once before,' she said, her voice croaking slightly. 'Has anything changed since then to make you think it'll be different this time?'

Carter didn't reply for a minute, ensuring he provided an honest answer.

'I reckon so,' he said at last, smiling at her.

A slight smile appeared. 'And what will you do if you're staying?'

Carter slapped the seat beside him. 'I reckon the first thing I'll do is restore this stage. It'll need a fresh lick of paint and the burnt wood will need replacing, but we've been through a lot in here and I think it deserves it.'

'Then I'm pleased you found something to stay here for.'

He looked at her. 'I sure have.'

He waited until he saw her smile widen then shook the reins to trundle the stage on to complete the final leg of its journey to Lonesome.

THE END

We do hope that you have enjoyed reading this large print book.

Did you know that all of our titles are available for purchase?

We publish a wide range of high quality large print books including:
Romances, Mysteries, Classics General Fiction Non Fiction and Westerns

Special interest titles available in large print are:
The Little Oxford Dictionary Music Book, Song Book Hymn Book, Service Book

Also available from us courtesy of Oxford University Press:
Young Readers' Dictionary (large print edition) Young Readers' Thesaurus (large print edition)

For further information or a free brochure, please contact us at:
Ulverscroft Large Print Books Ltd., The Green, Bradgate Road, Anstey, Leicester, LE7 7FU, England. Tel: (00 44) **0116 236 4325 Fax:** (00 44) **0116 234 0205**

Other titles in the
Linford Western Library:

RUNNING CROOKED

Corba Sunman

Despite his innocence, Taw Landry served five years in prison for robbery. Freed at last, his troubles seemed over, but when he reached the home range, they were just beginning. He was determined to discover who'd stolen twenty thousand dollars from the stage office in Cottonwood. But Taw's resolution was overtaken by events. Murder was committed and rustling was rife as Taw tried to unravel the five-year-old mystery. As the guns began to blaze — could he survive to the final showdown?

JUDGE PARKER'S LAWMEN

Elliot Conway

'Hanging' Judge Parker orders Marshal Houseman and his green-horn deputy, Zeke Butler, to deal with raiders who are burning out Indian farmers in the Cherokee Strip in Indian Territory. House-man begrudgingly sets off with Zeke, doubting he could be of any help at all. But with the aid of Bear Paw, and some of his kin, the two lawmen face the raiders in a series of shoot-outs, which prove Zeke to be one of the Judge's toughest manhunters.

DEAD MAN'S JOURNEY

Frank Roderus

The Civil War took everything from Alex Adamley. He was once the captain of the blockade runner the *Savannah Belle*. He'd been crippled; left penniless; his ship destroyed and his home and family gone. Yet his dead brother had left him some property in the distant West. Alex determined to go and see this property. He started walking ever westward . . . on a journey that would end in the toughest fight of his life. He was on a Dead Man's Journey.

A RECKONING AT ORPHAN CREEK

Terrell L. Bowers

When Sandy Wakefield, Flint's uncle, dies in a mining mishap, Flint and Johnny Wakefield suspect foul play. Sandy was trying to improve the miners' lot, who work long hours in dangerous conditions for a pittance. Then, Flint and Johnny discover the stripped body of an unknown man and seek to learn his identity. But life above ground gets as dangerous as below. Ultimately, it seems, Flint will have to die before there can be a reckoning at Orphan Creek!

MONTANA 1948

Born in Rugby, North Dakota, Larry Watson received his BA
and MA in English from the University of North Dakota and
his Ph.D. in creative writing from the University of Utah. He
is the author of the novel *In a Dark Time* and a chapbook
of poetry, *Leaving Dakota*, both published in the US. *Montana 1948* won the US Milkweed National Fiction Prize, and
marks Larry Watson's debut novel in the UK. He currently
teaches English at the University of Wisconsin and lives in
Plover, Wisconsin.

Also by Larry Watson

In a Dark Time

Leaving Dakota

Justice

Montana 1948

A Novel

LARRY WATSON

PAN BOOKS

First published 1993 by Milkweed Editions, Minneapolis

First published in Great Britain 1995 by Macmillan
This edition published 1996 by Pan Books
an imprint of Macmillan Publishers Ltd
25 Eccleston Place, London SW1W 9NF
and Basingstoke

Associated companies throughout the world

ISBN 0 330 33679 7

1 3 5 7 9 8 6 4 2

A CIP catalogue record for this book is available from
the British Library

Typeset by Intype London Ltd
Printed by Mackays of Chatham

For Susan

Montana 1948

Prologue

✿ ✿ ✿

Fʀᴏᴍ the summer of my twelfth year I carry a series of images more vivid and lasting than any others of my boyhood and indelible beyond all attempts the years make to erase or fade them. . . .

A young Sioux woman lies on a bed in our house. She is feverish, delirious, and coughing so hard I am afraid she will die.

My father kneels on the kitchen floor, begging my mother to help him. It's a summer night and the room is brightly lit. Insects cluster around the light fixtures, and the pleading quality in my father's voice reminds me of those insects—high-pitched, insistent, frantic. It is a sound I have never heard coming from him.

My mother stands in our kitchen on a hot, windy day. The windows are open, and Mother's lace curtains blow into the room. Mother holds my father's Ithaca twelve-gauge shotgun, and since she is a small, slender woman, she has trouble finding the balance point of its heavy length. Nevertheless, she has watched my father and other men often enough to know where the shells go, and she loads them until the gun will hold no more. Loading the gun is the difficult part. Once the shells are in, any fool can figure out how to fire it. Which she intends to do.

There are others—the sound of breaking glass, the odor of rotting vegetables. . . . I offer these images in the order in which they occurred, yet the events that produced these sights and sounds are so rapid and tumbled together that any chronological sequence seems wrong. Imagine instead a movie screen divided into boxes and panels, each with its own scene, so that one moment can occur simultaneously with another, so no action has to fly off in time, so nothing happens before or after, only during. That's the way these images coexist in my memory, like the Sioux picture calendars in which the whole year's events are painted on the same buffalo hide, or like a tapestry with every scene woven into the same cloth, every moment on the same flat plane, the summer of 1948. . . .

Forty years ago. Two months ago my mother died. She made, as the expression goes, a good death. She came inside the house from working in her garden, and a heart attack, as sudden as a sneeze, felled her in the kitchen. My father's death, ten years earlier, was less merciful. Cancer hollowed him out over the years until he could not stand up to a stiff wind. And Marie Little Soldier? Her fate contains too much of the story for me to give away.

A story that is now only mine to tell. I may not be the only witness left—there might still be someone in that small Montana town who remembers those events as well as I, but no one knew all three of these people better.

And no one loved them more.

One

❀ ❀ ❀

I N 1948 my father was serving his second term as sheriff of Mercer County, Montana. We lived in Bentrock, the county seat and the only town of any size in the region. In 1948 its population was less than two thousand people.

Mercer County is in the far northeast corner of Montana, and Bentrock is barely inside the state's borders. Canada is only twelve miles away (though the nearest border crossing is thirty miles to the west), and North Dakota ten miles. Then, as now, Mercer County was both farm and ranch country, but with only a few exceptions, neither farms nor ranches were large or prosperous. On the western edge of the county and extending into two other counties was the Fort Warren Indian Reservation, the rockiest, sandiest, least arable parcel of land in the region. In 1948 its roads were unpaved, and many of its shacks looked as though they would barely hold back a breeze.

But all of northeastern Montana is hard country—the land is dry and sparse and the wind never stops blowing. The heat and thunderstorms in summer can be brutal, and the winters are legendary for the fierceness of their blizzards and the depths to which temperatures drop. (In one year we reached 106 degrees in July and 40 below in January.) For those of you who automatically think of Montana and snow-capped

15

mountains in the same synapse, let me disabuse you. Mercer County is plains, flat as a tabletop on its western edge and riven with gullies, ravines, and low rocky hills to the east because of the work the Knife River has done over the centuries. The only trees that grow in that part of the country, aside from a few cottonwoods along the riverbank, have been planted by farmers and town dwellers. And they haven't planted many. If the land had its way, nothing would grow taller than sagebrush and buffalo grass.

The harshness of the land and the flattening effect of wind and endless sky probably accounted for the relative tranquility of Mercer County. Life was simply too hard, and so much of your attention and energy went into keeping not only yourself but also your family, your crops, and your cattle alive, that nothing was left over for raising hell or making trouble.

And 1948 still felt like a new, blessedly peaceful era. The exuberance of the war's end had faded but the relief had not. The mundane, workaday world was a gift that had not outworn its shine. Many of the men in Mercer County had spent the preceding years in combat. (But not my father; he was 4-F. When he was sixteen a horse kicked him, breaking his leg so severely that he walked with a permanent limp, and eventually a cane, his right leg V-ed in, his right knee perpetually pointing to the left.) When these men came back from war they wanted nothing more than to work their farms and ranches and to live quietly with their families. The county even had fewer hunters after the war than before.

All of which made my father's job a relatively easy one.

Oh, he arrested the usual weekly drunks, mediated an occasional dispute about fence lines or stray cattle, calmed a few domestic disturbances, and warned the town's teenagers about getting rowdy in Wood's Cafe, but by and large being sheriff of Mercer County did not require great strength or courage. The ability to drive the county's rural roads, often drifted over in the winter or washed out in the summer, was a much more necessary skill than being good with your fists or a gun. One of my father's regular duties was chaperoning Saturday night dances in the county, but the fact that he often took along my mother (and sometimes me) shows how quiet those affairs—and his job—usually were.

And that disappointed me at the time. As long as my father was going to be a sheriff, a position with so much potential for excitement, danger, and bravery, why couldn't some of that promise be fulfilled? No matter how many wheat fields or cow pastures surrounded us, we were still Montanans, yet my father didn't even look like a western sheriff. He wore a shirt and tie, as many of the men in town did, but at least they wore boots and Stetsons; my father wore brogans and a fedora. He had a gun but he never carried it, on duty or off. I knew because I checked, time and time again. When he left the house I ran to his dresser and the top drawer on the right side. And there it was, there it always was. Just as well. As far as I was concerned it was the wrong kind of gun for a sheriff. He should have had a nickel-plated Western Colt .45, something with some history and heft. Instead, my father had a small .32 automatic, Italian-made and no bigger than your palm. My father didn't buy such a sorry gun; he confiscated it from a drunken transient in one of his first arrests. My father kept the gun but in fair exchange bought the man a bus ticket to Billings, where he had family.

The gun was scratched and nicked and had a faint blush of rust along the barrel. The original grips were gone and had been replaced by two cut-to-fit rectangles of Masonite. Every time I came across the gun it was unloaded, its clip full of the short, fat .32 cartridges lying nearby in the same drawer. The pistol slopped about in a thick, stiff leather strap-and-snap holster meant for a larger gun and a revolver at that. Since it looked more like a toy than the western-style cap guns that had been my toys, I wasn't even tempted to take my father's gun out for play, though I had the feeling I could have kept it for weeks and my father wouldn't have missed it.

You're wondering if perhaps my father kept his official side arm in his county jail office. If he did, I never saw it there, and I wandered in and out of that jail office as often as I did the rooms of our home. I saw the rack of rifles and shotguns in their locked case (and two sets of handcuffs looped and dangling from the barrel of a Winchester 94) but no pistols.

We lived, you see, in a white two-story frame house right across the street from the courthouse, and the jail and my father's office were in the basement of the courthouse. On occasion I waited for my father to release a prisoner (usually a hung-over drunk jailed so he wouldn't hurt himself) or finish tacking up a wanted poster before I showed him my report card or asked him for a dime for a movie. No, if there had been a six-shooter or a Stetson or a pair of hand-tooled cowboy boots around for my father to put on with his badge, I would have known about it. (I must correct that previous statement: my father never *wore* his badge; he carried it in his suit-coat or shirt pocket. I always believed that this was part of his self-effacing way, and that may be so. But now that the badge is mine—my mother sent it to me after my father's death and I have it pinned to my bulletin board—I realize there was another reason, connected not to character but to practicality. The badge, not star-shaped but a shield, is heavy and its pin as thick as a pencil's lead. My father would have been poking fair-sized holes in his suits and shirts, and the badge's weight could have torn fabric.)

If my father didn't fit my ideal of what he should be in his occupation, he certainly didn't fit my mother's either. She wanted him to be an attorney. Which he was; he graduated from the University of North Dakota Law School, and he was a member of both the North Dakota and Montana State Bar Associations. My mother fervently believed that my father—indeed, all of us—would be happier if he practiced law and if we did not live in Montana, and her reasons had little to do with the potentially hazardous nature of a sheriff's work compared to an attorney's or the pay scale along which those professions positioned themselves. She wanted my father to find another job and for us to move because only doing those things would, she felt, allow my father to be fully himself. Her contention is one I must explain.

19

My father was born in 1910 in Mercer County and grew up on a large cattle ranch outside Bentrock. In the early twenties my father, with his parents and his brother, moved to Bentrock, where my grandfather began his first of many terms as county sheriff. My grandfather kept the ranch and had it worked by hands while he was in office, and since Mercer County had a statute that a sheriff could serve only three consecutive terms, he was able to return to the ranch every six years. When Grandfather's terms expired, his deputy, Len McAuley, would serve a term; after Len's term, Grandfather would run again, and this way they kept the office in the proper hands. During his terms as sheriff, Grandfather brought his family into town to live in a small apartment above a bar (he owned the bar and building the apartment was in). My father often spoke of how difficult it was for him to move from the ranch and its open expanses to the tiny apartment that always smelled of stale beer and cigar smoke. He spent every weekend and every summer at the ranch and when he had to return to the apartment where he and his brother slept on a fold-out couch, he felt like crying.

(And now that it is too late to ask anyone, I wonder: Why did my grandfather first run for sheriff? This one I can probably answer, from my memory and knowledge of him. He wanted, he needed, power. He was a dominating man who drew sustenance and strength from controlling others. To him, being the law's agent probably seemed part of a natural progression—first you master the land and its beasts, then you regulate the behavior of men and women.)

When my grandfather finally decided to retire for good

and return to the ranch, he found a way to do this yet retain his power in the county: he turned the post over to my father. Yes, the sheriff of Mercer County was elected, but such was my grandfather's popularity and influence—and the weight of the Hayden name—that it was enough for my grandfather to say, as he had earlier said of his deputy, now I want my son to have this job.

So my father set aside his fledgling law practice and took the badge my grandfather offered. It would never have occurred to my father to refuse.

There you have it, then, a portrait of my father in those years, a man who tried to turn two ways at once—toward my grandfather, who wanted his son to continue the Hayden rule of Mercer County, and toward my mother, who wanted her husband to be merely himself and not a Hayden. That was not possible as long as we lived in my grandfather's domain.

There was another reason my mother wanted us to leave Montana for a tamer region and that reason had to do with me. My mother feared for my soul, a phrase that sounds to me now comically overblown, yet I remember that those were precisely the words she used.

My mother was concerned about my values, but since often the most ordinary worldly matters assumed for her a spiritual significance, she saw the problem as centered on my mortal being. (My mother was a Lutheran of boundless devotion; my father was irreligious, a path I eventually found and followed after wandering through those early years of church, Sunday School, and catechism classes.)

The problem was that I wanted to grow up wild. Oh, not

in the sense that wildness is used today. I wasn't particularly interested, on the cusp of adolesence, in driving fast cars (pickup trucks, more accurately in Bentrock), smoking (Sir Walter Raleigh roll-your-owns the cigarette of choice), drinking (home-brewed beer was so prevalent in Mercer County that boys always had access to it), or chasing girls (for some reason, the girls from farms—not town or ranch or reservation—had the reputation of being easy). In fact, I came late to these temptations.

Wildness meant, to me, getting out of town and into the country. Even our small town—really, in 1948 still a frontier town in many respects—tasted to me like pabulum. It stood for social order, good manners, the chimed schedules of school and church. It was a world meant for storekeepers, teachers, ministers, for the rule-makers, the order-givers, the law-enforcers. And in my case, my parents were not only figurative agents of the law, my father *was* the law.

In addition to my discomfort with the strictures of town (a common and natural reaction for a boy), I had another problem that seemed like mine alone. I never felt as though I understood how town life *worked*. I thought there was some secret knowledge about living comfortably and unself-consciously in a community, and I was sure I did not possess that knowledge. When the lessons were taught about how to feel confident and at ease in school, in stores, in cafes, with other children or adults, I must have been absent. It was not as though I behaved badly in these situations but rather that I was never sure how to behave. I was always looking sneakily at others for the key to correct conduct. And instead of attributing this social distress to my own shy and too-serious character I simply blamed life in town and sought to escape it as often as I could.

And that was an easy enough matter. Though we lived in the middle of town, I could be out in minutes, whether I walked, biked, ran, or followed the railroad tracks just on the other side of our backyard. With my friends or on my own, I spent as many of the day's hours as I could outdoors, usually out at my grandfather's ranch or along the banks of the Knife River. (How it got its name I've never known; it's hard to imagine a duller body of water—in dry summers it could barely keep its green course flowing and sandbars poked up the length of it; it froze every year by Thanksgiving.)

I did what boys usually did and exulted in the doing: I rode horseback (I had my own horse at the ranch, an unnaturally shaggy little sorrel named Nutty); I swam; I fished; I hunted (I still have, deep in a closet somewhere, my first guns from those years—a single-shot bolt action Winchester .22 and a single-shot Montgomery Ward .410 shotgun); my friends and I killed more beer cans, soda bottles, road signs, and telephone pole insulators than the rabbits, squirrels, grouse, or pheasants we said we were hunting; I explored; I scavenged (at various times I brought home a snakeskin, part of a cow's jawbone, an owl's coughball, a porcupine quill, the broken shaft and fletch of a hunter's arrow, an unbroken clay pigeon, a strip of tree bark with part of a squirrel's tail embedded in it so tightly that it was a mystery how it got there, a perfectly shaped cottonwood leaf the size of a man's hand, and a myriad of river rocks chosen for their beauty or odd shape).

But what I did was not important. Out of town I could simply *be*, I could feel my *self*, firm and calm and unmalleable as I could not when I was in school or in any of the usual human communities that seemed to weaken or scatter me. I could sit for an hour in the rocks above the Knife River, asking for no more discourse than that water's monotonous gabble. I was an inward child, it was true, but beyond that, I felt a contentment outside human society that I couldn't feel within it.

Perhaps my mother sensed this, and following her duty to civilize me, wished for a larger community to raise me in, one that I couldn't get out of quite so easily and that wouldn't offer such alluring chaos once I was out. (The impression is probably forming of my mother as an urban woman disposed by background to be suspicious of wild and rough Montana. Not so. She grew up on a farm in eastern North Dakota, in the Red River valley, flat, fertile, prosperous farming country.)

That was our family in 1948 and those were the tensions that set the air humming in our household. I need to sketch in only one more character and the story can begin.

Because my mother worked (she was the secretary in the Register of Deeds office, also in the courthouse across the street), we had a housekeeper who lived with us during the week. Her name was Marie Little Soldier, and she was a Hunkpapa Sioux who originally came from the Fort Berthold Reservation in North Dakota. She was in her early twenties, and she came to our part of Montana when her mother married a Canadian who owned a bar in Bentrock. The bar, Frenchy's, was a dirty, run-down cowboy hangout at the edge of town. Among my friends the rumor was that Frenchy kept locked in his storeroom a fat old toothless Indian woman whom anyone could have sex with for two dollars. (One of my friends hinted that this was Marie's mother, but I knew that wasn't true. Marie's mother once came to our house, and she was a thin, shy woman barely five feet tall. She reminded me of a bird who wants to be brave in the presence of humans but finally fails. When Marie introduced her to my mother, Marie's mother looked at the floor and couldn't say a word.)

Marie was neither small nor shy. She loved to laugh and talk, and she was a great tease, specializing in outrageous lies about everything from strange animal behavior to bloody murders. Then, as soon as she saw she had you gulled, she would say, "Not so, not so!"

She was close to six feet tall and though she wasn't exactly fat she had a fleshy amplitude about her that made her seem simultaneously soft and strong, as if all that body could be ready, at a moment's notice, for sex or work. The cotton print dresses she wore must have been handed down or up to her because they never fit her quite right; they were either too short and tight and she looked about to pop out of them, or they were much too large and she threatened to fall free or be tangled in all that loose fabric. She had a wide, pretty face and cheekbones so high, full, and glossy I often wondered if they were naturally like that or if they were puffy and swollen. Her hair was black and long and straight, and she was always pulling strands of it from the corner of her mouth or parting it to clear her vision.

And I loved her.

Because she talked to me, cared for me. . . . Because she

was older but not too old. . . . Because she was not as quiet and conventional as every other adult I knew. . . . Because she was sexy, though my love for her was, as a twelve-year-old's love often is, chaste.

Besides, Marie had a boyfriend, Ronnie Tall Bear, who worked on a ranch north of town. I was not jealous of Ronnie, because I liked him almost as much as I liked Marie. *Liked* Ronnie? I worshipped him. He had graduated from Bentrock High School a few years earlier, and he was one of the finest athletes the region had ever produced. He was the Mustangs' star fullback, the high-scoring forward in basketball; in track he set school records in the discus, javelin, and 400-yard dash. He pitched and played outfield on the American Legion baseball team. (I realize now how much I was a part of that era's thinking: I never wondered then, as I do now, why a college didn't snap up an athlete like Ronnie. Then, I knew without being told, as if it were knowledge that I drank in with the water, that college was not for Indians.) During the war Ronnie was in the infantry (good enough for the Army but not for college). Marie told me he was thinking of trying his hand on the rodeo circuit.

Marie's room, when she stayed with us during the week, was a small room off the kitchen. My bedroom and my parents' were on the second floor. (And as I go back in my memory I realize we had a third bedroom on the second floor. Who decided that room should not be Marie's? I had long known that I was destined to be an only child.) I mention Marie's room because it was there, and with her, that this story began.

26

It was mid-August 1948. Our corner of the state had been, as usual, hot and dry, though even in the midst of all the heat there were a few signs of autumn—a cottonwood leaf here and there turning yellow and sometimes letting go, and nights cool enough for a light blanket.

Marie stayed in her room all that morning, and when I passed the door I heard her coughing. I peered in once and saw her lying on the bed. She came out only long enough to set out lunch. At our house meals were never fancy, but the food was always abundant and varied. Marie probably brought out cottage cheese, perhaps some leftover ham or chicken or sausage, a wedge of cheddar cheese, a loaf of bread, butter, pickles, canned peaches, cold milk, and something from the garden—carrots or radishes or cucumbers or tomatoes.

The noon whistle blew and within five minutes my mother was walking through the door, and if my father was in town, he would soon follow.

I stopped my mother in the living room and whispered to her, "I think Marie's sick."

"What's wrong?" My mother was instantly alarmed. She feared nothing more than disease, but she was not cowardly or meek in its presence. No disease, common or exotic, faced a fiercer foe than my mother. She spent a good deal of energy avoiding it or keeping it away from herself and her family. She would not accept or extend invitations if she knew it meant someone sick might get too close. If we were walking down the street and someone ahead of us coughed or sneezed, my mother slowed her pace until she thought those germs had dissipated in the air. It all sounds silly, but it must have worked.

We were seldom sick, and I did not get the usual childhood diseases until I left home. (And then they hit me hard. I had to drop a French class my freshman year in college because measles laid me up and put me too far behind. Years later my fever ran so high when I had chicken pox that my wife took me to the emergency room, where they packed me in ice.)

"I'm not sure," I told my mother. "She's been in her room all morning."

My mother walked quietly through the living room and kitchen to the door of Marie's room. I followed close behind.

The door wasn't shut tight, and my mother knocked hard enough so it swung open. "Marie? Are you all right?"

Just then Marie had another coughing fit, and she couldn't answer. She rolled onto her side, brought her knees up, and barked out a series of dry coughs. When the spasm subsided, she nodded. "A cold. I have a little cold."

My mother would have none of it. She went to the bedside and put her hand on Marie's forehead. "Come here," my mother commanded me. When I came close, she put her hand on my forehead. The comparison confirmed what she suspected.

"You have a temperature, all right."

If my father had been there he would have been quick to correct my mother's choice of words. "A fever, Gail. She has a *fever*. Everyone has a temperature."

My mother gave my forehead a tiny little push as she took her hand away, a signal that I was supposed to get back—there was illness here.

I didn't go far. I stood in the doorway and watched Marie while my mother went through her routine of questions.

"How long have you been feeling sick?"

Marie rolled onto her back and brushed her hair from her face. Her cheeks now glowed so brightly they looked painful, as if they had been rubbed raw. Her eyes seemed darker than ever, all pupil, black water that swallowed light and gave nothing back. Her lips were pale-dry and chapped. Her dress had ridden up over her knees and the sight of her sturdy brown legs and bare feet was strangely shocking, a glimpse of the sensual in the sickroom. (But nothing new. I had once seen Marie naked, or nearly so. In our basement laundry room we had a shower, nothing fancy—a shower head, a tin stall, and an old green rubber curtain with large white sea horses on it. I came galloping downstairs one day—obviously when Marie thought I would be out of the house a while longer—and caught her just as she was stepping out of the shower. She was quick with her towel but not quick enough. I saw just enough to embarrass us both. Dark nipples that shocked me in the way they stood out like fingertips. A black triangle of pubic hair below a thick waist and gently rounded belly. And above it all, shoulders that seemed as broad as my father's. I stammered an apology and backed out as quickly as possible. Neither of us ever said anything about the incident.)

After another brief coughing fit, this time nothing more than some breathy, urgent *chuffs*, Marie answered, "I don't know. A couple days maybe."

"Have you been eating?"

Marie shook her head.

"Are you sick to your stomach?"

Another head shake.

29

"Have you been throwing up?"

Marie whispered no.

"Do you know anyone else who is sick? Someone you might have caught this from?"

I felt so bad for Marie having to put up with this interrogation that I finally said something. "Mom. She doesn't feel good."

My mother turned and said sharply, "You wait in the other room. I'm trying to find out something here."

I took a few steps back into the kitchen, but I still saw and heard what went on in Marie's room.

My mother brought two wool blankets down from the closet shelf and spread them over Marie. "The first thing," my mother said, "is to bring your temperature down. We should be able to sweat that out of you in no time."

To this day many Sioux practice a kind of purification ritual in which they enclose themselves in a small tent or lodge and with the help of heated stones and water steam themselves until sweat streams from them. My mother believed in a variation of that. A fever was to be driven away by more heat, blankets piled on until your own sweat cooled you.

Marie must have agreed with the course of treatment because she made no protest.

"David will be here this afternoon if you need anything," my mother said. "You rest. I'll come over again around three o'clock, and if you're not feeling better we'll give Dr. Hayden a call."

This remark brought Marie straight up in bed. "No! I don't

need no doctor!" With that outburst she began coughing again, this time harder than ever.

"Listen to you," my mother said. "Listen to that cough. And you say you don't need a doctor."

"I don't go to him," said Marie. "I go to Dr. Snow."

"Dr. Hayden is Mr. Hayden's brother. You know that, don't you? He'll come to the house. And he won't charge anything, if that's what you're worried about." Marie's frugality was legendary. She hated waste, and on more than a few occasions she claimed what we were going to throw away—food, clothing, magazines—saying she would find a use for them. Finally we caught on. Before we planned to throw anything away, we checked with Marie first. Our old issues of *Collier's* probably found their way out to the reservation.

Marie closed her eyes. "I don't need no doctor." Her voice was no louder than a whisper.

My mother left the room, closing the door halfway. "Keep an eye on her, David," she told me. "If she gets worse, call me."

"Is she very sick?"

"She has a temperature. And I don't like the sound of that cough."

I stayed out, as my mother ordered, but I walked past Marie's room often. Marie slept, even when she coughed. I heard her voice on one of my passings and stopped, but it soon became obvious that she was not calling me but talking in her fevered sleep. "It's the big dog," she said. "Yellow dog. It won't drink." And then a word that sounded like *ratchety*. And repeated, "Ratchety, ratchety." I didn't know if it was a word from Sioux or from fever.

Later, as I was sitting at the kitchen table, Marie shouted for me. "Davy!" I ran to her door.

I stopped. Marie was lying on her back, gazing at the doorway. "I don't need no doctor, Davy. Tell them."

"My mom doesn't want you to get worse."

"No *doctor*."

"It's just my uncle Frank. He's okay."

Marie's forehead and cheeks shone with sweat. "I'm feeling better," she said. She pulled back the blankets and sat up, but as she did she began to cough again. Soon she was gasping for breath in between coughs. This frightened me. I went to the bed and held Marie's shoulders until the coughing subsided, something I remembered my mother doing for me. I felt Marie trembling all over, as your muscles do after great exertion.

When she was done I helped her lie down again. "Maybe I should go get my mother."

"No doctor."

"Okay, okay. I'll tell her you don't want a doctor."

Marie's eyes closed and she seemed to be breathing evenly again.

"Marie?"

She nodded weakly. "I'm okay."

I backed slowly away but hesitated in the doorway. Marie's eyes remained closed and her breathing was deep and regular. My hands were damp from gripping Marie's shoulders. Was the sweat mine or hers?

My mother and father came home together at five o'clock. If the evening followed its usual pattern, my father would read the *Mercer County Gazette*, have supper, and go out again for an hour or two if the evening was peaceful. He would be gone longer if it was not.

My father dropped his hat and briefcase (another lawyer's touch—and a gift from my mother) on the kitchen table. "David," he said, "I hear you're baby-sitting the baby-sitter."

How naive I was! Until that moment I believed that we had hired Marie to care for our house, to keep it clean and prepare the meals since my mother, unlike most mothers, worked all day outside our home. We called Marie our "housekeeper," and I thought that was her job—to keep the house. It never occurred to me that she had been hired to look after me as well.

My mother headed for Marie's room.

"I think she's still sleeping," I said.

Within minutes my mother came back out. She said, "She's burning up, Wes. You'd better call Frank."

My father did not question my mother's judgment in these matters. He went for the phone.

"Wait!" I called.

Both my father and mother turned to me. I did not often demand my parents' attention because I knew I could have it whenever I wanted it. That was part of my only-child legacy.

"Marie said she didn't want a doctor."

"That's superstition, David," said my father. "Indian superstition."

This is as good a place as any to mention something that I would just as soon forget. My father did not like Indians. No, that's not exactly accurate, because it implies that my father disliked Indians, which wasn't so. He simply held them in low regard. He was not a hate-filled bigot—he probably thought he was free of prejudice!—and he could treat Indians with generosity, kindness, and respect (as he could treat every human being). Nevertheless, he believed Indians, with only a few exceptions, were ignorant, lazy, superstitious, and irresponsible. I first learned of his racism when I was seven or eight. An aunt gave me a pair of moccasins for my birthday, and my father forbade me to wear them. When I made a fuss and my mother sided with me, my father said, "He wears those and soon he'll be as flat-footed and lazy as an Indian." My mother gave in by supposing that he was right about flat feet. (Today I put on a pair of moccasins as soon as I come home from work, an obedient son's belated, small act of defiance.)

"She said she doesn't need one," I said.

"What does she need, David? A medicine man?"

I shut up. Both my parents were capable of scorching sarcasm. I saw no reason to risk receiving any more of it.

My father was already on the phone, giving the operator my uncle's home phone number. "Glo?" he said into the receiver. "This is Wes. Is the doctor home yet?" Gloria, my uncle's wife, was the prettiest woman I had ever seen.

34

(Prettier even than my mother—a significant admission for a boy to make.) Aunt Gloria was barely five feet tall, and she had silver-blond hair. She and Frank had been married five or six years but had no children. I once overheard my grandfather say to my uncle: "Is she too small to have kids? Is that it, Frank? Is the chute too tight?"

In the too-loud voice he always used on the telephone, my father said, "We've got a sick Indian girl over here, Frank. Gail wants to know if you can stop by."

After a pause, my father said to my mother, "Frank wants to know what her symptoms are."

"A high temperature. Chills. Coughing."

My father repeated my mother's words. Then he added, "I might as well tell you, Frank. She doesn't want to see you. Says she doesn't need a doctor."

Another short pause and my father said, "She didn't say why. My guess is she's never been to anyone but the tribal medicine man."

I couldn't tell if my father was serious or making a joke.

He laughed and hung up the phone. "Frank said maybe he'd do a little dance around the bed. And if that doesn't work he'll try beating some drums."

My mother didn't laugh. "I'll go back in with Marie."

As soon as Uncle Frank arrived, his tie loosened and his sleeves rolled up, I felt sorry for my father. It was the way I always felt when the two of them were together. Brothers naturally invite comparison, and when comparisons were made between those two, my father was bound to suffer. And my father was, in many respects, an impressive man. He was tall, broad-shouldered, and pleasant-looking. But Frank was all this and more. He was handsome—dark, wavy hair, a jaw chiseled on such precise angles it seemed to conform to some geometric law, and he was as tall and well built as my father, but with an athletic grace my father lacked. He had been a star athlete in high school and college, and he was a genuine war hero, complete with decorations and commendations. He had been stationed at an Army field hospital on a Pacific island, and during a battle in which Allied forces were incurring a great many losses, Uncle Frank left the hospital to assist in treating and evacuating casualties. Under heavy enemy fire he carried—carried, just like in the movies—three wounded soldiers from the battlefield to safety. The story made the wire services, and somehow my grandfather got ahold of clippings from close to twenty different newspapers. (After reading one of the clippings, my father muttered, "I wonder if he was supposed to stay at the hospital.")

Frank was witty, charming, at smiling ease with his life and everything in it. Alongside his brother my father soon seemed somewhat prosaic. Oh, stolid, surely, and steady and dependable. But inevitably, inescapably dull. Nothing glittered in my father's wake the way it did in Uncle Frank's.

Soon after the end of the war the town held a picnic to celebrate his homecoming. (Ostensibly the occasion was to honor all returning veterans, but really it was for Uncle Frank.) The park was jammed that day (I'm sure no event has ever gathered as many of the county's residents in one place), and the amount and variety of food, all donated, was amazing: a roast pig, a barbecued side of beef, pots of beans, brimming bowls of coleslaw and potato salad, an array of garden vegetables, freshly baked pies and cakes, and pitchers of lemonade, urns of coffee, and barrels of beer. Once people had eaten and drunk their fill, my grandfather climbed onto a picnic table.

He didn't call for silence. That wasn't his way. He simply stood there, his feet planted wide, his hands on his hips. He was wearing his long buckskin jacket, the one so tanned and aged that it was almost white. He assumed that once people saw him, they would give him their attention. And they did.

He said a few words honoring all the men who served (no one from Mercer County was killed in action—not such an improbability when you consider the county's small population—though we had our share of wounded, the worst of whom, Harold Branch, came back without his legs). Then after a long, reverent pause, Grandfather announced, "Now I'd like to bring my son up here."

My father was standing next to me when Grandfather said that. My father did not move. Grandfather did not say, "my son the veteran," or "my son the war hero," or "my son the soldier." He simply said, "my son." And why wouldn't the county sheriff be called on to make a small speech?

But my father didn't move. He just stood there, like every other man in the crowd, smiling and applauding, while his brother stepped up on the table. Uncle Frank had not hesitated either; he knew immediately that Grandfather was referring to him.

Uncle Frank made a suitably brief and modest speech, saying that the war could not have been won without the sacrifices of both soldiers and those who remained at home.

At one point I looked up to see how my father was reacting to his brother's speech. My father was not there. He had drifted back through the crowd and was picking up scraps of paper from the grass. With his bad leg, bending was difficult. He had to keep the leg stiff and bend from the waist. Then he carried these bits of paper, a piece at a time, to the fire-blackened incinerator barrel.

Uncle Frank's talk must not have been enough for my grandfather. He climbed back up on the table and, after urging the crowd on to another minute of applause, held up his hands for silence again. "This man could have gone anywhere," he said. "With his war record he could be practicing in Billings. In Denver. In *Los Angeles*. There's not a community in the country that wouldn't be proud to have him. But he came back to us. My son. *Came back to us.*"

My father kept searching for paper to pick up.

Uncle Frank put his black bag on the kitchen table. "How about something to drink, Wes? I was digging postholes this morning and I've been dry all day."

My father opened the refrigerator. "Postholes? Not exactly the kind of surgery I thought you'd be doing."

"I'm going to fence off the backyard. We've got two more

houses going up out there. Figured a fence might help us keep what little privacy we've got."

I wondered what Grandpa Hayden would say about that. Though his land was fenced with barbed wire as most ranchers' were, he still had the nineteenth-century cattleman's open range mentality and hatred of fences. Our backyard bordered a railroad track (trains passed at least four times a day), but my father refused to put up a fence—as all our neighbors had—separating our property from the tracks.

"I've got cold beer in here," said my father. "It's old man Norgaard's brew." Ole Norgaard lived in a tar-paper shack on the edge of town. He had a huge garden and sold vegetables through the summer and early fall. His true specialty, however, and the business he conducted throughout the year, was brewing and selling beer. My father swore by everything Ole Norgaard produced.

Uncle Frank made a face. "I'll pass."

My father brought out a bottle with a rubber stopper and a wire holding it in place. "You can't buy a better beer." He held out the bottle.

Uncle Frank laughed and waved my father away. "Just give me a glass of water."

My father persisted. "Ask Pop. He still drinks Ole Norgaard's beer."

"Okay, okay," Frank said. "It's great beer. It's the world's greatest goddamn beer. But I'll drink Schlitz, if it's okay with you."

My father nodded in my direction. "Not in front of the

boy." That was one of my father's rules: no one was supposed to swear in front of my mother or me.

Uncle Frank picked up his bag. "Okay, Wes. I'll tell you what. Let me see the patient first and then I'll drink a bottle of Ole's beer with you. Maybe I'll drink two."

Just then my mother came out of Marie's room. "She's in here, Frank."

"Hello, Gail. How is the patient?"

"She's awake. Her temperature might be down a bit."

Frank went in and shut the door behind him. Within a minute we heard Marie shouting, "Mrs.! Mrs.!"

My mother looked quizzically at my father. He shrugged his shoulders. Marie screamed again. "No! Mrs.!"

This time my mother went to the door and knocked. "Frank? Is everything okay?"

My uncle opened the door. "She says she wants you in here, Gail." He shook his head in disgust. "Come on in. I don't give a damn."

This time the door closed and the room remained silent.

"David," my father said to me. "Why don't we go out on the porch while the medical profession does its work."

Our screened-in porch faced the courthouse across the street. When I was younger I used to go out there just before five o'clock on all but the coldest days to watch for my parents.

My father put his bottle of beer down on the table next to the rocking chair. I didn't sit down; I wanted to be able to maneuver myself into the best position to hear anything coming from Marie's room. I didn't have to wait long. I soon

40

heard—muffled but unmistakable—Marie shout another *no*.

I glanced at my father but he was staring at the courthouse. Then two more *no*'s in quick-shouted succession.

My father pointed at one of the large elm trees in our front yard. "Look at that," he said. "August, and we've got leaves coming down already." He heard her. I knew he did.

Before long Uncle Frank came out to the porch. He put down his bag and stared around the room as if he had never been there before. "Nice and cool out here," he said, tugging at his white shirt the way men do when their clothes are sticking to them from perspiration. "Maybe I should put up one of these."

"Faces east," my father said. "That's the key."

"I'll drink that beer now."

My father jumped up immediately.

Uncle Frank lowered his head and closed his eyes. He pinched the bridge of his nose and worked his fingers back and forth as if he were trying to straighten his nose. I heard the smack of the refrigerator door and the clink of bottles. I wanted my father to hurry. After what had just happened with Marie I didn't want to be alone with Uncle Frank.

Without opening his eyes Frank asked, "You playing any ball this summer, David?"

I was reluctant to answer. My uncle Frank had been a local baseball star, even playing some semipro ball during the summers when he was in college and medical school. I, on the other hand, had been such an inept ball player that I had all but given it up. But since Frank and Gloria had no children I always felt some pressure to please them, to be like the son

41

they didn't have. I finally said, "I've been doing a lot of fishing."

"Catching anything?"

"Crappies and bluegill and perch out at the lake. Some trout at the river."

"Any size to the trout?" He finally looked up at me.

"Not really. Nine inches. Maybe a couple twelve-inchers."

"Well, that's pan size. You'll have to take me out some afternoon."

Before I could answer, my father returned, carrying a bottle of beer. "Now drink it slow," he said. "Give it a chance."

Frank made a big show of holding the bottle aloft and examining it before drinking.

"What was the problem with Marie?" asked my father.

"Like you said on the phone. They're used to being treated by the medicine man. Or some old squaw. But a doctor comes around and they think he's the evil spirit or something."

My father shook his head. "They're not going to make it into the twentieth century until they give up their superstitions and old ways."

"I'm not concerned about social progress. I'm worried they're not going to survive measles. Mumps. Pneumonia. Which is what Marie might have. I'd like to get an X-ray, but I don't suppose there's much chance of that."

"Pneumonia," said my father. "That sounds serious."

"I can't be sure. I'll prescribe something just in case."

From where I stood on the porch I could see into the living room, where my mother stood. She was staring toward the porch and standing absolutely still. Her hands were pressed together as they would be in prayer, but she held her hands to her mouth. I looked quickly behind me since her attitude was exactly like someone who has seen something frightening. Nothing was there but my father and my uncle.

"Should she be in the hospital?" asked my father.

Frank rephrased the question as if my father had somehow said it wrong. "*Should* she be? That depends. Would she stay there? Or would she sneak out? Would she go home? If she's going to be in some dirty shack out on the prairie, that's no good. Now if she were staying right here. . . ."

Bentrock did not have its own hospital. The nearest one was almost forty miles away, in North Dakota. Bentrock residents usually traveled an extra twenty miles to the hospital in Dixon, Montana.

My mother came out onto the porch to answer Frank's question. "Yes, she's staying here. She's staying until she gets better." Her voice was firm and her arms were crossed, almost as if she expected an argument.

"Or until she gets worse. You don't want an Indian girl with pneumonia in your house, Gail."

"As long as she's here we can keep an eye on her."

Frank looked over at my father. If my mother said it, it was so, yet my father's confirmation was still necessary. "She can stay here," he said.

"She's staying *here*," my mother said one more time. "Someone will be here or nearby."

I couldn't figure out why my mother seemed so angry. I had always felt she didn't particularly care for Frank, but I had put that down to two reasons. First, he was charming, and my

43

mother was suspicious of charm. She believed its purpose was to conceal some personal deficit or lack of substance. If your character was sound, you didn't need charm. And second, Uncle Frank was a Hayden, and where the Haydens were concerned my mother always held something back.

Yet her comportment toward Frank had always been cordial if a little reserved. My parents and Frank and Gloria went out together; they met at least once a month to play cards; they saw each other regularly at the ranch at holidays and family gatherings. When either my father or I were hurt or fell ill, we went to see Frank or he came to see us. (My mother, however, went to old Dr. Snow, the other doctor in Bentrock. She said she would feel funny seeing Frank professionally.)

Whatever the source of her irritation, Frank must have felt it too. He abruptly put down his half-finished beer and said, "I'd better be on my way. I have the feeling I might be called out to the Hollands tonight. This is her due date, and she's usually pretty close. I'll phone Young Drug with something for Marie. Give me a call if she gets worse."

The three of us watched Frank bound down the walk, his long strides loose yet purposeful. After he got into his old Ford pickup (an affectation that my father made fun of by saying "If a doctor is going to drive an old truck, maybe I should be patrolling the streets on horseback") and drove away, my mother suggested I go outside. "I have to talk to your father," she said. "In private."

If I had gone back into the house—to the kitchen, to my room, out the back door, if I had left the porch and followed Frank's steps down the front walk—I would never have heard

44

the conversation between my father and mother, and perhaps I would have lived out my life with an illusion about my family and perhaps even the human community. Certainly I could not tell this story. . . .

I left the porch and turned to the right and went around the corner of the house. From there I was able to crouch down and double back to the side of the porch, staying below the screen and out of my parents' line of vision. I knew my mother was going to say something about Marie yelling when Uncle Frank was there, and I wanted to hear what she had to say.

I didn't have to wait long.

My mother cleared her throat, and when she began to speak, her voice was steady and strong, but her pauses were off, as if she had started on the wrong breath. "The reason, Wesley, the reason Marie didn't want to be examined by Frank is that he—he has . . . is that your brother has molested Indian girls."

My father must have started to leave because I heard the clump of a heavy footstep and my mother said quickly, "No, wait. Listen to me, please. Marie said she didn't want to be alone with him. You should have seen her. She was practically hysterical about having me stay in the room. And once Frank left she told me all of it. He's been doing it for years, Wes. When he examines an Indian he . . . he does things he shouldn't. He takes liberties. Indecent liberties."

There was a long silence. My mother's hollyhocks and snapdragons grew alongside the house where I was hiding, and the bees that flew in and out of the flowers filled the air with their drone.

Then my father spoke. "And you believe her."

"Yes, I do."

Footsteps again. Now I knew my father was pacing.

"Why would she lie, Wesley?"

My father didn't say anything, but I knew what he was thinking: She's an Indian—why would she tell the truth?

"Why, Wes?"

"I didn't say she was lying. Maybe she's simply got it wrong. An examination by a doctor. . . . Maybe she doesn't know what's supposed to go on. My gosh, I remember when I had to go see Doc Snow for my school checkups. He would poke me and tickle me and check my testicles and have me cough, and I might have felt funny about the whole business, but I knew it was part of the exam. But if I *didn't* know and. . . ."

"It's not like that. Marie told me. That's not the case."

"And if you'd never seen a doctor in your life. . . . Why, you wouldn't know what was going on."

"No, Wes."

"Think if you'd never had a shot, an injection. If you'd never seen a needle. You'd think he was trying to kill you. To stab you."

"Wesley, would you *listen* to me?"

"And Marie. For God's sake, you know how she likes to make up stories. She's been filling David's head with them for years. She's got a great sense of drama, that one—"

"*Wesley!*" My mother shouted my father's name exactly the way she would shout a baby's to stop him from doing something dangerous—toddling toward the stairs, extending his finger toward the electrical outlet—anything to stop him. I flinched and a part of me said leave, get away, run, now before it's too late, before you hear something you can't unhear. Before everything changes. But I pressed myself closer to the house and hung on.

"All right," my father said. "All right. Let's have it."

There was a shuffling, and I wondered if my mother was moving closer to my father. Her voice became lower. "I told you. When he examines Indian girls he does things to them."

"Things, Gail? He does *things* to them? I'm sure he does *things* to all his patients."

His tone must have angered her, because her voice went right back to where it had been earlier, and though it seemed each word was the product of effort it also seemed born out of absolute determination. "What things? I'll tell you what things. Your brother makes his patients—*some* of his patients—undress completely and get into indecent positions. He makes them jump up and down while he watches. He fondles their breasts. He—no, don't you turn away. *Don't!* You asked and I'm going to tell you. All of it. He puts things into these girls. Inside them, *there*. His instruments. His fingers. He has . . . your brother I believe has inserted his, his penis into some of these girls. Wesley, your brother is *raping* these women. These *girls*. These Indian girls. He offers his services to the reservation, to the BIA school. To the high school for athletic physicals. Then when he gets these girls where he wants them he. . . . *Oh!* I don't even want to say it again. *He does what he wants to do.*"

The shock of hearing this about Uncle Frank was doubled

47

because my mother was saying these words. *Rape. Breasts. Penis.* These were words I never heard my mother use—never—and I'm sure her stammer was not only from emotion but also from the strain on her vocabulary.

I waited for my father to explode, to shout a defense of his brother, to scream a condemnation of Marie and her lies. Instead, he said as quietly as before: "Why are you telling me this?"

"*Why?*"

"That's right. Why? Are you telling me this because I'm Frank's brother? Because I'm your husband? Because I'm Marie's employer?" He paused. "Or because I'm the sheriff?"

"I'm telling *you,* Wes. I'm just telling *you.* Why? What part of you doesn't want to hear it?"

"I wish," my father said, "I wish you wouldn't have told the sheriff."

Did he laugh softly, ironically, then? I thought I heard a chuckling noise, but it might have been the heavy heads of the snapdragons leaning and rustling against each other.

Neither of them spoke for a long time. I wanted to stand up, to look at them. Were they embracing? Glaring at each other? For some reason I imagined them staring off in different directions, my father toward the front lawn and the leaves that fell before they should and my mother the other way, back into the house and toward the bedroom where Marie lay sweating in her fever and her shame.

My father asked, "Did any of this happen to Marie?"

"Yes. Some. Not the worst. But her friends. People she knows."

48

"Would she be willing to talk to me?"

"She might be. If you approach her the right way."

"I only have the one way."

"I know," my mother said.

My father clapped his hands, his usual prelude to action—time to put up the storm windows, to rake the leaves, to shovel the walk, to shake the rugs. To this day, when I hear the first clap of applause in a theater, a lecture hall, a banquet, I reflexively think of my father and his call to chores. "Let's see if she's awake," he said, "and get on with it."

As they left the porch, I ran around the house and went in the back door just as they were heading into Marie's room. Neither of them said a word to me. They went in and closed the door behind them. I lingered nearby but couldn't make out a word, only the steady low murmur of voices punctuated occasionally by Marie's coughs.

On the kitchen table was Uncle Frank's beer bottle. I examined it closely, searching for the lines and whorls of his fingerprints. (One of the ways my father kept the respect and admiration of the boys in our town during the war was by fingerprinting every child who stopped by his office. I must have been fingerprinted fifteen times myself.) I was beginning already to think of Uncle Frank as a criminal. I may not have been entirely convinced of his guilt, but the story my mother told was too lurid, too frightening, for me to continue thinking of my uncle in the way I always had. Charming, affable Uncle Frank was gone for good.

49

My parents were in Marie's room for a long time, and when they came out both of them were grim-faced and silent.

"How's Marie?" I asked my mother.

"She's going to sleep a while. That's what she needs now."

Our supper was soup and sandwiches, a meal usually reserved for lunches or Sunday evenings when we got home late from spending the day at the ranch. After eating, my father went back out on the porch and simply stood there, staring out at the evening's lengthening shadows. My mother was finishing the dishes when he came back in and announced, "I'm going over to talk to Len."

Len McAuley was my father's deputy and our next-door neighbor, and before he was my father's deputy he had been my grandfather's deputy. I once heard a story about how Len, without a weapon, ran down on foot and disarmed a cowboy who shot up a bar on Main Street, but the story was hard to believe about the Len McAuley I knew. He was tall, gaunt, stoop-shouldered, shy, and soft-spoken. Len and his wife Daisy (who made up for Len's taciturnity with both the quantity and the volume of her talk) were in their sixties, and they were more like grandparents to me than my own. When I was younger, Len used to carve little animals for my play, and Daisy never stopped baking cookies for me.

As my father went out the door, my mother called after him, "If Daisy's home tell her I've got a fresh pot of coffee!"

Moments later they were off on their own, my father and Len standing in the McAuley front yard and my mother and Daisy sitting at our kitchen table. But there were similarities. All four were drinking coffee. In each pair one talked while the other listened. (My mother and Len were the listeners.) And both my father and mother were, I knew, conducting investigations.

I wandered in and out of the house, catching fragments of both conversations, until my mother finally said, "David. Either go out or stay in." Daisy laughed and said, "He's like Cuss"—her cat—"when he's out, he wants to go in. When he's in he wants to go out."

Both my parents were discreet about their investigations. Neither came right out and repeated Marie's story about Uncle Frank, yet they used the same strategy: to mention Marie's perturbation and then to pretend mystification—"I don't know why she would act that way," my mother said, while my father shook his head in puzzlement. They both left openings for Len or Daisy to contribute what they could.

And my mother struck pay dirt.

On one of my passes through the kitchen, Daisy was hunched over the table, her white hair bobbing in my mother's direction and her tanned plump arm reaching toward my mother. Daisy's usually loud, brassy voice was lowered, but I heard her say, "The word is he doesn't do everything on the up-and-up." Then she noticed me. She straightened up and smiled at me but stopped talking. That meant I was supposed to leave the room, and I did. But slowly. As I crossed into the living room, Daisy whispered, "Just the squaws though."

Later that night, right before we all went to bed, my

mother checked on Marie once more. When she came out my father and I were in the kitchen, drinking milk and eating the rhubarb cake that Daisy had brought over.

My mother shut Marie's door quietly and then leaned her back against it, almost as if she were using her weight to keep the door closed. She looked tired. She was still wearing her work clothes—she usually changed into dungarees or slacks and a gingham shirt as soon as she got home. Her glasses were off and her eyes were ringed with fatigue. Her lipstick had faded, and she hadn't brushed out her hair.

My father asked without looking up, "How's Marie?"

My mother's gaze was fixed upon my father. "You're eating," she said.

"Daisy's cake. It's delicious."

"You can eat. . . ."

At some point my father must have become aware that she was staring at him. His cake unfinished, he set down his fork. "I don't hear her coughing."

"She's sleeping again." I couldn't tell if she was actually looking at him or if she was simply staring off and his form intersected her vision.

Then I knew. She saw him now as she hadn't before. He was not only her husband, he was a *brother,* and brother to a man who used his profession to take advantage of women, brother to a *pervert!* And how did I know these were my mother's thoughts? I knew because they were mine. I put down my glass of milk but I did not look at my father. I didn't want to notice the way he combed his hair straight back. I didn't want to see the little extra mound of flesh between his eyebrows. I didn't want to see the way the long line of his nose was interrupted by a slight inward curve. I didn't want to see any of the ways that he resembled his brother.

"What did Len say?" asked my mother.

"That we need rain."

My mother hung her head.

"That's what we talked about, Gail."

She brought her head up quickly. "That's not what Daisy and I talked about."

"I don't want this all over town, Gail. We don't have proof of anything."

Now they were falling into familiar roles. My father believed in *proof*, in evidence, and he held off on his own convictions until he had sufficient evidence to support them. My mother, on the other hand, was willing to go on a lot less, on her feelings, her faith.

My mother said, "It's around town more than you realize."

"I don't want this getting back to my father."

That was what my father believed in. If he could not sufficiently fear, love, trust, obey, and honor God—as we were told in catechism class we must—it was because he had nothing left for his Heavenly Father after declaring absolute fealty to his earthly one.

"Is that what you're concerned about?"

"Gail. . . ."

My mother pointed at me. "He won't be going to him again. I guarantee that."

"For God's sake, Gail."

"He *won't*."

I was afraid I would give myself away—by blushing or failing to react the way I should. I wasn't supposed to know what they were talking about.

"Let's not discuss this in front of him."

My mother continued to stare at him.

"I'll handle this, Gail. In my fashion."

After another long silence, my mother finally left her post at Marie's door. She was almost out of the kitchen when she turned and said to my father in the calmest voice she had used all evening: "Just one thing, Wes. You never said you didn't believe it. Why is that? Why?"

She waited for his answer. I waited too, breathlessly, looking down at our floor's speckled linoleum and holding my sight on one green speck until my father said, of course I don't believe it; of course it isn't true.

But he didn't say a word. He simply picked up his fork and continued to eat Daisy McAuley's rhubarb cake.

That was when it came to me. Uncle Frank was my father's brother, and my father knew him as well as any man or woman.

And my father knew he was guilty.

Two

❀ ❀ ❀

THE next day my father began investigating the accusation Marie had made against his brother. How did I know this? I made my guess from three facts. Before he left for his office in the morning he asked my mother if she needed any honey. He was driving out to the reservation, and if she liked he could stop at Birdwells' and buy her some honey. My mother had a passion for honey. She spread it on toast and biscuits; she sweetened her tea with it; she used it in baking; she ate spoonfuls of it right from the jar. And the best honey, she said, came from the Birdwells' bee farm. Mr. Birdwell's place was on the highway that led to the reservation.

My father's inquiry about the honey was, first of all, an overture of peace to my mother. Let's not quarrel, my father was saying. (The phrase he often used with both my mother and me was, "Let's not have this unpleasantness between us," as if the problem, whatever it might be, resided not *in* us but *outside* of us.)

And, second, the offer to buy honey was also an offhand way for my father to announce that he was going out to the reservation. He had no jurisdiction there, and the reservation police hadn't called him in on a case, so he could be going there for only one reason: to look into the accusations Marie had made.

Later that day I saw my father at the Coffee Cup, a popular diner in downtown Bentrock. There was nothing uncommon about my father (or any other citizen) being in the Coffee Cup on a summer afternoon, but my father usually sat at the large table in the center of the cafe, drinking coffee with his regular group: Don Young, the pharmacist; Rand Hutchinson, the owner of Hutchinson's Greenhouse; Howard Bailey, who ran an oil abstracting company; and other members of the Bentrock business community. On that day, however, he sat at a table for two over against the far wall. With him sat Ollie Young Bear, the most respected—even beloved—Indian in northeastern Montana, perhaps even the whole state.

Ollie Young Bear was also a war hero (he was wounded in action in North Africa), a graduate of Montana State University in Bozeman, a deacon at First Lutheran Church, an executive with Montana-Dakota Utilities Company, the star pitcher on the Elks' fast-pitch softball team—runner-up in the Silver Division of the state tournament (though he probably could not have been admitted to the Elks as a member). He did not smoke, drink, or curse. He married Doris Strickland, a white woman whose family owned a prosperous ranch south of Bentrock, and Ollie and Doris had two shy, polite children, a boy and a girl. All of these accomplishments made Ollie the perfect choice for white people to point to as an example of what Indians *could* be. My father liked to say of Ollie Young Bear, "He's a testimony to what hard work will get you."

And it was not as though Ollie had forsaken his own

58

people. Though he was not from the reservation, he drove out there every weekend with bats and balls, equipment he paid for out of his own pocket, and organized baseball games for the boys.

Because my father obviously liked and respected him—held him up, in fact, as a model—I tried to feel the same way about him. But it was difficult.

Mr. Young Bear, as my father insisted I call him, was a stern, censorious man. He was physically imposing—tall, barrel-chested, broad-shouldered, large-headed—and he never smiled. His lips were perpetually turned down in an expression both sad and disdainful. He seemed to find no humor in the world, and I have no memory of hearing him laugh.

He and my father went bowling together, and I was sometimes allowed to tag along. I didn't particularly care for the sport, but I loved Castle's Bowling Alley, a dark, narrow (only four lanes), low-ceilinged basement establishment that smelled of cigar smoke and floor wax. I loved to put my bottle of Nehi grape soda right next to my father's beer bottle on the scorecard holder and to slide my shoes under the bench with my father's when we changed into bowling shoes. I loved the sounds, the heavy clunk of the ball dropped on wood, its rumble down the alley, the clatter of pins, and above it all, men's shouts—"Go, go, gogogo!" "Get *in* there!" "Drop, *drop!*" Then the muttered curses while they waited for the pin boy to reset the pins. When I was in Castle's Alley I felt, no matter how many women or children might also be there, as though I had gained admittance to a men's enclave, as though I had *arrived*.

When Ollie Young Bear was with us, however, I felt like a

child. Ollie could not keep from giving me instruction or correcting my game. Make sure you bring the ball straight back, he would say. Follow through. Use a five-step approach, keep your eye on the spot and not the pins. He was relentless in his criticism, and my father would simply say, "Now listen to what Ollie's telling you. Do you know what kind of average he's carrying in league play? Two-ten. You listen to what he's telling you." I know my father was trying to show his esteem for Ollie and his lack of prejudice, but the only thing that was accomplished was that going bowling began to seem an awful lot like going to school.

When I saw my father and Ollie Young Bear sitting together at a table away from the others in the café, I knew my father was asking Ollie if he had heard anything about Uncle Frank molesting Indian girls. Was he asking the right man? I wondered. Although Ollie Young Bear was much admired by the white population, he had no special status among the Indians. In fact, I once heard Marie say of Ollie, "He won't be happy until he's white." Both Ollie and my father leaned over the table, their coffee cups between them, their voices low.

I left my friends at the counter and crossed the room to say hello to my father.

As I walked toward them, Ollie Young Bear was the first to notice me. He stopped talking and sat up straight, and then both of them stared at me. Neither smiled nor gave any sign of recognition, and I felt as if I were moving down a long chute, as if I were livestock, a horse, a sheep, a calf, being inspected as I walked. At that moment I knew that as long as this business was going on with his brother, my father had no use for a son. I could come and go as I wished; he wasn't about to notice me.

When I got to the table, my father said, "What can I do for you, David?"

By way of explanation I pointed to my friends at the counter. "We were fishing. . . ."

My father reached for his billfold. "You need some money."

"No, that's okay." I backed away. "I just wanted to say hi."

He managed a smile. "Are you going home? Look in on Marie, will you? Make sure she's taken her medicine."

When I got home Marie's door was open slightly but she was sleeping, as she almost always seemed to be since she'd gotten sick. Her bottle of pills and a glass of water were beside the bed, so I assumed she had taken what she was supposed to. I didn't want to wake her.

I was in the house for a few minutes when I felt something was wrong, yet I wasn't sure what it was. Then it struck me. It was the silence.

On our kitchen counter was a small Philco radio, its once-shining wood case now dull and riven with tiny hairline cracks in the varnish (on the top there was a darker brown ring where something—either a tube inside or a hot object out-side—had burned a perfect circle). The radio wasn't on and probably hadn't been for a couple days, and when Marie was there she always had the radio on, usually tuned to a Canadian station that played Big Band music. To this day when I hear one of those television commercials urging us to send in $19.95 to get all the hits of the Big Band era—The Glen Miller Band, Artie Shaw and His Orchestra, Paul Whiteman, Kay Kaiser, Duke Ellington—or when I hear even a few bars of that music—"String of Pearls," "Tuxedo Junction," "Satin Doll"—I think of Marie. But I do not send my money in. My memories are strong enough—and painful enough—without prodding them further.

I turned the radio on and raised the volume, hoping that Marie would be able to hear her music when she woke.

That night, after we had eaten dinner and my mother had fixed soup for Marie, my father stood at the kitchen table and said, "Gail, maybe you and David would like to go for a walk. I want to speak to Marie again."

My mother began to stack dishes but my father stopped her. "Those can wait. I want to talk to Marie right now. While she's awake."

"She might want me here. She might feel more comfortable."

"Yes, she might, but I'm afraid Marie's comfort isn't what's important now. This is something that has to be done. You and David go outside."

Since he had questioned Marie before when I was in the house I figured that this time it was my mother he didn't want around. But she didn't seem to understand, and she persisted.

62

She said, "There might be some ways I can help."

By this time my father had retrieved a small notebook from the pocket of his suit coat. He stopped flipping its pages to say to my mother, "Did you hear me, Gail? Some of this I'd just as soon you didn't hear."

Was he being gallant—sparing his wife from hearing the particulars of his brother's alleged crimes? Or was he protecting his brother and keeping the number of witnesses to the accounts of his crimes to a minimum?

My mother and I didn't go far. That was all right. She wasn't much for taking walks and I was child enough to think I was too old to go for walks with my mother. We stayed in the backyard, though it was big enough that if we did nothing but walk up and down its length we could have gotten our exercise.

We stood in the middle of the yard while a gusty wind that lowered the temperature twenty degrees in less than an hour whipped my mother's hair in front of her face and wrapped her skirt tight against her legs. A cool front was moving through—sure to ruin the fishing, the local fishermen would say. My mother shivered and folded her arms. "I should have brought a sweater," she said.

"Do you want me to get you one?"

"*No*," my mother said sharply. "No. You stay out of there. Your father's doing . . . official business."

I swallowed hard. I had already decided that I was going to ask my mother, once we were alone out there, why my father was talking to Marie. I knew the reason, of course, yet I wanted my knowledge out in the open. I wanted to be included, to know more than what my eavesdropping brought me. I supposed I wanted adult status, to have my parents discuss this case in front of me, not to have to leave rooms or to have people shut up when I came near, or worst of all, have them speak in code as if I were a baby who could be kept in ignorance by grown-ups spelling words in his presence.

Yet now that I had the opportunity, alone with my mother, my courage was running out. I wasn't sure which prospect was more unsettling: that she wouldn't tell me anything and would scold me for prying, or that she would reveal everything and I would have to hear that story coming from my mother's lips.

Finally I emboldened myself enough to ask a quick, awkward, suitably vague question: "What's going on, anyway?"

My mother kept her face turned to the wind but had closed her eyes against the blowing dust.

"Oh, there's some trouble going on with the Indians. Possible trouble, I should say." Now she was as cautious as my father.

"Why does he have to talk to Marie? When she's sick."

She took a long time in answering. Obviously her mind was elsewhere, somewhere off with the wind. "He thinks Marie might have some information."

"I thought the BIA handled Indian problems."

"He's just helping, dear. It's not so much."

"It's not so much" was a phrase my mother inherited from her mother. I had heard Grandma Anglund use it for occasions ranging from a scraped knee (mine) to a family burned out of its farm. It was her Norwegian way of keeping all our earthly affairs from achieving too much importance.

My mother wandered a few steps away and stopped next to the one tree we had in our backyard, a towering, spreading oak exactly in the center of the lawn—precisely in the spot that kept the yard from being a boy's perfect football field.

"I love the wind," she said, tilting her head up to catch as much of it on her face as she could. "It reminds me of North Dakota. My goodness, how Dad used to curse the wind. 'Carrying away the topsoil,' he'd say. 'Giving it to South Dakota.' But I always loved it, that feel of rushing air. Bringing something new, was the way I felt."

"Makes good fishing," I said. "Riffles the water so the fish can't see you."

She turned a slow circle. "But the wind has a different smell here. In North Dakota it always smelled like dirt. Even in the middle of winter with all that snow there could still be the smell of dirt in the air. As if the wind came from some open place that never froze. But here the wind smells like the mountains. Like snow. Like stone. No matter how far away the mountains are, I still feel them out there. I can't get used to it. I never will. I guess I'm a flatlander at heart."

Had I any sensitivity at all I might have recognized that all this talk about wind and dirt and mountains and childhood was my mother's way of saying she wanted a few moments of purity, a temporary escape from the sordid drama that was playing itself out in her own house. But I was on the trail of something that would lead me out of childhood.

"Is Marie in trouble?" I asked. "Is Ronnie?"

"What? Oh, no. No, nothing like that. Your dad just wants

to see if she can give him some information. Answer some questions."

I looked back at the house. I could see, in the kitchen window, my father's form. I wondered how long he had been watching us. "He's out," I said. "We can go back in."

My mother turned and waved in my father's direction. If he saw he gave no sign, yet he remained in the window.

"The sun must be in his eyes," she said.

"Let's go in."

"You go ahead. I'm going to stay out here for awhile."

"And sniff the wind?"

She laughed. "Something like that."

The following Sunday the wind that my mother loved was still blowing as we drove out to my grandparents' ranch. We were traveling in our new Hudson that my father bought that year, and even that big, heavy boat rocked slightly in the wind once we were out in open country. It was a hot day, yet we had to keep the windows rolled up to keep the dust and grit from blowing into the car.

Marie felt a little better, so we thought it might be all right to leave her for the day. Besides, Daisy was right next door, and she would look in on Marie. Later in the afternoon Doris Looks Away, a friend of Marie's, was going to stop by the house.

Neither of my parents spoke as we rode, and the silence in the car was as oppressive as the heat. I knew why they weren't talking. My mother wanted to refuse the dinner invitation because Uncle Frank and his wife would be there. My parents tried to keep their quarrels from me, but that morning I had heard my father say, "For Christ's sake, Gail. They're my parents. What am I supposed to do—break off with them too?" "You don't have to curse," was my mother's only response. The next thing I knew, we were getting into the car. The excursion was all right with me. I hadn't been out to the ranch in a while, and I was eager to see my horse and to spend as much of the day riding as I could.

As soon as we turned off the highway and onto the rutted, washboard road that led to my grandparents', loose gravel and scoria began to clatter under the car. A thick cloud of red-tan dust rose behind us. Almost shouting, my father said, "I've been thinking. What would you two think of taking a few days later this month and going down to Yellowstone? Camp out. See the geysers."

"A real vacation," my mother said. "The mountains."

"Why not," my father said, as he held the jiggling steering wheel with both hands. "Why not us?"

It wasn't much of an exchange, but I knew what it meant: my parents were no longer fighting. I also knew we wouldn't go to Yellowstone. My father disliked conflict so much that he would frequently make a promise or a suggestion—like a family vacation—intended to make everyone feel better. Unfortunately, often he did not keep the promises.

When we pulled up in front of the ranch house, Uncle Frank's truck was already there. Covered with the day's dust, the Ford looked even older and more battered than usual.

"They're here," my mother said softly.

My grandparents' house was built of logs, but it was no cabin; in fact, there was nothing simple or unassuming about it. The house was huge—two stories, five bedrooms, a dining room bigger than some restaurants, a stone fireplace that two children could stand in. The ceilings were high and open-beamed. The interior walls were log as well. And the furnishings were equally rough-hewn and massive. Leather couches and armchairs. Trestle tables. Brass lamps. Sheepskin rugs on the floors and Indian blankets on the walls. Hanging in my grandfather's den were two gun cases, racks of antlers from deer, elk, bighorn sheep, and antelope, and a six-foot rattlesnake skin. One of the few times I heard my father say anything disparaging about his parents was in reference to their home. He once said, as we drove up to the house, "This place looks like every Easterner's idea of a dude ranch." (For a Montanan there was no greater insult than to have your name associated with the term "dude.") My mother, who disliked ostentation of any sort, was especially offended by the house's log construction—usually symbolic of simplicity and humility. (Her parents' house was a very modest two-story white farmhouse—neat, trim, pleasant, but revealing nothing of the occupants' prosperity.)

And I?—I loved that house! It was large enough that I could find complete privacy somewhere no matter how many others were in there. The adults might be downstairs playing whist while I crept around upstairs, toy gun in hand, searching from room to room for the men who robbed the Bentrock First National Bank.

When I slept over I was given a second-floor bedroom with wide, tall windows that faced north, and I sat at those windows and picked out the Big and Little Dippers, the only constellations I could identify. Or I imagined that the wide porch was the deck of a ship and the surrounding prairie the limitless sea.

Grandpa stood on the porch to greet us. He was dressed in his Sunday rich ranch owner best—white Western shirt and string tie, whipcord trousers, and the boots that were hand-made in Texas. He was alone, and while we got out of the car he watched us as impassively as he would strangers. He had his hands thrust in his back pockets, and his big belly stuck out like a stuffed sack of grain. His legs were spread wide, as if he were bracing himself. He wore his white hair longer than most men—over the tops of his ears, curling over his shirt collar, and with bushy sideburns almost to his jowls. As he stood there the wind lifted his hair and made his large head seem even larger.

It was the first time I had seen Grandpa Hayden since I heard about Uncle Frank, and when I saw him towering there like a thundercloud I thought, he won't let anything happen to his beloved son. He won't. But what if it's his *other* son who's trying to do something. . . .

"Can I go down to the stable?" I asked.

"You certainly may not," my mother said. "You come in first and greet your grandparents and find out how long until dinner."

My mother lifted a cake pan from the front seat. When he saw it, Grandpa Hayden said in his booming voice, "What have you got in there? Damn it, Enid said you didn't have to bring a thing."

"Hello, Julian," my mother said as she stepped onto the porch. "I thought you liked chocolate cake."

Grandfather took the pan from her. "Don't even take it in there. Hell, they don't have to know about it. I'll take care of it myself."

"What are you doing out here, Pop?" asked my father. "Acting as the official welcoming committee?"

"Came out here to fart. I had sausage for breakfast, and I'm not going to stay in the house any longer and squeeze 'em in. Can't do it."

My mother took the cake pan back and went into the house. She hated talk about bodily functions even more than she hated swearing. Both were specialties of my grandfather.

My father took up a position at the porch rail next to Grandfather. "That wind's something," my father said.

"If you don't like wind," Grandfather replied, "you don't like Montana. Because it blows here 360 days a year. Better get used to it."

That was another of my grandfather's specialties—turning casual remarks so they became opportunities for him to pass on his judgments or browbeating opinions. I was about to go when my father turned around, stared at the house, and asked softly, "Pop, where's Frank?"

"He's in there poking and twisting your mother's shoulders. Trying to figure out if she's got bursitis. Hell, I know she's got bursitis."

"Can I ask you something, Pop?"

I had my hand on the handle of the screen door while my father watched me, waiting for me to go in before he continued. I went in the house but stayed right by the door so I could hear what my father said.

"It's about Frank. . . ."

Yes, tell him, I thought. Tell Grandfather. Tell him, and he'll take care of everything. He'll grab Uncle Frank by the shoulders and shake him so hard his bones will clatter like castanets. He'll shake him up and shout in Frank's face that he'd better straighten up and fly right or there'll be hell to pay. And because it's Grandfather, that will be the end of it. Frank would never touch a woman like that again. *Tell him.*

My father cleared his throat. "About him and Gloria not having kids. . . . You've got to go easy on that, Pop. They want kids. They're trying."

"You know that, do you? Frank tell you that?"

"Not right out, but—"

"They sure as hell look healthy. Glo might be tiny but she's got enough tit for twins. What's the problem? He's a goddamn doctor. He ought to be able to figure it out."

"Pop. Listen to yourself."

My grandfather's boot heels thunked on the porch planks. "Your mother and I thought we'd have more to show than the one grandchild. Nothing against Davy. But Christ—just the one? From both of you?"

"You know what she went through with David. After that we decided—"

"—and white," Grandfather interrupted. "We want them white."

The silence was so sudden and complete I thought at first that they saw me and that was why they quit talking. But I didn't move; if I did they'd see me for sure.

My father said something I barely heard: "What do you mean by that?"

Grandfather laughed a deep, breathy *cuh-cuh-cuh* that sounded like half cough and half laugh. "Come on, Wesley. Come on, boy. You know Frank's always been partial to red meat. He couldn't have been any older than Davy when Bud caught him down in the stable with that little Indian girl. Bud said to me, 'Mr. Hayden, you better have a talk with that boy. He had that little squaw down on her hands and knees. He's been learnin' from watching the dogs and the horses and the bulls.' I wouldn't be surprised if there wasn't some young ones out on the reservation who look a lot like your brother."

One of them approached the screen door, and I quickly slipped away from my hiding post and into the living room. I picked up the first thing at hand—a cigarette lighter that looked like a derringer—and began to squeeze the trigger over and over, each time scraping the flint and throwing up a small, pungent flame. I tried to make my concentration on the lighter seem so total that no one would suspect me of eaves-dropping.

It was my father coming through the door, and as he did he said over his shoulder to Grandfather, "I suspect you might be right on that." To me he said, "Put that down, David. It's not a toy."

72

It was the second time I had heard my grandfather say something about my uncle and Indian girls. . . .

Neither my father nor my uncle married women from Bentrock, or from Montana, for that matter. (That was probably another reason for people to resent the Haydens. I could imagine someone from town saying, "Weren't any of the local girls good enough for the Hayden boys?") My mother, as I mentioned, was from North Dakota, and Gloria was from Minnesota. My father met my mother while he was in law school, and Frank met Gloria while he was in medical school at the University of Minnesota. My parents were married soon after they met; Frank and Gloria, however, had an on-again, off-again romance for years.

They were finally married in Minneapolis, Gloria's hometown. This was during the war, and Frank was home on leave. The wedding took place right after Christmas, and it was a small, quiet affair, with only a few friends and family in attendance. Grandfather paid for all of us to travel by train to the wedding and to stay in a hotel in Minneapolis. It was the first time I was on a train and the first time I stayed in a hotel.

The night before the wedding my father, Grandfather, Uncle Frank, an old college friend of his, and two of Gloria's brothers went out together for Frank's bachelor party.

They didn't return to the hotel until quite late. I was already asleep, but I woke up when my father came in. He was drunk—which made another first for me. I had never seen my

73

father take more than one drink. I lay quietly in bed while my mother helped my father undress. She also tried to keep him quiet, but it was no use; he was too drunk and too excited to keep his voice low.

"You should have seen it, Gail," he said. "By God, it was something. This Minneapolis big shot, this city boy, wouldn't let up. Kept saying to Pop, 'Mighty fine boots. Mighty fine. Just hope you're not tracking in any cow shit with those boots.' Wouldn't stop."

"Shhh. Watch your language. David can hear you."

"Just reporting. That's all. Just saying how it was. Finally Pop says, 'You don't let up, I'm going to stick one of these boots up your ass. Then I'm going to track *your* shit all over this bar.' "

"Oh, Wesley!"

He laughed. Giggled would be more accurate. "I've got to say what happened, don't I? This city fellow thinks he's heard enough. He plops his hat down on the bar, takes off his glasses and sets them down too. He starts for our table. But by the time he gets there Pop has pulled out that little .32 revolver of his. Chrome-plated so it's the shiniest thing in the place. Hell, I didn't know he had it with him. Anyway, he's got that gun right in the fella's face, and the guy goes white. He's just white as a sheet. Pop holds it there for a minute, and then he says, 'Out in Montana you wouldn't be worth dirtying a man's hands on. Or his boots. So we'd handle him this way. Nice and clean.' And he keeps holding the gun on him. I thought maybe I should say something, but Frank reaches over and puts his hand on my arm. Frank's laughing to beat the band, so he must know something. Finally Pop says, 'Now you head on out of here and you better hope the snow covers your tracks because I'm going to finish this whiskey and then I'm coming after you.' By God, Gail, you should have seen that fella hightail it out of there! Left without his hat and glasses. And Pop just sits back down and finishes his whiskey. Doesn't say a word. Meanwhile Frank's laughing so hard he gets *me* going and then neither one of us can stop. People are leaving the bar right and left—probably afraid of these wild and woolly cowboys from Montana—and Frank and I are howling our heads off. Then when we leave we notice that Minneapolis hasn't even *got* any snow. And that sets Frank and me off all over again. Oh, Gail, I wish you could've been there. The Hayden boys all over again. The Hayden boys and their old man."

By that time, my mother had gotten him into bed and was covering him. "I don't think you'll find this so funny tomorrow morning. You're lucky you weren't all arrested."

"They couldn't arrest us—we *are* the law!" My father found that idea hilarious. He started laughing so hard he could barely breathe. Soon he was coughing and choking, and then he had to rush to the bathroom. The next thing I heard was my father vomiting. He was in there so long I fell asleep before he came out.

After the wedding the next day on the train going back to Montana, my grandfather offered a box of chocolates to my mother, Grandmother, and me. My father couldn't even look at them, a fact that my grandfather found amusing. My grandfather had a sweet tooth, and he insisted those were the best chocolates in the world, available only from a small confectionary in downtown Minneapolis.

Soon they were all talking about Frank and Gloria and the wedding, how nice the ceremony was, what a lovely woman Gloria was, how they hoped for a happy life for the two of them. Then Grandfather said, "Now he's got himself a good-looking white woman for a wife. That better keep him off the reservation."

No one said another word. Every one of us turned to the window as if there were actually something to look at besides wind-whipped, snow-covered prairies.

At dinner I sat between my grandmother and Aunt Gloria. My grandmother, a thin, nervous woman who seldom spoke when my grandfather was present, concentrated during the meal on cutting her ham into small perfect triangles before she ate them. Whenever she passed a dish to me she asked quietly, "Do you like this, David?" and her questions seemed so eager and pathetic that I said yes to everything. As a result, my plate was piled high with sweet potatoes and cooked carrots and sliced tomatoes and cottage cheese and kidney beans and corn bread and ham. And I had no appetite.

Aunt Gloria chattered throughout the meal. She talked about the weather and the price of milk. She talked about how, even though the war had been over for three years, she still felt funny about throwing out a tin can. She taught first grade, and she talked about how she was going to make little construction paper Indian headbands for all her students, with their names on the feathers. She talked about her little brother who was in college in Missoula and who told her how the ex-GI's pushed the professors around.

I loved Aunt Gloria—she was sweet and beautiful and good to me—yet that day I couldn't bear to look at her. How could she act normal, I wondered, when she was married to Uncle Frank? How could she not *know?*

Those were the cleanest thoughts I had. The ones I tried to suppress went something like this: Why would Uncle Frank want another woman when he had a wife like Gloria? And this line of thought was nudged along by my own desire. I thought Aunt Gloria was more than pretty. . . .

A year earlier I had stayed with Frank and Gloria when my parents were in Helena for a law-enforcement convention. I usually stayed home with Marie or with my grandparents at the ranch when my parents were out of town, but during that time Marie was doing something with her family and Grandmother was recovering from gall-bladder surgery.

While my parents were gone, I came down with a case of tonsilitis, as I frequently did as a child. Uncle Frank gave me a shot of penicillin, and Aunt Gloria took better care of me than my own mother. She made me chicken soup and Jell-O, she brought me comic books and ginger ale, and she never let more than an hour pass without checking on me.

She came in late one night to make sure I was covered. I kept my eyes closed and pretended to be asleep, but when she bent down to feel my forehead I could smell her perfume. The scent itself seemed warm as it closed in on me. She backed away and went to the window, and I opened one eye. She was wearing just the top of a pair of pajamas, and as she stood before the window just enough light came in from the street lamp to silhouette her breasts perfectly. I closed my eyes again, out of both shame and fear of being caught looking.

From the doorway came Uncle Frank's whisper. "Is he asleep?"

"Shhh," Aunt Gloria whispered back. "Yes." She tiptoed out of the room. In the hall Uncle Frank said aloud, "So this is what it's like to have kids. Damn."

Before long, I heard them through the wall in their own bedroom. Their bedsprings squeaked rhythmically; I thought I could her breathing—a sound spreading through the house as if it were more than sound, as if it were a presence, like perfume, like darkness itself. Later I heard them in the bathroom together. I couldn't make out anything they said, but that didn't matter. By then I was concentrating on only one thing: one more reason to envy Uncle Frank.

It was shame again that Sunday that kept me from looking at Aunt Gloria during our meal. And the day had one more similarity to that night. As Gloria leaned toward me to take a plate of tomatoes from Grandmother, I smelled my aunt's perfume again. But the lush sweet floral scent—so out of place in that rough-timbered room and among all those odors of food—did not excite me this time. This time it made me so sad I wanted to cry.

As soon as the meal was over, I asked if I could be excused to go riding. My parents gave me permission so quickly I wondered if they were planning to bring up the accusations against Uncle Frank as soon as I was out of the house. No, not in front of Grandmother. My father might have said something to Grandfather, but they would have gone to any extreme to keep that from Grandmother. It was often said that she was "nervous," a term that did not merely mean, as it does when it is applied to someone today, that she fidgeted, bit her nails, or worried too much (though she did all three); no, it meant that Grandmother had a condition that could strike her down at any time, as if a virus lived quietly in her but could suddenly run loose on a moment's notice if something upset her. Everyone knew the importance of shielding Grandmother from shocks of any kind.

Before I left the dining room, my grandfather stopped me. "Hold on there, David. Wait up a minute." He got up from the table and went into his den.

He came back in just a moment, and he was carrying a gun, a Hi-Standard automatic .22 target pistol and a box of cartridges.

"Goddamn coyotes," he said. "They're getting worse than ever. You see any out there, blast away."

Like almost every kid in Montana I had my own little arsenal—a .22 for plinking at prairie dogs and snakes; a .410-gauge shotgun for hunting pheasant, grouse, ducks, and geese; and a 30-30 for hunting deer. But in my case, all were single-shot. My father believed there was nothing worse than sloppy marksmanship and wasting ammunition. Having only one shot was a great incentive for learning to make that shot count. The theory was a good one, but it did not prove out in my case. I was never a very good shot but I was awfully quick at reloading.

Handguns were different, however. They were somehow not serious, not for bringing down game but for shooting as an activity in and of itself, and therefore slightly suspect.

I looked eagerly at my parents for their permission. My mother didn't care for guns of any kind but she had long ago seen the futility of trying to keep them out of the hands of a Montana boy. She simply shrugged. My father might have been troubled by my having both a pistol and a gun that could burn so much ammunition, but he only said, "Coyotes. Just coyotes."

I took the gun and shells from my grandfather and walked slowly out of the house, but once I was outside I ran to the stable. Within minutes I had saddled Nutty and was riding at a brisk trot out to some sagebrush hills and rimrock ravines where I often played. I didn't actually think I'd see any coyotes out there, but I'd be far enough from the ranch that I could fire off as many rounds as I wanted without anyone hearing.

I shot up that entire box of bullets. There was so much gunfire out there that afternoon that the ground glittered with my casings and Nutty became so accustomed to the shots that he grazed right through the barrage. After a while his ears didn't even twitch at the continual *pop-pop-pop*.

The .22 had very little recoil but after firing clip after clip, my hand and arm felt the effects. My hand tingled as if a low-level electrical current was passing through it, and my arm felt pleasantly loose and warm from the wrist to the shoulder.

I could have used all that ammunition to improve my marksmanship, aiming carefully at my targets and slowly squeezing off one shot at a time, but I didn't. Instead I tried to see how fast I could fire off a whole clip, shooting into the ground just to see the dirt fly. When I had a target (pinecones, branches, knotholes) I often fired at it from the hip or threw a hasty shot as I was whirling around. Most of the time I missed.

But once. I shot and killed a magpie.

He was teetering on a branch, his black feathers glistening like oil and his long tail wavering to steady him in the wind.

Less than forty yards away, I brought the .22 quickly up to shoulder height and snapped off a shot with no more care than pointing my finger.

The bird toppled from the branch, but in the instant of its fall it had enough life left—or perhaps it was only the wind— to open its wings and in so doing slow its descent.

To confirm my kill I walked over to where the magpie lay. Its half-open, glassy green eye was already beginning to dust over. This wasn't the first time I had killed something and it wouldn't be the last, and I felt the way I often did, that extraordinary mixture of power and sadness, exhilaration and fear. But there was something new.

I felt strangely calm, as if I had been in a state of high agitation but had now come down, my pulse returned to normal, my breathing slowed, my vision cleared. I needed that, I thought; I hadn't even known it but I needed to kill something. The events, the discoveries, the secrets of the past few days—Marie's illness, Uncle Frank's sins, the tension between my father and mother—had excited something in me that wasn't released until I shot a magpie out of a piñon pine.

I felt the way I did when I woke from an especially disturbing and powerful dream. Even as the dream's narrative escaped—like trying to hold water in your hand—its emotion stayed behind. Looking in the dead bird's eye, I realized that these strange, unthought-of connections—sex and death, lust and violence, desire and degradation—are there, there, deep in even a good heart's chambers.

With my boot heel I dug a shallow depression in the hard-baked dirt and nudged the magpie into it. I kicked some dirt over the bird, just enough to dull the sheen of its feathers.

I took a different route back to the ranch, riding slowly along a pine-covered ridge that looked down on McCormick Creek, a stream I sometimes fished. I was scouting for places where the water was high enough to give the trout pools to gather in.

Less than a mile from the ranch, where the creek widened and was bordered by an expanse of rocky, sandy beach, on the near side I saw two men. I pulled up Nutty and watched until I could see who it was. Uncle Frank and my father were standing on the riverbank, and they seemed to be arguing. I was too far away to hear what they said, but they were gesturing angrily at each other and speaking over the other's words.

It was strange. From that height I noticed something I had never noticed before. I noticed how the two men were brothers in posture and attitude. Two men in dress pants and white shirts, each bent forward slightly at the waist almost as if he were leaning into the wind. Each pointed at the other like a schoolteacher scolding a pupil. And when each was done talking he leaned back, squared his shoulders, and put his hands on his hips—exactly the way my father stood while he listened to one of my excuses for not cutting the grass or doing some chore.

I figured my father must have been confronting his brother over Marie's accusations, and I wanted to get closer so I could hear what they were saying. I dismounted and, as quietly as I could, began to weave my way down the hill. About halfway down the trees thinned, so I had to stop or be seen. I hid behind a thick pine.

I still couldn't hear them, but I wasn't sure if it was the distance or the fact that they had lowered their voices. Now they were barely speaking. Uncle Frank was backing away and muttering something. My father picked up a rock, wound up as if he were going to throw it as far as he could, then simply tossed it into the creek. I watched the splash to see if a trout rose to check it out as they sometimes will. Nothing. I wasn't surprised. You weren't likely to get a trout out in the middle of a shallow creek on a hot day.

Then Frank took a sudden step toward my father. Frank's arms were spread wide, beseechingly, yet his movement was so quick it seemed threatening.

I still had my grandfather's pistol, tucked inside the waistband of my jeans. I took it out, thumbed off the safety, and rested the gun against the stub of a branch. My view of Uncle

83

Frank was unobstructed, and I steadied the sights on his head, right in front of his ear.

The gun was unloaded, of course, but I wondered at that moment what might happen if it weren't. And my first question wasn't, could I pull the trigger; it was, could I, from that distance, with that weapon, under those conditions—the wind, the slope of the hill—hit my target. Only after I decided, probably not—an unfamiliar gun, its small caliber, my poor marksmanship—did I wonder what might happen if I killed my uncle. Would everyone's problems be solved? Would my father be relieved? Could I get away with it?

While these thoughts were gusting through my brain, my father and his brother had come closer to each other. The next thing I knew they were shaking hands. I put the gun back inside my waistband. My father and Uncle Frank walked off together, their broad shoulders almost touching.

We left for Bentrock after dark, and I took my customary place in the backseat, where I could lean back and watch the stars out the back window. The wind had died and the night was clear. My parents were silent in the front seat until we were halfway to town. Then my father said without prelude, "I talked to Frank."

"Wes!" My mother whispered sharply and looked in my direction. I didn't move.

"It's okay," my father replied. Whether he thought I was asleep or that he wasn't going to reveal anything, I wasn't sure.

84

My father went on. "I think the problem's been taken care of. Frank said he's going to cut it out."

"Oh, *Wes*-ley!" Her words came out in a moan, and I almost gave myself away by leaning forward to see if my mother was in pain.

"What?" my father replied, his confusion apparent and sincere. "What is it?"

"What about what's already been done? What about that, that . . . *damage?*"

"It can't be undone. That's passed. That's over and done."

My mother's voice became so low and tender it seemed better suited for an expression of love than what she actually said. "That's not the way it works. You know that. Sins—crimes—are not supposed to go unpunished."

Even then I knew what the irony of the conversation was: the secretary lecturing the lawyer, the law-enforcement officer, on justice.

My father was silent for such a long time I thought the conversation was over. At last he said, "He'll have to meet his punishment in the hereafter. I won't do anything to arrange it in this life."

When we arrived home Doris Looks Away was still there, and she and Marie were sitting in the living room drinking coffee. Marie was wrapped in a blanket, but she said she felt stronger. She still had a cough, but it was not as tight and wracking as it had been. My mother felt Marie's forehead and pronounced the fever still present, but obviously it had gone down. Her eyes had lost that unfocused, feverish gleam, and her cheeks no longer looked inflamed but merely ruddy.

Uncomfortable in our presence, Doris left almost immediately. Marie announced that she was going back to bed. Before she left the room she turned to me and asked, "Did you ride today, Davy?"

I nodded.

"Did you ride far?"

I nodded again.

"And did you see a coyote?"

How did she know I was given a pistol for hunting coyotes? "No," I said, "but I was looking."

"He's hard to see when you look for him."

Those were the last words Marie spoke to me. The next day, Monday, August 13, 1948, Marie Little Soldier was dead. My mother came home from work at 5:15 and found Marie lying dead in her bed. By the time I came home at 6:00 (I had spent the day fishing with Georgie Cahill), the hearse—a Buick station wagon from Undset's Funeral Parlor —was backing out of our driveway and carrying Marie's body away. Uncle Frank's pickup was parked in front of the house. On the courthouse lawn across the street stood a few onlookers, and Mr. and Mrs. Grindahl next door were on their porch, staring at our house as if it might burst into flames at any second. From somewhere on the block came the steady *ratcheta-ratcheta* of a lawn mower—someone who didn't know that for the moment all usual activity had ceased.

When I saw the car from Undset's, I did not run to our house in fear or curiosity. I didn't have to. I knew, I knew immediately what had happened. What's more, I could have walked right past our house, down the length of Green Avenue and right out of Bentrock. I could have kept going and never returned, out of my town, away from my family, away from my childhood. I could have kept going and taken with me the truth of what had happened in that house. No one else knew, and I could keep going until I found a place where I could bury that secret forever.

But I didn't. I walked slowly up the driveway and into the garage. I hung up my fishing pole and tackle box and the stringer of freshly caught perch and bluegills and went into the house.

Everyone was still in the kitchen. My father was on the telephone. "Yes, that's right," he was saying. "Could you please tell her that. That's right. She's at Undset's now." My mother sat at the table. She was slumped and staring at the floor, but she had one hand on the tabletop and her fingers were tapping rapidly. Those two actions—the body slumped and the fingers tapping—seemed so mismatched it was as if they belonged to separate bodies. Uncle Frank leaned over the table, filling out a form of some kind. His medical bag was on the table too, and seeing it there where we ate our meals I realized how large it was, how if its black mouth opened, it could swallow all the light in the room.

The door to Marie's room was partially open, and I saw

her bed. The blankets and sheets had been stripped, and the mattress was tilted up off the box springs and rested on its edge on the floor.

My mother saw me and reached out to me with one arm; the hand with the drumming fingers remained on the table as if her arm was paralyzed.

I stepped into my mother's embrace, and as I did she leaned her head against my torso in a way that made it clear I was the one offering comfort.

"It's Marie," she said. "She didn't make it, David."

My father hung up the phone, and I looked at him. "She's dead, David. That's what your mother means. Marie died this afternoon."

I smelled like fish. That's what I kept thinking. I smelled like fish, and that was the reason I didn't belong in this room. It was that and not the secret I held, the fearful knowledge. . . .

The back screen door slammed and Daisy McAuley burst into the kitchen. "My God! My God! What is going on here?"

My father repeated the words he spoke to me. "Marie's dead, Daisy. She died this afternoon."

"Oh, my Lord! Oh no! Why, I looked in on her yesterday afternoon. She was doing much better."

Uncle Frank finished his form and stood up so straight he seemed to be at attention. "This happens," he said to Daisy. "Pneumonia patients can have a sudden relapse, their lungs fill quickly. . . . Or the heart can fail from the strain of dealing with the disease. And there may have been a preexisting condition. We don't know. I see this much more often, however, in older patients."

I saw the document that Uncle Frank had been filling out. Across the top it said in bold letters "Mercer County Certificate of Death."

"I also have the feeling," Uncle Frank continued, "that she may not have been doing as well as she wanted us to believe. I think the Indian way is to deny illness, to try to push through in the face of it."

"Her fever was down, I know that," said my mother.

Uncle Frank shrugged. "A fever can fluctuate dramatically."

Daisy sunk down so hard onto a kitchen chair that it scraped a few inches across the linoleum. "That poor thing. That poor young thing."

"Pneumonia is still a serious disease," Uncle Frank said sternly. "Very serious. We mustn't lose sight of that."

My father stood by the refrigerator with his back to us. He ran his index finger up and down the woven basket that covered the motor on top of the refrigerator. "I couldn't reach any of Marie's family. No answer at home or at the step-father's bar." He turned around and I saw he had been crying. "I'm going to drive out there. They have to be notified as soon as possible. . . ."

"What about Ronnie?" my mother asked.

My father nodded. "I'll get in touch with him too. And Doris. But Marie's mother first. She has to be the first."

He moved toward the door, car keys in hand. "Do you need anything?" he asked my mother.

She shook her head. "Just hurry back."

"I won't take any longer than I have to."

89

This was my chance. I could ride along with my father and, when we were alone, tell him what I knew. But my mother still had her arm around me, and until she let go it didn't seem right to leave. Besides, he was going to face more grief, and this room held all I could handle. (I hadn't realized until that moment how large a part of my father's job this was. When someone's son rolled his pickup on a county highway, or someone's father shot himself climbing over a fence when he was deer hunting, or when some woman's husband dropped dead of a heart attack in a hotel down in Miles City, it was my father's duty to notify the family. Or when a drunk lay down on the tracks right in the path of a Great Northern freight train, it was my father's job to find out if he *had* any family. To this day I cannot hear that phrase—"pending notification of next of kin"—without thinking that someone out there, someone like my father, is toting around a basket of grief, looking for a doorstep to deposit it on. To think I once believed the hardest part of his job would be the dangerous criminals he might face.)

Right after my father left, Uncle Frank excused himself, saying he had to look in on Janie Cassidy, who had an unusually severe case of chicken pox. My mother did not get up to see him out.

Daisy reached out toward my mother and patted the back of my mother's hand. "You took good care of her," said Daisy. "That girl got the best care she could get right here in this house."

My mother released me and put her hand on top of

Daisy's. "I could have stayed home from work. I could have looked in on her earlier. . . ."

Daisy urgently placed her other hand on top of my mother's so it looked as though they were playing that baby's game of mounding hands, pulling the bottom one out and placing it on top. "You don't talk like that," Daisy told my mother. "You took good care of that girl. *Good* care."

Then Daisy must have seen something in my mother's eyes, because she turned to me and said, "David, are you hungry? You must be hungry. . . . Why don't you go over to our house and help yourself to pie. I've got a fresh blueberry pie on the kitchen table. You go get yourself some before Len eats it all."

I didn't move. The next time Daisy spoke it was not a suggestion but a command. "Go. And help yourself to ice cream. Have all you like."

Because Daisy kept the curtains drawn and windows closed to keep the heat of the day out, the McAuley house was dark and stuffy. The house always had a strange smell, as though Daisy had found some vegetable to boil that no one else knew about.

I stood over the pie, wondering how I could make myself eat a slice when I had no appetite.

From another room a voice called out, "Who's there?" It was Len.

I went into the living room, where Len sat in an over-stuffed chair, his long legs extended. In the room's dimness Daisy's white lace doilies on the sofa and chairs glowed white, as if they were hoarding all the available light.

On the table beside Len was a glass of whiskey. I recognized its brown color and smelled its smoky-sweet odor in the room. This was a bad sign. At one time Len had been a heavy drinker, given especially to week-long benders when he would plunge so deeply into a drunken gloom that it seemed unlikely he would ever climb out. In Bentrock Len McAuley was so well liked and respected that everyone was relieved when he quit drinking. I felt as bad seeing that glass of whiskey as I had when I'd first heard Marie cough.

He turned his gaze to me. It seemed, to my untrained eye, steady and clear. But it remained on me a little too long before he greeted me.

"David. Quite a commotion over at your place."

"Marie died." The words—and the fact they conveyed—popped out so easily they startled me.

Len nodded solemnly. "Yes. I believe I'm aware of that. Yes."

The room's heavy, dusky air seemed to insist on silence, and speaking was a struggle. "My dad's going out to talk to her family."

Len continued to nod. "Yes. Your father would do that. Yes."

I wanted to get away, but I couldn't think of anything to say that would serve as an exit line. And then it was hopeless. Len kicked their old horsehair hassock—the first sudden move he had made—and as it tumbled my way he said, "Sit down, David." I couldn't refuse.

Len stared at me for a long time, and though his gaze was steady there was something unfocused about it, as if an unseen dust in the room was clouding his vision.

He took a swallow of whiskey and that seemed to start his tongue. "You know, David, how I feel about your family."

"Yes, sir."

"I have this job. Deputy sheriff." He looked down at his shirt as though he expected to see his badge there. "Which I owe to your granddad and your dad. You know what your granddad said it means to be a peace officer in Montana? He said it means knowing when to look and when to look away. Took me a while to learn that." Len leaned forward and pointed a long, gnarled finger at me. "Your dad hasn't quite got the hang of it. Not just yet."

He slumped back in his chair and looked intently around the room at floor level as if he were watching for mice or insects. I had heard about drunks and their pink elephants and I wondered if he was hallucinating. I wanted more than ever to get away, but there was something tightly wound even in Len's casual posture—slumped shoulders and long legs extended—that made me think he was feigning repose and inattention, and as soon as I made a move to leave, his booted foot would suddenly trip me up or a long-fingered hand would pull me down.

He stopped looking around the room and fixed his eye on the carpet in front of his feet. "Long time ago I wanted to say something to your granddad. . . . I wanted to tell him, don't let those boys run wild. Just because we're out here, a thousand miles from nowhere, you think it doesn't matter. Out here, nothing but rimrock and sagebrush. You think no one's going to care. But those boys have to live in the world. Rein 'em in a little. Don't break them, but pull 'em back. But I didn't. Never said a word. Now look at them." He jerked his head up as if he actually saw my father and uncle in the room. "A lawyer and a doctor. College and the whole kit. Sheriff and a doctor. . . . Your granddad could tell me a thing or two. . . ."

For an instant something parted, as if the wind blew a curtain open and allowed a flash of sunlight into the room. Did Len know what I knew?

I leaned forward. "Did you see something, Len?"

He sat up straight and peered at me as if he weren't sure of my identity. "Did you?" he asked.

There it was, my opening! Now I could unburden myself, find someone else to carry this freight. Certainly Len could be trusted. But there was that glass of whiskey and its odor of sweet decay on his breath. . . . What if we *weren't* talking about the same thing?

I jumped to my feet. "I forgot the pie! I was supposed to get the pie!"

Len smiled wearily. "Look after your mother. This'll be a hard time for her."

Was Len in love with my mother? The thought never occurred to me until I wrote those words. But now I remember all the small chores and favors he did for her around our house—planing a sticking door or fixing a leaky faucet, bringing her the pheasants he shot or the fish he caught. The way he removed his hat when he came into our house and fiddled with it, creasing and denting the crown, running his finger around the sweatband. Well, why not. Why not say he loved her? Why not say his was one more heart broken in this sequence of events?

That night I thought I felt death in our house. Grandmother Hayden, a superstitious person, once told me about how, when she was a girl, her brother died and for days after, death lingered in the house. Her brother was trampled by a team of horses, and his blood-and-dirt-streaked body was laid on the kitchen table. From then until the day he was buried my grandmother said she could tell there was another presence in the house. It was nothing she could see, she said, but every time you entered a room it felt as though someone brushed by you as you went in. Every door seemed to require a bit more effort to open and close. There always seemed to be a sound—a whisper—on the edge of your hearing, something you couldn't quite make out.

As I had so often been advised by my parents, I never believed any of my grandmother's supernatural stories. Until the day Marie died. That night I lay in bed and couldn't breathe. The room felt close, full, as though someone else was getting the oxygen I needed.

I turned on the light and got slowly, cautiously, out of bed and opened my window wider. That brought no relief. The curtain stuck tight to the screen as if the wind was in the house blowing out.

Close to panic, I went to my parents' room. From the doorway I called softly, "Dad?"

In a voice so prompt and calm I wondered if he had really been asleep, my father answered, "What is it, David?"

"I thought I heard something."

"What is it you thought you heard?"

I peered into the darkened room. My father was still lying down.

"I don't know. Nothing, I guess."

The sheets rustled and my mother sat up. "Is something wrong?"

"I thought I heard something. Nothing. It wasn't anything."

"Come here, David," said my father.

As I approached the bed he sat up and swung his legs to the floor. He patted the bed beside him. "Sit down."

I sat down and my father rubbed my back, massaging the thin band of muscle on either side of my spine. "What's the trouble? Can't sleep?"

Just that little gentleness, that little thumb-rub below my neck, was all it took, and the words spilled out of me. "I saw something. . . ."

"Really?" His voice was steady and low. "I thought you said you heard something."

"I mean earlier. This afternoon."

"What did you see?"

"Uncle Frank. Uncle Frank was here."

"Of course he was. Your mother called him right away when she found Marie."

●

"No, I mean before. Earlier."

His hand stopped rubbing. "What time was that, David?"

"I'm not sure exactly."

"A guess. Take a guess, David."

"Around three."

My mother crawled quickly across the bed to the other side of me. "What are you saying, David?"

"Shh, Gail. Let David tell it."

I drew a deep breath and with its exhale let the secret out. "I was going fishing with Charley and Ben and we had just come from Ben's house and we were riding our bikes along the tracks. We were going out to Fuller's gravel pit. Then I had to go to the bathroom. I didn't want to go all the way back to our house to go, so I used Len and Daisy's outhouse." (In 1948 most, but not all, of the houses in Bentrock had indoor plumbing, yet many homeowners chose to keep their outhouses operational. They saved water, for one thing, and they were useful in case of emergency—if the pipes froze in the winter, for example.) "I told Charley and Ben to go on ahead and I'd catch up. While I was sitting there I saw someone cutting across our backyard. There's a knothole you can see out of. I was pretty sure it was Uncle Frank. Then I got out and watched him go down the tracks. He was going toward town. I'm pretty sure it was him."

"You're *pretty* sure, David?" my father asked abruptly. "What do you mean, you're pretty sure?"

"I mean I'm sure. I know it was."

"Did he have his bag with him?"

"I think so. Yeah. Yes, he had it."

97

"Was he in the house? Can you be sure? Did you see him come out of the house?"

Next to me, my mother had pulled together a tangled handful of sheets and bedspread and brought it toward her face.

"I just saw him coming from that direction."

"So you didn't actually see him come out of our house?"

"Oh, Wesley," my mother said in a sobbed half-plea, half-command. "Don't. You've heard enough. No more."

My father stood stiffly and limped toward the window. His bad leg always bothered him most when he first got up. "And you say this was around three o'clock?"

He had long since stopped being my father. He was now my interrogator, my cross-examiner. The sheriff. My uncle's brother.

"I think that's what time it was."

"Think, David. Think carefully. When did you last notice the time? Work from there."

"At Ben's. He had to watch his little brother and couldn't go until his mom came back. She was supposed to be back at two o'clock, but she was late. So maybe it was a little before three."

"Did anyone else see Frank? Charley or Ben?"

"No. They didn't wait for me."

My father looked at my mother. "And you got home when—at five?"

She got up from the bed and put on her robe. "I told you that before. I came right home at five."

My father muttered softly to himself. "He could have been

looking in on her. Checking on a patient. Doctors look in on their patients. . . . She was fine when he left her. . . . Fine. Used the back door because the front was usually locked. . . ."

My mother tried to interrupt him. "Wesley."

But my father's reverie continued. "On foot? Truck wasn't working. Truck was parked down the street at another patient's house. Gloria dropped him off."

"Stop, Wesley."

My father gently rapped his knuckles on the window. He stood like that for a long time, tapping the glass and staring out at the night.

My mother rested her hand on my shoulder, and I took advantage of that kindness to ask, "Is this bad?" I still couldn't reveal what I knew about Uncle Frank, but again I wanted my parents to let me in. I wanted to know that what I was doing was right and that I wasn't simply ratting on my uncle. But my mother didn't answer me. She patted my shoulder reassuringly, and it was my father who finally said, "Bad enough."

I pushed a little harder. "Does this mean—"

My father cut me off. "Does anyone else know? Are you sure no one else saw him? Did you tell anyone else?"

"I didn't tell anyone, but. . . ."

"But what, David?"

"Maybe Len saw him."

My father took a backward step as if he were trying to avoid a punch. "Len?"

I nodded.

"Oh, God. God*damn*. Len saw Frank."

"Maybe. . . ."

My mother asked me, "What makes you think Len saw, David?"

"He said. . . . I don't know. He was acting funny. I just think he might have."

"That tears it," said my father. "If Len saw Frank. . . ."

"It doesn't change anything," my mother said. "Not a thing."

"Oh really? Maybe. If Len knows, he'll keep his mouth shut if I ask him. Or if Dad asks him. But he'll know. There he'll be, day after day. With that look. I'm not going to live with that look."

My mother turned on the lamp beside the bed. In its sudden brightness the first thing I saw was my father's bad knee. He was wearing boxer shorts and a T-shirt, and his knee looked inflamed, swollen, scarred, and misshapen, as if his kneecap had been put back in the wrong spot. I saw my father limping every day but I seldom saw the reason. I realized the pain he must have been in constantly, and that pain seemed strangely to connect with the anguish he felt over his brother.

As if he were suddenly self-conscious in the light, my father put on his trousers.

"One more thing, David," my father said as he buckled his belt, the only bit of western regalia he wore—a hand-tooled ranger belt with a silver buckle and keeper. "Why didn't you say something before?"

"I don't know."

"Well, you can go back to bed. Now *you* can get some sleep." In his voice I thought I heard both jealousy and resentment.

Unfortunately, I couldn't sleep well either. Half-asleep and half-awake, I lay in bed and thought about Indians. In my daily life in Montana I saw Indians every day. There were Indian children in school, their mothers in the grocery store, their fathers at the filling station. Objects of the most patronizing and debilitating prejudice, the Indians in and around our community were nonetheless a largely passive and benign presence. Even the few who were not—Roy Single Feather, for example, who seemed intent on single-handedly perpetuating the stereotype of the drunken Indian and who, when drunk, walked down the middle of Main Street lecturing passersby, cars, and store windows on the necessity of giving one's life over to Jesus Christ—were regarded as more comedic or pathetic than dangerous.

But that night Marie's death and too many cowboy and Indian movies combined to bring me a strange half-dreaming, half-waking vision. . . .

To the east of Bentrock was a grassy butte called Circle Hill, the highest elevation around. It was treeless, easy to climb, and its summit provided a perfect view of town. That night I imagined all the Indians of our region, from town, ranches, or reservation, gathered on top of Circle Hill to do something about Marie's death. But in my vision, the Indians were not lined up in battle formation as they always were in the movies, that is, mounted on war ponies, streaked with war paint, bristling with feathers, and brandishing bows and arrows, lances, and tomahawks. Instead, just as I did in my daily life I saw them dressed in their jeans and cowboy boots, their cotton print dresses, or their flannel shirts. Instead of shouting war cries to the sky they were simply milling about, talking low, mourning Marie. Would they ever come down from Circle Hill, rampage the streets of Bentrock, looking for her killer, taking revenge wherever they could find it? My vision didn't extend that far, and finally I fell completely asleep, still watching Ollie Young Bear and Donna Whitman and George Crow Feather and Simon Many Snows and Verna Bull and Thomas Pelletier and Doris Looks Away and Sidney Bordeaux and Iris Trimble all walking the top of Circle Hill.

Three

✿ ✿ ✿

W had planned, of course, to attend Marie's funeral, but when my father asked Mrs. Little Soldier about when and where it would be, he was told that Marie would not be buried in Montana. Her family was coming from North Dakota and they would take Marie and her mother back to their home in North Dakota. When my father told my mother about this conversation, he said, "I tried to tell Mrs. Little Soldier that this was Marie's home also and that we thought of her as a member of the family, but she didn't want to hear. She wants to get out of Montana as quickly as possible."

My mother nodded knowingly. "Try to find out where we can send flowers. It's the least we can do. And we have to do something."

Quietly my father replied, "I am doing something, Gail. You know that."

I knew what he meant. In the days right after Marie's death my father was working all the time. He left early in the morning, and he did not return until late at night. When he was home, he was on the phone. (He left his office a few times to come home and use the telephone; there were some matters he didn't want to discuss in his office.)

His work habits were familiar enough to me that I knew

what was going on: he was building a case, and my father did this the same way he ran for reelection—by gathering in friends and favors. I suppose he was collecting evidence as well, but that part was never as obvious to me. What he seemed intent on doing—just as boys at play do, just as nations at war do—was getting people to be on his side.

Earlier in the year there had been a controversial arson case. Shelton's Hardware Store burned to the ground, and my father suspected Mr. Shelton, a well-liked businessman, of setting the fire himself to collect the insurance money. While my father conducted his investigation I was amazed at the change in him. I saw him on the street or in the Coffee Cup, telling jokes and laughing at the jokes of others. He passed out cigars like a new father. He inquired about families; he asked if there were favors he could do for people. Then, when he felt he had garnered enough good will, he made his arrest, exactly at the moment when his popularity was highest in the county. Naturally the consequent community feeling was, "Well, if Sheriff Hayden says it's so, it must be so." That feeling frequently carried juries as well. Mr. Shelton was convicted of arson and sent to Deer Lodge State Penitentiary for five years.

In short, rather than become grim and dogged when closing in on a suspect, my father became good-humored and gregarious. He became charming. He became more like his brother.

In the few days following Marie's death there was one significant change in this usual pattern. . . .

Three days after my mother found Marie dead in our home, around four o'clock on a rainy Thursday afternoon, my father brought Uncle Frank to our house. I had had something planned for the day with my friends, but the rain changed my plans, so I passed the day indoors, working on a balsa-wood model of a B-29 bomber. When my father and Uncle Frank came in the back door, I was at the kitchen table, my fingers sticky with glue and a hundred tiny airplane parts spread out on a newspaper in front of me. Uncle Frank walked in first, and he greeted me jauntily. "Good afternoon, Davy me boy. Wet enough for you?" He was carrying a small satchel, but it was not his medical bag.

He saw what I was doing and asked, "What's that you're working on?"

I showed him the box the model came in. "B-29."

"The B-29," he said. "I saw a few of those overhead. Always a welcome sight."

My father came in right behind Frank, and about him there was nothing of Frank's good cheer. Unsmiling and mute, my father simply pointed toward the basement stairs, and the two of them crossed the room and descended, my father closing the door behind them.

They were down there a long time, but I didn't move from the kitchen. I strained to hear what was going on in the basement, but I heard nothing. Finally, when slow, heavy steps began to climb the stairs, I pretended to be concentrating on my model, though I hadn't fitted a single piece since they came in.

My father came through the door—and he came through

alone. He closed the door tightly behind him.

He looked exhausted, as though climbing the stairs had taken all his energy. His face was pale, and he simply stood still for a moment, his back against the basement door. Then he went to the cupboard under the kitchen sink, rummaged around for a moment, and came out with a bottle of Old Grand-Dad. He took a juice glass from the shelf, poured it half full of whiskey, then held the glass to the rain-streaked window as if he were examining the liquid for impurities. He tilted his hat back on his forehead, raised the glass to his lips, closed his eyes, and took a small sip.

I watched him and discovered that adults could, like kids, be there yet not be there (as I often was in school). As my father took another drink of whiskey, this time a longer one that shuddered through him, I could tell that he was making a long journey while he stood in our kitchen. I waited until I thought he was back and then asked as softly as I could, "Dad?"

He put his finger to his lips. "In a minute, David. All right? Your mother will be home soon, and I only want to tell this once. We have a new development here."

So my father and I remained silent. He continued to sip his whiskey, and I packed up all the tiny pieces of my model plane. The rain clattered and gurgled through the gutters around the house. Once—only once—I thought I heard a noise from the basement that could have been Uncle Frank moving around.

But was that possible? How could Uncle Frank make any noise when my father had killed him?

I almost believed that.

I almost believed my father had taken his brother to a corner of the basement and—and what? Strangled him? Clubbed him? Shot him with a pistol equipped with a silencer? He had somehow killed him soundlessly. My father had tried to find a way to bring his brother to justice for his crimes, but finally, inevitably, unable to do that, he had opted instead for revenge. He had taken his brother into the basement and killed him. What else could explain that look on my father's face?

When my mother came home from work, she took one look at my father and asked, "Wes, what's wrong?"

He pointed to the basement door. "Frank's down there."

Both my mother and I stared at him, waiting for him to go on.

My father took off his hat and sailed it hard against the refrigerator. "He's in the *basement*. Goddamn it! Don't you get it—I've arrested him. He's down there now."

He stared at us as if there was something wrong with us for being more mystified than ever. Then he turned around, and instead of explaining to us he addressed the rain. "He didn't want to go to jail. Not here in town."

"Frank's in the *basement*?" my mother asked.

My father turned back to us but didn't speak. He walked over and picked up his hat. He looked it over and began to reshape it, denting it just so with the heel of his hand, pinching the crown, restoring the brim's roll with a loving brush-and-sweep. He dropped his hat in the center of the table and said solemnly to me, "My brother—your uncle—has run afoul of the law. I had to arrest him. You understand that, don't you? That I had no choice?"

He looked close to tears. "I understand," I said.

My mother had her purse open and was looking frantically through it as though she could find among its contents the solution to this problem. Without looking up from her search, she asked, "Where in the basement?"

"In the laundry room. I've locked that door." He held up the key for proof.

Our basement was unfinished, but the laundry room and its adjoining root cellar were closed off from the rest of the basement by a heavy wooden door (the door used to be in a rural schoolhouse; my father rescued it when the school was going to be torn down). The room where Uncle Frank was locked had a wringer washer, an old galvanized sink, the shower where I had once seen Marie naked, a toilet, and a couple of old dressers for storing blankets and winter clothes. The root cellar had wooden slats over a dirt floor, and shelves stacked deep with jars of home-canned pickles, tomatoes, rutabagas, applesauce, and plum and cherry jam. In another section of the laundry room was our ancient furnace, a huge, silver-bellied monster sprouting ductwork like an octopus's tentacles.

"In the basement?" repeated my mother.

"I wheeled the roll-away in there. He can sleep on that. I'll take him something to eat after we've had our supper."

"You've turned my laundry room into a *jail*!"

"Look," said my father, "Frank said he'd come with me

110

without a fuss. But he'd like to keep this quiet. He didn't want to be locked up in the jail. I said I'd respect that, and he's going to cooperate. Cooperate—hell, he's acting as if this is all some kind of joke."

"Who knows he's here? Have you talked to Mel?" She was referring to Mel Paddock, the Mercer County state attorney. If my uncle were formally charged with a crime, it would be up to Mr. Paddock to bring those charges on behalf of the state. Mr. Paddock and my father were good friends; during every election they pooled their resources and campaigned together for their respective offices.

"No one knows about this but the people in this house. I talked around it with Mel, but I didn't name any names. First I'm going over to tell Gloria." He looked at his watch. "I should go over there now. I figure she has a right to know—"

"—that you have her husband locked up in our basement." My mother groped for a chair as if she were blind. She sat down heavily and let her head rest on the heel of her hand.

"I'm not saying this is the best—"

My mother stopped him with her question. "How long?"

"I'm not sure," my father replied. "I'm going to call Helena in the morning. Talk to the attorney general's office and see if we can't get him arraigned in another county. Or maybe I'll check with Mel, see if we can do it quickly, get bond set—"

Again my mother interrupted him. "What are you going to tell Gloria?"

"Maybe that Frank's in some trouble. . . ."

"Tell her the truth. She's going to hear it anyway. Don't lie to her."

111

He nodded gravely but made no move to leave the kitchen.

"Go *now*, Wesley," urged my mother. "She has a right to know where her husband is."

My father took out his handkerchief and blew his nose—had he been crying quietly and I hadn't noticed? He put on his hat and went out the back door.

After a moment he was back, calling me outside. "David, could I see you out here?"

I went out immediately, thinking that now my father was going to tell me, man to man, what Uncle Frank's offense was.

The rain had almost stopped, and my father was waiting for me along the west side of the house. He stood back under the eaves and seemed to be examining the house's wood.

"Look here, David." He pointed to a section of siding. I looked but couldn't see anything.

"What?"

"The paint. See how it's blistered and peeling?" With his fingernail he flicked a small paint chip off the house. "It flakes right off."

I didn't understand—was there something I was supposed to have done?

"We're going to have to paint the house," he said. "But before we do, we're going to have to scrape it and sand it right down to bare wood. Then prime it good before we paint it. And we might have to put two coats on." He picked off another paint chip. "It's going to be hard work. Think you're up to it?"

"I think so."

He looked closely at me as if he were inspecting me for signs of peeling, chipping, or flaking. I must have passed inspection, because he clapped me on the shoulder and said, "I think so too. As soon as we get this business with your uncle straightened out, you and I are going to tackle this job." Was this another of his promises—like a trip to Yellowstone—to make me feel better? Was this the best he could do?

Then, as if it really were houses and paint that he wanted to talk about, he turned back to the wall. "Though if it was up to me, I'd probably just let it go. Let it go right down to bare wood. If I had my way, I'd let every house in town go. Let the sun bake 'em and the north wind freeze 'em until there isn't a house in town with a spot of paint on it. You'd see this town from a distance and it would look like nothing but firewood and gray stone. And maybe you'd keep right on moving because it looked like nothing was living here. Paint. Fresh paint. That's how you find life and civilization. Women come and they want fresh paint." He looked up at the eaves and gutters, judging perhaps how tall a ladder we'd need. Then he rapped sharply on the wall, three quick knocks to warn it that Wesley Hayden and his son were coming with scrapers, sandpaper, paintbrushes, and white paint, paint whiter than any bones bleaching out there on the Montana prairie.

"One more thing, David."

"Yes."

"If there's any trouble and I'm not here, you run for Len. Understand? Get Len."

"What kind of trouble?"

113

"Any kind. You'll know."

"Len's drinking again."

"You just get him. Drunk or sober. Understand?"

"Yes."

My father held out his hand to test if the rain was still falling. It came back dry. "No putting it off. I'll go talk to Gloria. Remember what I said."

"Wait," I said. "Does Len know?"

"He knows."

At about nine o'clock that night my grandparents came to our house. My father, mother, and I had been sitting in the living room, paging through the *Saturday Evening Post* or the *Mercer County Gazette*, listening to the radio, trying not to think about the fact that a relative was being held captive in our basement. When I think now of how calm we all looked, how natural and domestic this scene was, I find it more disturbing than if we had been crawling around on our hands and knees, howling like wild dogs. When the knock came on the front door, all three of us jumped.

"David," said my mother, "see who's here, please."

I opened the door and saw my grandparents dressed as though they had just come from church. My grandfather wore a double-breasted brown suit, white shirt, and tie. My grandmother's dress was such a pale yellow that I noticed how deeply tanned she was from working long hours in her garden.

She said hello to me, but my grandfather pushed right past me.

My father smiled widely when he saw his parents. "Well, look who's here. This is a nice surprise—"

Grandfather looked swiftly and suspiciously around the room. "Where's Frank?"

My father creased his newspaper and set it gently down on the table. "Gloria told you."

Grandfather took another step forward. "Where is he? Where have you got him? I want to see him."

My father simply shook his head. "I don't think that would be a good idea. Not at this point."

Meekly my grandmother said, "Gloria was concerned. She wanted us to make certain Frankie's all right."

The muscles of my father's jaw bounced rhythmically. "He's all right. I told Gloria that."

Without my having noticed her movement, my mother had come around behind me. She rested her hands on my shoulders.

"Bring him out here," Grandfather demanded. "Now. Right goddamn now."

My mother's voice rose and cracked as she asked, "Wouldn't you like to sit down? I have some coffee. . . ."

Grandmother smiled sympathetically at my mother. She nodded toward her husband. "He gets so upset."

"Wesley," repeated Grandfather. "Get your ass in gear and get your brother out here now."

I suddenly felt sorry for my father—not as he stood before me at that moment, but as a boy. What must it have been like to have a father capable of speaking to you like that?

"This isn't about family," my father said. "This is a legal matter."

"Bull*shit*. Then why have you got him locked up here and not over at the jail? This is your brother here. My *son!*"

I looked at my grandmother. Didn't she want to say that Frank was her son too?

My father replied, "I wanted to save Frank some embarrassment. I don't know how long that's going to be possible."

My grandfather began to dig furiously through his coat pockets, and I suddenly remembered the incident in Minneapolis when he pulled a gun on a stranger. Why was my father just standing there, his hands hanging defenselessly at his sides? Didn't he know that his father was going for a weapon?

"Dad!" I said.

My father turned to look at me. My mother squeezed my shoulders hard, and my grandmother pleaded, "Julian, the boy."

My grandfather was the only one who wasn't staring at me. He pulled out a cigar and ripped off the cellophane.

My mother whispered sharply in my ear, "Go on upstairs, David. Right away." She pushed me away from her.

I was glad to get away, and I ran upstairs. But I also wanted to hear how this confrontation would play out, so I hurried to the spare bedroom, the one right over the living room. In that room was a hot-air register in the floor that, when opened, let you hear what was being said in the room below. I crouched down by the register, slowly eased open the metal flap so it wouldn't rattle or squeak, and laid my ear against the grate.

"Sit down, Dad," my father was saying. "Please. Let's all sit down and talk about this calmly and reasonably. Please."

They must have agreed, because my father next said, "That's better. There. Gail, why don't you get us some of that coffee. And get Dad an ashtray. We don't want him to have to put his ashes in his pants cuff."

I could tell my father was trying desperately to put everyone in as good a mood as possible. His voice had risen just as it did when he tried to tell a joke. (He was terrible at it—he'd get the parts out of sequence and often mangle the punch line.) My grandfather was grumbling—it sounds, I know, like a trite thing to say about an older man, but in my grandfather's case it was literally true. When he wasn't talking he continued to make noise, a sound like a combination of throat-clearing and humming, as though he was keeping himself ready to talk, keeping the apparatus oiled and ready to go.

"Now," said my father. "Do you want to hear my side of it?"

That struck me as an odd phrase. I hadn't thought of my father as being against his brother, not in any personal way. I preferred to think of it as though the law had taken a curve in its course, and as a result these two brothers had ended up on opposite sides of the road.

"He's supposed to have beaten up some Indian," Grandfather said.

"What?" asked my father. "What are you saying?"

117

"That's what Gloria said. Something about assaulting a goddamn Indian. Since when do you get arrested in this part of the country for taking a poke at a man, red or white, that's what I—"

"Whoa!" my father interrupted. "Wait. What did Gloria say?"

My grandmother's faint, quavering voice answered him. "She said you arrested Frank for assaulting an Indian."

My father must have gotten up, because his voice grew louder and softer as if he were moving back and forth in the room. "Mom. Dad. I didn't arrest Frank for simple assault. I don't know what Gloria told you. This is for sexual assault. I arrested Frank for . . . for taking liberties with his patients. With his Indian patients."

"Oh, for Christ's sake!" Grandfather said. "What kind of bullshit is this?"

"There's cause. I've done some investigating, Dad."

"You—*investigating?*" In those two words I heard how little respect my grandfather had for my father and anything he did.

"I've even found some women who are willing to testify. And some others who aren't quite ready to talk. Yet. But I'm betting that once they see their friends come forward, they will too. There are a lot of them, Pop. A lot."

The living room fell so silent I checked to make sure the register hadn't flapped shut.

Then my mother spoke, in the accomodating, eager-to-please way that she used only with Grandfather and Grandmother Hayden: "We could hardly believe it ourselves."

Misinterpreting what my mother said, Grandmother quickly, hopefully, said, "A girl could be so easily mistaken. A trip to the doctor. The fear. The confusion. An Indian girl especially—"

"Please, Mom," said my father. "Not *a* girl. *Many.* There's something to this. Please. Don't make me say more."

"Go on," Grandfather said, "get on out of here. Let him say it to me."

My mother said, "Come on, Enid. Let's go out to the kitchen."

For a moment I thought of changing my station, of running to a different register so I could hear what my mother and grandmother would talk about, but since the conversation in the living room promised to be more revealing, I stayed put.

"Ever since the war," Grandfather began, "ever since Frank came home in a uniform and you stayed here, you've been jealous. I saw it. Your mother saw it. The whole goddamn town probably saw it. But I thought you'd have the good sense not to do anything. Now you pull a fucking stunt like this. I should've taken you aside and got you straightened out. If it meant whipping your ass I should've got you straightened out."

There was another long silence before my father said softly, "Is that what you think?"

"That fucking uniform. If I could've got you in one, maybe we wouldn't have this problem."

"Is that what you think." This time it was not a question.

"What the hell am I supposed to think? Screwing an Indian.

119

Or feeling her up or whatever. You don't lock up a man for that. You don't lock up your brother. A respected man. A war hero."

"Stop it, Dad. Just stop."

But I could tell Grandfather couldn't stop. He had his voice revved up—after all the grumbling, the motor caught and couldn't be shut off. "Is this why I gave you that goddamn badge? So you could arrest your own brother?"

"Don't try to tell me law. Don't."

"Some Indian thinks he put his hands where he shouldn't and you're pulling out your badge."

"It's not that. If it was only that. . . ." Here my father's voice faded. I couldn't tell if he was walking away or if he had come up against something he didn't want to talk about.

Grandfather continued to press. "Well, what is it? What the hell's so big you have to take an Indian's side and run your brother in?"

My father said something that I couldn't hear. Neither could Grandfather, because he said, "What? What are you saying? Goddamn, speak up!"

My father's single-word response boomed so loudly I pulled back from the register.

"Murder!" my father shouted. And a second time even louder: "*Murder!*"

What sounded like a gasp—it had to be Grandmother's, as she and my mother ran into the room at my father's shout— came rushing through the grate like a blast of hot air from the furnace. And then something occurred to me that made it difficult for me to put my ear back to the register.

120

On the other end of the house, in the basement, Uncle Frank might have been doing exactly what I was doing, listening to his family's voices boom through the ductwork and discuss his fate. And to hear the shouted word "murder," Uncle Frank wouldn't need the aid of the heating system.

I couldn't shake the image—my uncle Frank with his ear to the basement ventilator—and then it seemed to me that if I were to return to my listening post, Uncle Frank and I could be connected, two ears attached to the same sheet-metal system. And what if Frank should speak, should suddenly shout his innocence—his voice would travel the entire house unheard to arrive at my ear!

After a couple of moments I calmed down. The voices below were going on without me, like a furnace that doesn't care if anyone is there to feel its heat or not.

Grandmother was sobbing, a series of jerky breaths like hiccups.

Grandfather said, "My God, boy. Look at this. Look at what you've done to her."

My mother said, "Here. Let me."

"I'm sorry," said my father.

"Who the hell's dead anyway?"

"Marie."

"She was sick! She had pneumonia, for Christ's sake!"

"He didn't deny it, Pop. There's evidence—"

Grandmother's crying intensified, and I could tell she was having trouble breathing.

"Evidence? What kind of evidence? Go-to-court evidence or a wild hair-up-your-ass evidence?"

"That's for Mel Paddock to decide."

"You brought Mel in on this?"

"Not yet."

"My God. My God, boy. Stop this now. Stop this before I have to."

"This isn't for any of us to stop or start. This has to go its own way."

Not for any of us? I thought again of how I held my uncle in the sights of my pistol, of how I held, even tighter, the secret information that Uncle Frank had been in our house the afternoon Marie died.

"Oh, Wesley, Wesley," Grandmother said in that special tone that mothers use when pleading with their sons. Could my father withstand its power? I couldn't hear him make any response.

"Get up," said Grandfather in a calmer voice. "Let's go. We're not going to beg him."

There was a general rustling about, some footsteps, and I knew they were moving toward the front door and away from my hearing. I heard my mother's voice, but the only word I could make out was "please."

The front door closed, but I waited before going downstairs. I don't know what I was apprehensive about: my grandparents were gone, my uncle was locked in the basement, yet I had reached the point where I was afraid of being with my parents as well. There was so much unpredictable behavior going on that it seemed unwise to depend on anyone. For the moment it felt safer to remain alone on the bedroom floor, within earshot yet out of sight and reach.

What finally lifted me from the floor and moved me back down the stairs? It was trivial, yet it bore out what a boy I was when all this was going on. In the kitchen was chocolate cake. My father had stopped at Cox's Bakery the day before and bought a cake, and it was sitting on the counter. A murderer may have been locked up a floor below and the molecules of his victim's dying breath still floating in the air, yet these were not strong enough finally to stand up to my boy's hunger for chocolate cake.

As I approached the kitchen where my parents were, I heard my father say, "Help me with this, Gail," and a chair scraped across the linoleum. I thought he might be moving furniture or changing a light bulb and needed her help.

I was wrong.

I came into the kitchen and saw my mother sitting by the table. My father was on his knees before her, and his head was on her lap. She was rubbing the back of his neck in a way that was instantly recognizable to me: it was exactly the way she rubbed my neck when I had a headache. Overhead, insects flew frantic circles around the kitchen light.

Before I could speak my mother saw me and said so softly I wondered for an instant if my father was sleeping, "Hello, David."

My father lifted his head and I could tell by his red-rimmed eyes that he had been crying. But that was not what concerned me.

At that moment my father looked so *old* (he was only thirty-eight at the time), and I knew for the first time how this experience with his brother was ruining him physically. Was that the moment I realized my father would die someday? Perhaps. At any rate I knew that the puffiness around his eyes, the deepening creases of worry across his forehead and around his mouth, his pallor, his slow, stiffening gait were all signs that he was growing weaker. I also knew that to continue to stand up to Grandfather, my father needed all the strength he possessed. And perhaps that would still not be enough.

As if she could read my mind, my mother said, "Your father's just tired, David."

Using his good leg to brace himself, my father pushed himself to his feet. "We're all tired," he said. "Let's hit the hay."

I wasn't tired, and I didn't want to go to bed. I wanted my parents to tell me what happened when Grandfather and Grandmother were there. Though I knew exactly what was said, I wanted my parents to interpret it all for me. I wanted them to explain it so it wasn't as bad as the facts made it seem.

But since my father was embarrassed because I saw him on the floor, I had to go to bed. My mother gave me a sympathetic look but said nothing. I turned to go up to my room but my father stopped me.

"David."

"Yes."

"If Grandpa should come here when I'm not home, you're not to let him in, understand?"

"What should I say?"

"You don't have to say anything. Just don't answer the door. It'll be locked. Front and back both."

"What about Grandma?"

My father blinked and tilted his head back the way you do

124

when you're trying to keep tears from spilling over. "Not Grandma either."

"Not ever?"

"Not until I tell you different."

That night I cried for the first time since that whole sad, sordid, tragic set of events began. My tears, however, were not for Marie, whom I loved, or my uncle, whom I once idolized, or for my parents or grandparents or for my community or my life in it—all, all changed, I knew, by what had happened. But that night I cried myself to sleep because I believed that I would never see my horse, Nutty, again. I remembered the way he lowered and twisted his head when I approached, as if he were waiting for me to whisper something in his ear, that long ear whose touch reminded me of felt. I remembered how I used to rub my fingertips against the grain of the tight, short hair of his forehead and then smooth the hair back down again. I remembered how, when I first put my foot in the stirrup, he seemed to splay out his legs slightly, as if he were lowering himself and bracing for my mount. One of the great regrets of my childhood had always been that I couldn't live on the same grounds as my horse. Now the distance between us seemed too great for either Nutty or me to travel ever again.

The next day was hot and windy. My mother stayed home

from work, and though she said it was because she had a headache, I knew that was not the reason. She was staying home so I wouldn't have to be alone in the house with Uncle Frank. Early that morning my father took breakfast down to Frank and stayed down there about half an hour. When he came up he said to my mother, "I'm going to see what other arrangements we can make."

Around ten o'clock my mother sent me to the grocery store, and within a few minutes of walking out of the house that morning I noticed that a change had occurred.

I was a Hayden. I knew, from the time I was very young and without having been told, that that meant something in Bentrock. Because my grandfather was wealthy and powerful, because my father—like his father before him—enforced the law, because my uncle treated the sick and injured (and—am I wrong in mentioning?—because their wives were beautiful), people had an opinion about the Haydens. In their homes, in the cafes and bars and stores, they talked about us. When one of us passed on the street, there were sometimes whispers in our wake. They may not have liked us—perhaps Grandfather bought someone's foreclosed ranch cheap or let his cattle graze someone else's range, or perhaps he or my father sent someone's brother or cousin to the state penitentiary, or perhaps we were simply too prosperous for that luckless, hardscrabble region—but our name was no joke. We were as close as Mercer County came to aristocracy. I never consciously traded on the Hayden name, yet I knew it gave me a measure of respect that I didn't have to earn.

But as I walked down our tree-lined street that morning, I

imagined, behind every curtain or pulled shade, someone peering out and seeing a Hayden and thinking not of power, wealth, and the rule of law, but of perversion, scandal, family division, and decay. If the citizens of Bentrock didn't know yet that my father had arrested his own brother for sexually assaulting his patients and murdering Marie Little Soldier, they would know soon enough. Then being a Hayden would mean having an identity I didn't want but could do nothing to disown or deny.

By the time I got to Nash's Grocery Store, my shame over my family name was so great I didn't want to go in. I finally got my courage up by convincing myself that it was too early for all the details of our scandal to have made the rounds yet. Still, I picked up the items my mother wanted and left as quickly as I could.

On my way out I almost ran into Miss Schott, riding down the street on one of her big palominos. Miss Schott had been my second-grade teacher (everyone's second-grade teacher was probably more like it), and since she had retired from teaching she devoted herself full-time to what had been her hobby—breeding, raising, and showing blue-ribbon palominos that were as fine as any in Montana.

She was a strong, stout, cheerful woman who, now that she was no longer teaching, always dressed in boots, dungarees, a bandana-print shirt, and a sweat-stained short-brimmed cowboy hat that looked too small for her big head. She lived just outside town, and she rode one of her horses in every day to check her post office box or to run errands. No one in Bentrock was ever surprised to hear the heavy, slow *clop-clop* of Miss Schott riding down one of the town's streets, or to see one of her tall, golden palominos tied up along the side of Nash's Grocery or in the alley behind the Hi-Line Hotel, or to smell the horse's steaming turds in any of the town's gutters.

It is commonplace to refer to the narrowness and intolerance of small-town life, but it seems to me just the opposite is true, at least of Bentrock, Montana, in 1948. The citizens of that community tolerated all kinds of behavior, from the eccentric to the unusual to the aberrant. From Miss Schott and her palominos to Mrs. Russell, who was a kleptomaniac (storekeepers kept track of what she stole and then once a week Mr. Russell, the president of the bank, went around and reimbursed them), to Arne Olsen, a farmer, who never (*never*) bathed and was proud of the fact, to Mr. Prentice, the band director at the high school who liked his boy students better than he liked his girl students, to old Henry Sandstrom, who shot mourning doves in his backyard, cooked them, and ate them. To my uncle Frank who molested his patients. How many other secrets had our town agreed to keep?

When Miss Schott saw me, she greeted me cheerily, "Good morning, David. Is the summer flying by for you too?"

I couldn't answer her.

I remembered that she had once been Uncle Frank's patient. I couldn't recall the reason or how I had even acquired this knowledge—another overheard conversation, perhaps—yet it was the one fact at the moment that pushed aside all others. I looked up at her astride her horse, and all I could think of was—*What did Uncle Frank do to you? Did he touch you there? There? What did he put inside you?*

And then Loretta Waterman, a pretty high-school girl whose father owned the drugstore, walked by, her moccasins scuffing the sidewalk, and she waved to me or Miss Schott or Miss Schott's horse, and I forgot about what Uncle Frank might have done to my former teacher and instead I wondered about Loretta, *Did you go to Uncle Frank? Did he make you take off all your clothes? Did he look at you there? And there?*

I began to feel at once dizzy and ashamed and sick because this time, with Loretta, the thought of how Uncle Frank may have abused her did not disgust and anger me as it had with Miss Schott, but stirred me sexually.

I didn't want to feel any of what I was feeling. I hugged my sack of groceries and ran home.

Once I was in the house, my mother said, "Look at you. All red in the face."

I jerked my head in the direction of the basement door. "How long is he going to be here?"

"Not long. You know your father's working on that."

"Then what?"

"Then what *what?*"

"What's going to happen after he leaves?"

My mother put her finger to her lips and whispered her reply. "I imagine there will be a trial."

"Grandpa will just get him off. He can get everybody to do what he wants."

She shrugged and went back to slicing cucumbers. "You might be right about that." As an afterthought, she added, "But not everybody."

"So what's it all for?"

"We're—your father is doing what's right."

"But we're the ones getting the shitty end of the stick."

Usually language like that would get me sent to my room. My mother didn't even look up from her knife's work. "You might be right about that too."

I was the first to notice the truck circling the house. From my bedroom window I saw it drive through the alley in back, along the railroad tracks. Four men were in it, two in the cab and two standing in back.

After it went by a second time, slowly, I ran downstairs to see it go by in front as well. I crouched below the living room window and peeked over the sill—I didn't want them to see me—and when it went by this time I recognized one of the men. Dale Paris, the foreman at my grandfather's ranch, was in the passenger seat, his bare arm crooked out the window, his cap pulled low. Dale Paris was the only cowboy I knew who never wore a hat but instead a red-and-black checked wool cap, earflaps tied up in summer and down in winter. I didn't know much about the man. He was simply a lean, silent presence on the ranch. My only contact with him had occurred when I came back from riding Nutty long and hard one day, and because I was in a hurry or lazy or both I simply unsaddled him and put him back in the stall. I was on my way out when Dale Paris stepped out of the shadows, grabbed my arm hard, and said, "Your horse needs wipin' down."

The other men in the truck were probably also employees of my grandfather. If that were so, it didn't take much reasoning to figure out why they were in town. They had come for Uncle Frank. How did they plan to get him? I didn't care to speculate that far.

My mother caught me peeking out the window. "What are you so interested in out there?"

I felt I should protect her, though from what I wasn't yet sure. "Nothing," I replied.

My answer didn't satisfy her, and she pushed the curtain aside in time to see the truck pass, close to the curb and driving so slowly you could hear the engine lug in low gear.

"Who was that?" she asked.

"I'm not sure."

She looked at me a long time as though she knew I had the answer. When I couldn't resist the power of her gaze any longer, I said, "I think they're from Grandpa's ranch. I saw them drive down the alley."

Without a word, my mother spun and went toward the kitchen, where she could look out the back window. Each of us at our respective posts—I in front and she in back—we kept careful watch on the circling truck. It drove around the house two more times before stopping in the alley. That was when my mother called me to the kitchen.

"Who are they?" she asked again. "You know. Tell me."

I looked out the window again even though I knew who she was talking about. The truck was parked along the railroad tracks, at the end of our yard, and straight out from the house.

The men who had been riding on the truck's bed had gotten down and were standing by the cab, talking to the man in the passenger seat.

"I think that's Dale Paris," I said.

"Who?"

"He works for Grandpa."

One of the men standing by the truck pointed toward the house, and the other man nodded. I knew what they were noticing. The people who owned the house before us had once planned to finish the basement and rent it out as an apartment. Toward that end they had built a rear entrance, steps going down to a door into the basement. These men must have figured, with Grandpa's help, that Frank was in the basement, and that rear door was the way they were going in after him.

The two men in the pickup got out. My mother clapped me on the shoulder. "Call your father," she said. She remained at the window, as if it was important that she not take her eyes off the four men.

I gave the operator the number of my father's office—two, two, three, two—and when Maxine, my father's secretary, answered, I asked for him.

"He's not here, honey," she said in her Louisiana drawl. Maxine Rogers and her husband came to Montana in the 1920s, in one of the first waves of oil-drilling exploration. After her husband's death, Maxine went to work for my grandfather, and she had been in the sheriff's office ever since. She was a short, wiry woman full of what I took to be Southern charm. She had a streak of snow-white hair running from her forehead to the top of her head that I always

132

associated—totally without reason—with her husband's death. He was struck by lightning on a butte west of town. Maxine wasn't anywhere near him when it happened.

"It's important," I said. "Do you know where he is?"

"Couldn't say for sure. Haven't seen him for an hour or so. You might try Mr. Paddock's office."

"How about Len? Is he there?"

"Haven't seen him all morning."

"If my dad comes in, please tell him to come over to the house."

I turned to ask my mother the number of the state attorney's office, but she was gone. The wind gusted, the curtains reached into the room, and when I looked out the window I saw four men crossing our lawn.

They walked abreast of each other but spaced out so that together they took up almost the entire width of the yard. Three of the men were dressed identically in straw cowboy hats, white T-shirts, blue jeans, and boots, so they looked like some strange uniformed team crossing the lawn in formation.

They came on slowly, looking about, as if they expected to be stopped at any time. I looked for weapons—rifles or shotguns or pistols—but saw none. Dale Paris, however, had an axe, and he carried it loosely at his side, the axe head swinging close to his leg.

Before I could turn or call out to my mother that the men were approaching, she came back into the room.

She was carrying my father's shotgun and a box of shells. She put the box on the kitchen table, opened it, and took out two shells.

"Dad's not in his office. Len either."

She turned the shotgun over, looking for something, holding it awkwardly across her forearms and wrists, trying to cradle it, to balance it. When she found what she was searching for, the loading chamber, she tried to push in a shell. When she couldn't get it in, I said, "You have to pump it open."

She pulled back on the pump—the quick, smooth, oily clatter of steel on steel—and put in the shells. She pushed back up on the pump and the gun was ready to fire.

"It'll hold five," I told her.

She gestured to the box. "I've got more."

The sight of my mother loading that shotgun was frightening—yes—but also oddly touching. She was so clumsy, so obviously unsuited for what she was doing that it reminded me of what she looked like when she once put on a baseball glove and tried to play catch with me. I wanted to rush over to her, to help her, to relieve her of the awful duty she had taken up.

"It's got a tremendous kick," I said. "If you fire it you really have to brace yourself." I took a step forward. "Why don't you let me—"

"Get out of here!" she snapped. "Go! Go over to the courthouse. Find your father. Find *someone!*"

Before I left I looked out the window once more. The four men were closer, but they had not reached the house. They had closed their rank and were now side by side. I could see Dale Paris's face clearly, sharp, intent, wind-bitten. One of the other cowboys laughed about something, and Dale Paris shut him up with a word and a scowl as quick and definite as a coyote's snarl.

My mother still stood a few paces back from the window, but she hefted the shotgun up, holding it right below her breast, and pointed it toward the window.

"The safety," I said and reached up close—close enough to embrace her—and clicked the safety off. "You're ready."

She didn't take her eyes off the backyard.

"I'll be right back."

"Just *go!* Out the front door."

I ran across the street, took the stone courthouse steps two at a time, pulled open the door—everything, the steepness of the stairs, the weight of the door, seemed to slow me down. I ran up another flight of stairs to the opaque glass door with the stenciled black letters "Mercer County State's Attorney." I pulled the door open with such force the glass rattled in its frame.

Flora Douglas, the secretary, was there, stacking reams of paper inside a cabinet. She was perhaps in her sixties, a round-faced, large-jawed woman whose severe look was made even harsher by her rimless spectacles and her steel-gray hair pulled tightly back in a bun. In truth, she was a kind, gentle woman—unmarried and childless—who had doted on me since she baby-sat me as an infant.

"Hello, David." Her gold-backed teeth glistened when she smiled.

"Is my dad here?"

"He was here earlier. About an hour ago."

"Do you know where he went?"

135

"I'm sorry, I don't."

"Is Mr. Paddock here?"

She shook her head and shrugged helplessly.

"If my dad comes back, will you tell him to come home right away?"

"I sure will."

I ran from the house, down the stairs, and toward the jail in the basement. As fast as I was moving it seemed agonizingly slow when I thought of Dale Paris and the other men in our yard.

Maxine was at the counter out front where people paid their parking tickets. She was counting manila envelopes and whispering numbers to herself so she wouldn't lose count.

"My dad back?" I panted.

She popped her Beeman's gum before answering. "Not yet, honey." She went back to her count.

"Could you call him on the radio please?"

"He's not in his car. I thought he was someplace in the building."

"Is Len here?"

"Still haven't seen him." She finished the stack, and when she looked up at me she must have seen something she hadn't noticed before. "My God, David. What is it? Has something happened? Is it your mom?"

I was already backing away. "Just tell him to come home. Please. Right away."

I was running back across the street when the shotgun boomed, and its blast was so loud, so wrongly out of place along that quiet, tree-lined, middle-class American street that

136

the air itself seemed instantly altered, turned foul, the stuff of rank, black chemical smoke and not the sweet, clean oxygen we daily breathed.

I was panting hard anyway, and when the shotgun fired, my heart jumped faster and I was suddenly breathless, the air blown so far out of me I couldn't get it back for a second and I wondered—but didn't really—have I been shot?

Yet I kept moving and when I burst through the front door I let the screen door slam behind me and to my distorted hearing—both sharpened and dulled by the shotgun blast—it sounded like another gunshot.

My mother had fired out the kitchen window but from a few paces back so that the buckshot had a chance to spread slightly and not only tear a ragged hole in the screen but to pull in the path of its explosion the kitchen curtain.

I knew from where she stood, from the angle of the shotgun's barrel, and from where the buckshot flew that she hadn't shot anybody. She had simply fired in warning or general panic or both.

She raised the shotgun, pumped another shell into the chamber—the ejected empty shell skittered across the linoleum—as if she were as practiced with that weapon as she was with her typewriter.

She stepped to the window and shouted, "You get away from there! Get away from the house—do you hear me!"

I came up behind her—did she even know I was there?—and I planned on wresting the shotgun from her. The thought of my mother shooting someone seemed the worst possibility the moment held. It was not that I preferred being overrun and beaten or killed by those men, but they were still *out there*. My mother was there in front of me, now trying clumsily to poke the shotgun barrel out through the hole in the screen, and I wanted to protect her not only from Dale Paris but from herself and the life she'd have to lead with someone's blood on her hands.

But before I could stop her I saw something outside that made it unnecessary.

Len McCauley was stepping through the hedge that divided our property from his. He was hatless, barefoot, and his dungarees were riding low on his hips. His shirt was untucked and unbuttoned, flapping open in the wind. Even at a glance and from a distance, I could see how rib-skinny and pale his torso was, but there were ropey strands of sinew along his arms. Then I saw something that made the issue of muscle irrelevant.

In his right hand, held close to his side against his thigh, Len carried a gun, a long-barreled revolver, probably a .44 or .45.

Once he was in our yard Len broke into a long-legged lope. When he was about thirty feet from our house he dropped to one knee, brought his pistol up to eye level, rested the barrel in the crook of one arm, and aimed in the direction of the four men, who must have been by the back door leading to our basement. He said something quick and sharp. It sounded like "right there."

Was Len drunk? I don't know why I thought that. His shooting position may have been faintly comical—nothing like the cowboys in the movies—but his aim and his eye looked

138

rock-steady. Maybe it was simply the sight of that skinny bird-chested old man suddenly appearing in our backyard with a gun in his hand, ready to save us from marauders. And since there was nothing in the realm of logic or rational thought to explain his being there, the illogic of drunkenness seemed as ready as anything.

Len gestured with his gun, indicating that the men were to move away from the house.

As they came into view, walking slowly and watching Len closely, Len stood up. He kept his pistol aimed—right at Dale Paris's head, or so it looked. One of the men had his hands up. Len said something to them again, and though I couldn't hear what he said, all four men began to walk quickly back toward the truck.

Len turned toward the house and the window with the blown-out screen. "Okay in there?" he called.

"We're okay!" my mother shouted back. Then she was hurrying toward the door, still toting the shotgun. She banged open the screen door as if she couldn't wait to get outside. I followed her, wondering why we were leaving the house now that it was safe.

The sun was shining, an unremarkable fact except that I felt, standing on our lawn, as if I had just returned from a strange, hostile country where there was neither sunlight nor soft grass. At the end of the yard the black truck and its four riders sped off, sending up a spray of gravel and raising dust we could taste even from our distance.

My mother laid the shotgun down gently and ran to Len McAuley's side. Because you do not leave a shotgun lying in the grass, even hours after the dew has burned off, I picked up the gun. It smelled of gun oil and cordite.

"Oh, Len," she said and put her arms around him. He did not return her embrace, but he raised one arm to keep his gun hand free.

My mother noticed me and, still clinging to Len, reached out to me. "David," she said. I felt as though she were asking me to step over and become part of a new family consisting of Len our protector, my mother, and me. I remained in place, holding my father's shotgun.

At that moment, with those thoughts of betrayal and loyalty running through my brain, my father came around the side of the house. "What is it?" he asked. "What's going on? Maxine said. . . ."

My father was sweating, red-faced, and out of breath. With his bad leg, even walking fast exerted him. His hands were empty, and in our little armed enclave that made him seem out of place, almost naked.

Len took a step back, and my mother left his side to run to my father's arms.

When he had held her long enough to reassure both of them that everything would be all right, my father asked again, this time to Len: "What happened here?"

Len gestured toward the yard's end, where the truck had been parked. "Dale Paris. Mickey Krebs. Couple other men who work for your pa. They were here, looking to bust your brother loose, I suppose." He nodded at my mother. "She gave 'em a warning with a load of buckshot. Sent 'em packing."

My mother said, "If Len hadn't come. . . ."

"Any of them hurt?" asked my father.

Len shook his head.

"David," said my father. "Are you all right? I hear you were running all over trying to find me. What do you think about all this foolishness?"

"Where were you?" I asked.

"I was up in the third-floor court room. Sitting in there with Ollie Young Bear. He's been doing some work on this. Says he's found some women from the reservation, two anyway, who are willing to come forward and testify against Frank."

"Which charge?" asked Len.

"Assault. Sexual. That's the best we can do. Nothing's going to happen with Marie. No chance of an indictment there. That's long gone."

"You better move on it. Some sharp lawyer's going to raise hell about you keeping him locked up like this."

Since the moment this scandal had broken only a few days earlier, this was the most explicit anyone had been in my presence. My father actually said the word "sexual" in front of me!

My father nodded at Len. "It's moving ahead right now. We'll have him up for an arraignment later today or tomorrow."

Without taking his attention from Len, my father walked over to me and gently, wordlessly, took his shotgun from me.

Len looked down at his bare toes in the grass. "How about your pop? He's not going to stand for any of it. Today was just his first try. He'll come at you again."

"I'm going to see about heading that off."

As those two men coolly discussed their plans for prosecuting Uncle Frank and protecting our home, my mother gestured to me. "Let's go inside, David." Len and my father stayed behind, as I knew they would.

Back in the kitchen my mother fussed with the window screen, pulling and twisting a few of the loose wire strands as if the hole could somehow be mended the way a small tear in a sweater could be rewoven. She finally gave up and closed the inside window.

Moments later my father and Len came in. My father leaned his shotgun in the corner just as he did when he returned from hunting.

"From now on," he said, "if I can't be here, Len will be. He's not going to the office; he's going to stay right here. He'll keep an eye on things. And I'm calling Dad today. Tell him no more stunts like this. This is my family. My house."

As my father spoke, the words bouncing out of him like something falling from an overloaded truck, what struck me was that he seemed to be apologizing. For what? I wondered. For not being there when those men came? How could he have known? He was at work, where he was supposed to be. For being Frank Hayden's brother? Julian Hayden's son? Even then I knew we were not responsible for the circumstances of our birth or the sins of our fathers. For locking up Frank in our basement? For living in Montana? For not working as an attorney in Minneapolis?

Perhaps my mother also heard that apologetic tone in his voice, because she was looking at him queerly.

"No, Wes," she said. Her voice was strangely mild. "You

don't have to do any of that." She sat down slowly, carefully, as though she wasn't quite sure she could trust the chair to hold her weight. "You can simply open that door." She pointed to the basement door. "Go ahead. Let him go. That will take care of everything."

My father stared at her, waiting for her to say something more—to say she was joking or exaggerating to make a point. But when no other word was forthcoming, he said, "You don't mean that, Gail."

"Oh, yes I do. Yes. I most certainly do mean that. Let him go. Get him out of here. Then I won't have to walk around my own house thinking I hear him breathing down there. I won't have to worry about him breaking out—bursting into the kitchen like, like . . . like I don't know what. A crazy man! And I won't have to worry about strange men breaking *in* to break him *out*. I won't worry about my son, whether I should keep him close to me or as far from the house as possible. I won't wonder when men come threatening if David should pick up the gun to drive them away or if I should. But at least I know I can shoot the thing now. So, yes. I mean it. Let him go. Let him do whatever he wants to do to whomever he wants. I don't care anymore. I just want my house back. I want my family safe."

By the time my mother finished, tears were sliding down her face.

My father didn't speak for a long time, and when he did, it was to Len. "What do you think?"

Len looked embarrassed, as if he had intruded on a husband and wife's private quarrel. But since my father asked, there was no getting out. He sniffed and said, "She's right. Might as well let him go. Even on the lesser charge you're going to have a hell of a time getting a conviction. In this town. With your pop. With who's going to be testifying against him."

"At least the word will be out on him," said my father. "Maybe it will stop."

Len said, "I don't think you have to worry. He's got the message."

During this conversation two things struck me: first, that the man they were discussing (and whose crimes they kept alluding to but now did not specifically mention in deference to my supposed innocence) was not some outsider, some Kalispell cowboy or Billings tough who got in trouble up here in my father's jurisdiction, but was my uncle, a man who had only recently stopped lifting me and spinning me around in a dizzying whirl of affection and roughhouse play when he came to the house. He was *Uncle Frank,* who tried to teach me how to throw a curve ball, who gave me expensive gifts for my birthday and Christmas, who made bad jokes all through my grandmother's Thanksgiving and Easter dinners, who every year went up to Canada to buy the best fireworks for our Fourth of July celebration. Who was married to Aunt Gloria, beautiful Aunt Gloria. Who murdered my beloved Marie. And I couldn't make all those facts match the last one. Just as I couldn't get my mind to wrap itself around the knowledge that he was in our basement, and when I tried to think of that the floor beneath my feet suddenly seemed less solid, like those sewer grates you daringly walked over that gave a momentary glimpse of the dark, flowing depths always waiting below.

Len said, "Your pop's going to keep coming. You have to know that. It's not going to be safe around here. She's right to worry."

My father stared at the floor so intently it seemed as though he too was concentrating on his brother below.

"You've got an election coming up," continued Len. "You've got to think about how something like this is going to play with the voters. This county is going to get split three ways by this. Some will stand by you. Not many. There's the reservation. The Indians in town. Your pa. And he'll call in every marker he can. This county is going to get torn up over this. This will make Mercer County look like the Indian wars and the range wars combined. We'll be a long time coming back from this."

My father kept looking down. "Did my father talk to you, Len?"

"When?"

"Recently. The last day or so."

Len paused for a long time. "He talked to me."

"What did he want? What did he ask you to do?"

"You don't want to know that, Wes. Your pa's wild right now. He's not thinking right. He doesn't know what to do."

"Did he ask you to come over here, Len? Did he ask you to get Frank out yourself? Did he tell you how to do it?"

Len shook his head. "Don't ask me any more. Your pa talked to me. Let's leave it at that."

"And you turned him down. Or you wouldn't be standing here right now."

Len patted his head awkwardly as if he were checking to see if he had his hat on. "You're the sheriff. I'm the deputy."

I thought a saw a trace of a smile flicker across my father's lips. When he finally lifted his head he looked briefly at my mother, at Len, then settled his gaze on me.

I was still child enough to believe, as children do, that when adults were engaged in adult business children became invisible. That was why it was so unsettling to have my father staring at me. What did he want from me? Was he waiting for me to express an opinion—I was the only one in the room who hadn't. Didn't he know—I was a child and ineligible to vote? How dare he bring me in on this now—I wasn't even supposed to know the facts of the case!

Young people are supposed to be the impatient ones, but in most circumstances they can outwait their elders. The young are more practiced; time passes slower for them and they are constantly filling their hours, days, months, and years with waiting—for birthdays, for Christmas, for Father to return, for summer to arrive, for graduation, for the rain to stop, for the minister to stop talking, for girls to stop saying, "Not now, not yet; wait." No, when it comes to patience, even the enforced variety, the young are the real masters.

So it was easy to outwait my father. I simply put on my best blank face and kept its dim light beaming toward him. Soon he turned away and, without saying another word to any of us, crossed the room, opened the door to the basement, and descended the stairs.

When the thudding of his steps stopped, my mother calmly asked Len, "How do you think Frank did it?"

"Marie?"

She nodded.

"Wouldn't be hard, I suppose. A doctor. He's probably got the means right there in his bag. Pills. A shot of something or other. Maybe he put a pillow over her face. Weak as she was, it wouldn't have taken much."

Talk as brutal as this I would have thought would upset my mother, but she didn't flinch. Neither did she shoo me from the room so I would be spared this talk. She was too tired to care anymore. This was the day she had fired a gun in the direction of four men. From her own kitchen. There was no point in worrying about what children heard. There was no point in protecting them from words when evil and danger were so near at hand.

She said, "There should have been an autopsy."

Len shrugged. "Someone's got to ask for one. And someone's got to have a reason for asking."

"But at least we'd know."

"And then what? If you know something for sure, then you've got to act on that knowing. It's better this way. You know what you want Wes to do. It'll be a lot easier for him if he doesn't know too much."

"Yes," my mother replied, chastened.

It bothered me that Len and my mother could talk so easily, freely, almost intimately. That ease seemed to depend on my father's absence. He left the room, and they relaxed and talked about what was really on their minds.

Len went to the sink for a glass of water.

"I'm sorry," said my mother. "Would you like some

147

coffee? Or—I think we have something . . . stronger."

Len waved his hand. "Got to go. Daisy must be wondering what's going on."

"I'm surprised she didn't come over."

"That shotgun blast. That's what's keeping her away."

Len tapped the kitchen window right over the blown-out screen. "Might as well just put up the storm window. August. It's not that long until it's time anyway." He finished his water, drinking it all as if it was really thirst and not nerves that brought it to his lips.

He turned to me. "How about it, David. There's a project for you. Take that screen down and put up the storm window for your mother."

"Right now?" I asked.

"Not now, David," answered my mother.

"I better get moving," Len said again. On his way to the door he plucked his gun from the top of the refrigerator as casually as if he were picking up a garden tool. "Just holler if you need me." He glanced at the basement door. "I don't think you're going to have any more trouble. Not now."

He left, and my mother and I remained in the kitchen, waiting for my father and Uncle Frank to come up the stairs. Neither of us spoke, but the room's silence was not the usual kind. It felt stunned, still vibrating, the way the air feels in the silence immediately following a gunshot. And something else: I knew that all around us—in the houses up and down the block—human ears were tuned to our frequency, listening to our silence and wondering, was that a shotgun? Where did it come from? Did it come from the Haydens?

148

I didn't want to be there when Uncle Frank came up. What were we supposed to say to him? Did you miss your wife? How do you like our basement? Are you glad to be out? Yet I couldn't walk away. As long as my mother stayed, I felt I had to as well. I wasn't protecting her—I no longer had any illusions that I could play that role—but I stayed out of loyalty. I wasn't sure what our family had become in those troubled days, but I knew we had to stay close together. We had been under siege. We had to shore up the walls of the family as best we could.

Then the waiting was over. Footsteps thudded up the stairs, dull booms that could be mistaken, if one hadn't heard the real thing so recently, for a series of tiny shotgun blasts.

But two men did not come through the door. It was my father alone, sputtering as if he had come up from underwater. Before my mother could say anything, my father waved his hand in disgust.

"I'll move him over to the jail first thing in the morning," said my father.

My mother let her head drop forward.

"He's guilty as sin, Gail. He told me as much." My father struck himself on the thigh with his fist. "Goddamn it! What could I have been thinking of? Maybe a jury will cut him loose. I won't. *By God, I won't.*"

My mother got up from the table and began to work. She set the sugar bowl, the butter, and a loaf of bread on the table. She was on her way to the refrigerator when my father stopped her. "Did you hear me? This is the way it's got to be. I'm sorry."

She opened the refrigerator and peered inside. "I'm not arguing with you, Wesley."

"You don't think I wish it could be some other way?" my father asked belligerently. "He's my brother—we grew up together, sucked the same tit!"

She slammed the refrigerator. "Wesley—"

"I don't care. I tell you, if you could hear him talk. As if he had no more concern for what he did than if . . . if he had kicked a dog. No. He'd show more remorse over a dog."

"Marie?"

My father nodded grimly. "Don't ask how."

She pressed her hand over her mouth, to hold back a curse or because she was gagging on what my father told her. Or on what he wouldn't tell her and what her imagination filled in.

"Do you see?" asked my father. "I can't let him loose. Not and live with myself."

My parents' usual roles had neatly reversed themselves. My mother now represented practicality and expediency; my father stood for moral absolutism. Yet when I looked at my father his expression was so anguished that it didn't seem possible that he was arguing on principle.

"We understand, Wesley," my mother said gently, but I knew her words would do nothing to diminish his suffering.

"David," my mother said clearly and calmly, a different voice for a different world. "We don't have anything to eat. Why don't you run down to Butler's and get some of those frankfurters, and I'll boil them. That'll be quick."

She wanted me out of the house. That I knew. But she tried to soften that banishment with a little gift. The food I loved more than any other was the frankfurters from Butler's Butcher Shop. She gave me five dollars. "And when you go by Cox's, if you see one of those lemon cakes in the window, why don't you get one. Or anything else that looks good to you."

Before I left the house I turned back to look at my parents. They had not collapsed into each other's arms as I thought they might. They were simply standing in the kitchen. My father had his arms folded and stared blankly at the floor again. But my mother was looking at him, the expression in her eyes tender and loving and frightened, the same look she lowered on me when I was sick.

I suddenly felt a great distance between us, as if, at that moment, each of us stood on our own little square of flooring with open space surrounding us. Too far apart to jump to anyone else's island, we could only stare at each other the way my mother stared at my father.

That night the jars began to break.

I woke around 1:00 A.M., startled but unsure of what had roused me. Then I heard it, a distant *pop* and a faint clinking. I searched the dark, not because I thought the sound was in my room, but because I felt, in my sleepy groping, that activating any of my other senses might help my hearing.

There it was again—that ringing-tinkling—plainly glass breaking. But where? What was happening?

I got out of bed to look out my window but before I got

there I knew the noise wasn't coming from outside. No, this was in the house. It was coming from the basement! From Uncle Frank!

I ran to my parents' room. Their door was open and the light was on, so I had no reluctance about walking right in.

They weren't there. Their pillows still held the indentations of their heads, and the blanket and sheet formed an inverted V in the middle of the bed, suggesting that they had both thrown away the covers from their own side of the bed. I ran out of the room and to the head of the stairs.

I stood there waiting, listening.

Another faint shatter of glass.

Was it a window? Was Uncle Frank breaking one of the windows, hoping he could crawl out the high, narrow opening and escape through one of the window wells? Had my parents gone to stop him?

No, there was no possible way he could squeeze through one of those windows.

Another crash.

At the bottom of the stairs the darkness lost some of its thickness and strength—a light was on somewhere downstairs. Was it my parents? Uncle Frank? Someone come again to break him out, someone who broke our windows to get in?

I ran downstairs, hitting each step as hard and loud as I could, hoping to embolden myself as much as to frighten off whoever might be there.

My father and mother, in their pajamas, were sitting on the couch. They were not touching each other, and they looked frightened and tired, like children who have been awakened during the night for an emergency.

"Dad," I said, "I heard——"

"I know," he interrupted. "The canning jars."

"He's smashing them," my mother needlessly added.

"He's got into the root cellar," said my father. "He must be breaking every jar in there."

"All my jars of tomatoes and rutabagas. The pickles. The plum jelly. The applesauce. That corn relish you like so much."

Another jar popped below us, and now that I knew what the noise was from I could make some distinctions among the sounds. The higher-pitched pops were the small jelly jars— tightly packed and sealed tight with wax. The bass-note crashes were the large pickle jars, full of liquid and screwed tight with canning lids.

My mother pressed her fist to her face. "When I think of the work I did. And Marie did. And Daisy. . . ."

"I'm not going down there," my father explained to me. "That's just what he wants. No, let him get it out of his system. He'll run out of jars eventually."

Another one crashed.

"He's throwing them," said my mother. "I can tell. He's not just dropping them on the floor, he's *throwing* them as hard as he can."

My father patted her arm.

"Who's going to clean up that mess?" she asked.

"You can go back to bed, David," said my father. "I'm going to sit up until things calm down."

Another one. Was he spacing them at exact intervals?

"Get some sleep," my mother advised. "It's been such a long day."

My father stood and approached me. He put his hand on my shoulder. That gesture, along with an occasional back rub, was the only sign of physical affection he bestowed on me. My mother, on the other hand, still kissed and hugged me frequently. I knew and had known since I was very young that this difference between them had absolutely nothing to do with unequal qualities of love but only with their abilities to demonstrate it. Nevertheless, I wished at that moment that I could stay there, stay and feel the reassuring pressure of my father's hand upon my shoulder.

"One more night, David," my father said. "Just one more night and he'll be out of here. Things will be back to normal."

He was walking me toward the stairs, his hand no longer simply resting on my shoulder but gently pushing, giving me direction. "Sleep late," he said when we got to the stairs. "Sleep as late as you can, and when you wake up the worst of this will all be over."

But I didn't sleep late. I couldn't. I fell asleep listening for the crash of the jars and I woke the same way, straining to hear breaking glass.

Was it silence that finally woke me? At around six o'clock I came awake. The morning was overcast, dim, so there was no sunlight flooding my room. Birds do not sing at a gray sky with the same vigor as at a blue one, so their songs were not shaking me awake. From the basement there was no sound of Uncle Frank shattering jars. What else could it have been but silence?

I got up quickly and quietly, crept past my parents' closed bedroom door, and went downstairs. I was so happy to have our house's stillness restored that I wanted to enjoy it.

But I was startled when I entered the kitchen. My father was already up (or hadn't he gone back to bed?), sitting at the kitchen table. He was wearing a sleeveless T-shirt and the trousers to his light gray suit. He was barefoot, but his heavy black brogans were under the table. There was a copy of *Argosy* next to him, but it was unopened. He jerked his head up when I came into the room.

"David. You're up early."

"I didn't know anyone else was awake."

"I'm waiting until I hear him stirring down there. Then I'm going to hustle him out and across the street."

"And put him in jail."

"And put him in jail. That's right."

Perhaps because he was tired and I could see it—his hair uncombed, his beard unshaven, his eyes ringed with dark circles, his shoulders slumped—I finally realized what this day meant to my father: This was the day he would put his only brother in jail. There would never be another day like it in his life.

I wanted to say something to indicate that I understood and sympathized. And I did sympathize. But understand? I could not; no one could. The best consolation I could manage was, "Not a very happy day, I guess."

155

He shrugged, a gesture full of resignation and fatigue. "David, I believe that in this world people must pay for their crimes. It doesn't matter who you are or who your relations are; if you do wrong, you pay. I believe that. I have to." He pushed himself up stiffly from the table. "But that doesn't mean the sun's going to shine."

He began to make coffee, trying to be as quiet as possible while he filled the percolator with water and carefully spooned in the grounds. "It's funny, the story I keep thinking about this morning. I don't know if I ever told it to you. Can't even remember how old I was at the time. Nine or ten maybe, and Frank twelve or thirteen. We'd already moved into town, and Dad was sheriff. Anyway. A friend of mine—could that have been Cordell Wettering? I believe so—and I were playing out by the golf course one fall day. Back then that course wasn't much. Still isn't. But then it was really sad. It had sand greens and barely a tree on it. Except on the seventh hole where the fairway runs right along that old slough.

"Cordell and I were on our way somewhere, or back from somewhere, and we cut through the slough. I guess things were dried out just enough or matted down from a few freezes, but we started finding golf balls in the brush, dozens of them. I don't know why that was such a big deal for us— neither of us had ever golfed in our lives—but you know how it is. We couldn't have been more excited if it was gold nuggets we found in that slough. When we came up out of there we were just dripping golf balls. Our pockets were stuffed and we were trying to carry more than we could hold.

"But when we climbed out, there were the Highdog boys,

three Blackfoot brothers who were widely known as bad customers. The oldest brother must have been about fourteen; the youngest, he was a skinny little runt about our age but mean as a snake when he was with his big brothers. Over the years every one of them was in and out of trouble with the law, but the little one got life in the state pen for carving up a cowboy with a broken bottle over in Havre.

"Anyway, the Highdog brothers said the golf balls we were carrying were theirs. Said that slough was part of the territory they watched over—those were the words they used—so anything we found was their property.

"Now, Cordell and I were plenty scared—we'd heard our share of stories about those brothers—but neither one of us wanted to give up our golf balls.

"We took off, running as fast as we could, dropping golf balls as we ran. Those golf balls helped us keep a lead on them. Every one we dropped, they stopped to pick up.

"But they were gaining on us, and just when it looked as though they were going to catch us—over by the clubhouse, such as it was—we ran into your uncle Frank.

"He and some of his friends were hanging out in the parking lot of the golf course. They were with an older boy, Charley McLaughlin, who was rolling cigarettes for Frank and the others.

"Cordell and I weren't dumb. We ran over to Frank and the others and told them the Highdog brothers were on our tails. That was all they needed to hear. This was an excuse to get those Indians who had bullied so many kids. Now it was the Highdogs turn to run—with my brother right after them.

"Well, they didn't catch them but that was all right. The important thing was, they saved our bacon.

"When Frank heard we almost got ourselves scalped over golf balls, he couldn't stop laughing. For years afterward, he'd tease me about that day. 'Look out!' he'd say. 'Here come the Highdogs! Hide your golf balls!' I didn't care. I was so grateful to him just for being there that day—I mean, I felt it was a kind of miracle. My brother. Being in the one place in the world I needed him most. . . ."

When he finished his story my father was staring out the same window through which my mother had fired the shotgun.

"Would they really have scalped you?" I asked.

"Oh, no. No. I don't mean that literally. They were bad business but not. . . . They'd have worked us over, though. That's sure. Funny. I found out years later that they had a reason for wanting those golf balls. They were selling them back to the golf course. Those Highdogs. . . . I mentioned the little one ended up in the pen? The oldest Highdog was killed when he lay down on the railroad tracks just outside town. Drunk, trying to walk home. I remember Dad coming home after investigating the accident. He said it was the worst he ever saw."

The coffee stopped percolating, and the silence that abruptly followed seemed to startle my father out of the past and back to the kitchen. "Well. Did I hear him stirring down there?"

"I didn't hear anything."

"No? Maybe not. I'll take some coffee down. That should get him going. We'll get an early start."

He poured two cups of coffee and then put both cups on saucers, an action of such delicacy and formality that I almost laughed.

He had a cup and saucer in each hand, so he asked, "Could you please open the door for me, David?"

The door or its frame was warped so I had to push hard to get it open. When it came unstuck I deliberately did not look down.

"Do you want me to close it behind you?"

"You can leave it open. We'll be up in a few minutes."

How much time passed before I heard my father's cry—thirty seconds? A minute?

Certainly no more than that. Yet what I heard signalled such a breach in our lives, a chasm permanently dividing what we were from what we could never be again, that it seems some commensurate unit of time should be involved. Ten years after my father descended the basement steps. . . .

From out of the cellar's musty darkness, up the creaking steps, through the cobwebbed joists and rough-planked flooring came my father's wail—"Oh, no! *Oh my God, no!*"

I ran down the stairs. It felt as it sometimes does in dreams, as if I were falling yet still able to control myself, hitting each step for just the instant it took to keep me from tumbling headlong down toward the concrete floor.

I slowed when I reached the bottom, as though suddenly the fear of what I was running toward overtook my concern for my father.

The aroma of coffee was still in the air. In fact, it felt as if I were following that smell.

Then I turned into the laundry room and another odor replaced it. All those broken jars—the sharp vinegary smell of the pickling juices, the dill weed, the sweet apples and plums, the rotting, damp-earth smell of rutabagas and tomatoes, and another odor, sweeter, heavier, fouler than the others.

My father was on the floor of the root cellar, and when I first saw the blood swirled like oil through the other liquids, I thought he had cut his bare feet on the broken glass that was everywhere.

But I thought that only for an instant, for the split second before I saw the blood's real source.

Uncle Frank lay on the floor, his head cradled against my father's chest. The gash across Uncle Frank's wrist had already started its useless healing: the edges of the wound had begun to dry and pucker; the blood, what was left in him, had begun to blacken and congeal. I could see only his right arm, but I knew the cut there was one of a matching set.

I must have made a sound—a little gasp that cracked against my larynx—because my father turned toward me. His features were contorted for a sob, but his eyes were tearless.

"Go wake your mother, David. *Tell her to call Len.* Get him down here *right away.*"

I backed away quickly, glad to have a mission that would take me out of the basement. My father stopped me with one more command: "And David, don't let your mother come down here. *Don't let her!*"

Then my father's tears broke loose, one more briny fluid to mingle on the basement floor.

I didn't run up the stairs. I couldn't. But the reason is not what you might think. My legs worked fine. Oh, I was shaken. What I saw in the basement set my heart racing and soured my stomach but was not what slowed me down.

No, I took my time climbing the two flights to my mother because I needed time to compose myself, to make certain I could keep concealed my satisfaction over what had happened.

You see, I knew—I knew! I *knew!*—that Uncle Frank's suicide had solved all our problems.

My father would not have to march his brother across the street to jail.

There would be no trial, no pile of testimony for jurors to sift through, trying to separate the inevitable one-eighth, one-quarter, one-half truths from the whole truth. No pressure on anyone to come forward and bear witness, no reputations damaged, no one embarrassed, no one chastised. . . . The town would not have to choose sides over guilt or innocence.

Indian women could visit a doctor without fear of being assaulted, violated by a man who had taken a vow to do them no harm.

We would no longer have to worry that Grandfather would mount an attack of some kind on our home.

Certainly there would be sadness—Aunt Gloria was a widow, my father was suddenly, like me, an only child, Grandma's tears would fill a rain barrel—but this grief would pass. Once the mourning period passed, we would have our lives back, and if they would not be exactly what they had been earlier, they would be close enough for my satisfaction.

What more can I say? I was a child. I believed all these things to be true.

As I climbed the stairs, I felt something for my uncle in death that I hadn't felt for him in life. It was gratitude, yes, but it was something more. It was very close to love.

Epilogue

* * *

W̲ᴇ moved from Bentrock on a snowy day in early December 1948, a day, really, when we had no business traveling. It was bad enough in town, where snow covered the streets; out in the country nothing stopped the wind, so roads and highways could easily be drifted closed. But the car was packed, the moving van had left the day before with our furniture, we had said our good-byes to those who would hear them. Doors were locked; minds were made up.

They had been made up, in fact, for months. Since shortly after Uncle Frank's suicide, when my mother abruptly said to my father, "I cannot continue living here."

I knew she did not mean the house alone but Bentrock as well.

And I knew it was not the macabre discomfort of living in the same rooms where two people had recently died. That was not what made living there impossible for her. She had her religious beliefs to see her through that.

But she had no resources that enabled her to live with the lies concocted in the aftermath of Frank's death.

It was decided (my use of the passive voice is deliberate; I could never be exactly sure who was involved in the decision: my parents, certainly, but others were probably involved as well—my grandfather seems a good bet. Len? Gloria?) to explain Uncle Frank's death as an accident, to say that he had been helping my father build shelves in our basement, that he fell from a ladder, struck his head on the concrete floor, and died instantly. The only outsider to see Frank's body—and who could thus contradict this story—was Clarence Undset, owner of Undset's Funeral Home. What bribes were offered, what deals were struck to secure Mr. Undset's silence, I never knew, but everyone seemed confident that he would never reveal what he saw when he took Frank's body away: the gashes in Frank's wrists.

Similarly, it was decided not to reveal any of Frank's crimes. What purpose would it serve? He would never molest anyone again. The Indian women of Mercer County were safe from him. Besides, as my letter-of-the-law father said, Uncle Frank was never convicted of anything; there was no sense clouding the air with accusations.

As a consequence of these postmortem cover-ups, it was possible for Frank Hayden to be buried without scandal and to be eulogized in the usual blandly reverent way—decorated soldier, public servant, dedicated to healing, dutiful son, loving husband, still a youthful man, strong, vital. . . . Finally even the minister had to confess some bafflement over a life so rudely, inexplicably cut off. Who among us can begin to understand God's plans for any of us? Who indeed.

None of these precautions on behalf of Frank's reputation was enough however to restore harmony in the Hayden family. At the funeral, all of us—Grandpa and Grandma, Aunt Gloria, my father, mother, and I—sat together in the same pew (a surprisingly small group, considering the clan's power in the county), but neither my aunt nor my grandparents would speak to us. At the cemetery they made a point of standing on the opposite side of the grave from us. Even I understood the symbolism: Frank's death was an unbridgeable gulf between us. Although my parents seemed only hurt by this snubbing (they shuffled away from the cemetery and did not return with everyone else to the church for the meal in the church basement), it angered me. If there was any sense, any purpose at all in Uncle Frank's suicide, if he killed himself for any *reason*, it was so these people—his wife, his parents, his brother, his sister-in-law—could be reunited after his death. But there was the open grave, and not one of us would dream of leaping across it.

Therefore, when my mother made her pronouncement about living in Bentrock, my father understood exactly what she meant, and he simply nodded, as if he had known all along that was so but had been waiting for her to say the words. He didn't argue; he didn't say, "This is our home"; he didn't accuse; he didn't say, "You've never liked this town or this house, but it's my home." He agreed with my mother and began immediately to dismantle our lives in Bentrock.

He arranged, first of all, to withdraw from the upcoming election, citing as his reason "another job offer—an opportunity to practice law and put all that schooling to use." This was before he had lined up the possibility of a job with a law firm in Fargo, North Dakota. Len McAuley's name was substituted for my father's on the ticket. There was no doubt Len would be elected. He ran unopposed.

Next, our house was put up for sale, and my mother called her parents to tell them we would be staying with them on the farm while we looked for our own place.

My mother withdrew me from school and was given, in a manila envelope, my records to be conveyed to my next school.

My parents said their good-byes—to Len and Daisy, to the Hutchinsons. To Ollie Young Bear. The number of people seemed so small that it diminished my parents' years in Bentrock, as if their time there hadn't really amounted to much at all. I kept my own farewells to a minimum, and to ease the emotionalism (and perhaps to trick myself and make leaving easier), I told many of my friends that we would probably be moving back the following summer.

There we were, our car so loaded down it seemed ready to bottom out as my father backed out of the driveway. As we were about to pull away, I shouted, "Wait!", opened the back door, and jumped out of the car.

I ran to the house and clambered up a snowdrift to the living room window. I wanted one last look, to see what our house looked like without us in it. If my parents asked what I was looking for, I had already decided what I would answer. "Ghosts," I would say.

The frost on the window made it difficult to see in.

No, that wasn't it.

The emptiness inside made it difficult to see in. The blank

room had even less pattern than frosted glass. The bland gray carpeting, the once-white walls trying to turn yellow—snow should have been falling and drifting in *there*.

My parents, bless them, did not honk the horn or yell for me to get back in the car. They waited, and when I turned back to them and saw them through the screen of falling snow, I wondered again how it could have happened—how it could be that those two people who only wanted to do right, whose only error lay in trying to be loyal to both family and justice, were now dispossessed, the ones forced to leave Bentrock and build new lives. For a moment I felt like waving good-bye to them, signalling them to go, to move without me. It had nothing to do with wanting to stay in Montana; it had everything to do with wanting to stay away from those two hapless, forlorn people. What kind of life would it be, traveling in their company?

In fact, it was not a bad life at all. After spending the winter with my mother's parents on their farm, we moved the following spring to Fargo. There my father got a job with a small law office and within five years his name was listed as a partner with the firm: Line, Gustafson, and Hayden, Attorneys-at-Law. My mother got her wish: my father became a lawyer. He finally had a job to go with that briefcase she gave him.

For a while she tendered hopes that I would follow in my father's footsteps and pursue a career in law. "Wouldn't it be something," she once hopefully said to me when I was in my teens, "Hayden and Son, Law Partners?" "Wouldn't it be more appropriate," I answered, "for me to be elected sheriff of Mercer County, Montana, and carry on that Hayden tradition?" She never said another word about what I should do with my life. My remark was cruel, yet it was kinder than the truth: after what I observed as a child in Bentrock, I could never believe in the rule of law again. That my father could continue in his profession I attributed to his ability to segment parts of his life and keep one from intruding on another.

For myself, I eventually became a history teacher in a Rochester, Minnesota, high school. I did not—do not—believe in the purity and certainty of the study of history over law. Not at all. Quite the opposite. I find history endlessly amusing, knowing, as I do, that the record of any human community might omit stories of sexual abuse, murder, suicide. . . . Who knows—perhaps any region's most dramatic, most sensational stories were not played out in the public view but were confined to small, private places. A doctor's office, say. A white frame house on a quiet street. So no matter what the historical documents might say, I feel free to augment them with whatever lurid or comical fantasy my imagination might concoct. And know that the truth might not be far off. These musings, of course, are for my private enjoyment. For my students I keep a straight face and pretend that the text tells the truth, whole and unembellished.

Our only link with Montana was Grandma Hayden. She wrote to us regularly and even visited us a few times until she became too ill to travel.

As far as I know, she never spoke of the events of 1948, but she kept us up to date on some of those who played roles in the tragedy.

Aunt Gloria left Montana less than a year after we did. She moved to Spokane, where her sister lived, and Gloria eventually remarried.

Len McAuley was unable to complete his term in office. He had a stroke that left him partially paralyzed, and he had to turn the badge over to his deputy, Johnny Packwood, who had been in the military police. Thus, the Hayden-McAuley control of the Mercer County sheriff's office was broken.

Len lived on a number of years after his stroke, but ironically, less than a year after Len's cerebral hemorrhage my grandfather had one too. Which he did not survive. He was dead within three days.

Two strokes. I used to think, my interest in symbol and metaphor far surpassing my medical knowledge, that they died from keeping the secret about my uncle Frank. They held it in, the pressure built, like holding your breath, and something had to blow. In their case, the vessels in their brains. In my father's case, it was not only the secret he held in but also his bitterness. Which eventually turned into his cancer. Well, there I go, blaming an incident that happened over forty years ago for what was probably brought on by Len McAuley's whiskey, my grandfather's cigars, and my father's diet.

❁

My happiest memory of Marie, the one that gradually separated itself from the general tangle of pleasant, warm moments, was from the autumn before she died.

Unhappy with my general lack of success at team sports, I decided I would do something about it. By sheer disciplined practice, through diligence, I would overcome my lack of natural ability and become good at something. Football was the sport I chose, and I further narrowed my choice of skills by concentrating on just one aspect of football. I would become an expert dropkicker. Drop-kicking, of course, has long since ceased to be a part of football, but in 1947 players dropkicked field goals; they dropped the ball, let it hit the ground for the briefest instant, then tried to boot it through the goal posts. That fall I spent hours in the backyard, trying to dropkick a football over a branch of our oak, then shagging the ball and kicking it back the other way, back and forth, back and forth. . . .

One afternoon when I was practicing after school, Ronnie Tall Bear burst out the back door of our house, Marie close behind him. Although Marie was obviously chasing him, they were both laughing.

Ronnie ran across our yard. When he came to my football, he fell on it, rolled with it through the leaves, and came up running, exactly as he no doubt had done with recovered fumbles countless times in football practices or in actual games.

When Ronnie picked up my football, Marie was able to gain some ground, but now he began to run like the football

172

star he once was, tucking the ball under one arm, faking, spinning, stopping, starting, shifting direction. Ronnie turned when he came to the railroad tracks and doubled back toward me. Once he got close enough, he lateraled the ball to me. Now Marie, tiring and slowing but still pursuing, was after *me*.

For the next half hour we chased up and down the yard, throwing the football back and forth, running after each other. It was a game, yet it had no object and no borders of space or time or regulation. It was totally free-form, but we still tried to use our skills—throwing accurate spirals, leaping to make catches, running as fast as we could in pursuit or escape. I felt that what we played, more accurately *how* we played, had its origin in Ronnie and Marie's Indian heritage, but I had no way of knowing that with any certainty. All I could be sure of was that I never had more fun playing ball, any kind of ball, in my life.

When we were too tired to play any longer, we went back to the house by way of the garage. There my mother kept a gallon of apple cider. Was it Marie's idea to uncap it? No matter. We passed the cider around, each of us drinking from the heavy jug, the cool, sweet cider the perfect answer to the question, how do you follow an afternoon of running around in the warm autumn sun?

I believe I remembered that incident so fondly not only because I was with Marie and Ronnie, both of whom I loved in my way, but also because I felt, for that brief span, as though I was part of a family, a family that accepted me for myself and not my blood or birthright.

My wife, Betsy, lived in seven cities before she graduated from high school. All of the communities were in Minnesota, Wisconsin, and northern Illinois, and during one summer vacation we drove to each town so she could photograph her childhood homes. (My wife also teaches, and this trip was exactly the sort of thing that teachers, with all that time and so little money, are likely to come up with for their summers.)

Since Betsy was immersed in all this nostalgia, it was natural for her to suggest that we drive to Montana to see *my* boyhood home. No, I told her, that was all right; I had no desire to go back. This she couldn't understand, and I finally gave in and told her why I—why no one in my immediate family—wanted to return to Bentrock. I told her about what happened in the summer of 1948.

The story stunned her, but it also fascinated her. She couldn't wait for the next meeting with my parents, so she could ask them about their memories of that summer.

I could have warned her off. I could have told her that in my family that is a subject never discussed. We all know what happened—we know it is there, in our shared past, we don't deny it, but we don't talk about it, as if keeping quiet is a matter of good manners. But I didn't tell my wife any of this. I suppose I wanted to see what would happen when someone else brought out into the open a topic that had never been discussed in any detail in my presence.

A few months later we were all together, gathered at my parents' house for Thanksgiving dinner. We had been seated for only a few minutes when Betsy said, "David told me all about what happened when you lived in Montana. That sure was the Wild West, wasn't it?"

My father, at this time, had already had one cancer surgery, and he was not strong, but at Betsy's question he slammed his hand down on the table so hard the plates and silverware jumped.

"Don't blame Montana!" he said. "Don't ever blame Montana!"

He pushed himself away from the table, left the room, and never returned to the meal.

Later that night, after everyone was in bed, I came back down to the dining room. I sat in the chair where my father had sat and lightly put my hands on the table. For an instant I thought I felt the wood still vibrating from my father's blow.

All Pan Books are available at your local bookshop or newsagent, or can be ordered direct from the publisher. Indicate the number of copies required and fill in the form below.

Send to: Macmillan General Books C.S.
                Book Service By Post
                PO Box 29, Douglas I-O-M
                IM99 1BQ

or phone: 01624 675137, quoting title, author and credit card number.

or fax: 01624 670923, quoting title, author, and credit card number.

or Internet: http://www.bookpost.co.uk

Please enclose a remittance* to the value of the cover price plus 75 pence per book for post and packing. Overseas customers please allow £1.00 per copy for post and packing.

*Payment may be made in sterling by UK personal cheque, Eurocheque, postal order, sterling draft or international money order, made payable to Book Service By Post.

Alternatively by Access/Visa/MasterCard

Card No. | | | | | | | | | | | | | | | | | . | | | . |

Expiry Date | | | | | | | | | | | | | | | | | | | | |

Signature _____

Applicable only in the UK and BFPO addresses.

While every effort is made to keep prices low, it is sometimes necessary to increase prices at short notice. Pan Books reserve the right to show on covers and charge new retail prices which may differ from those advertised in the text or elsewhere.

NAME AND ADDRESS IN BLOCK CAPITAL LETTERS PLEASE

Name _____

Address _____

_____

_____

_____

8/95

Please allow 28 days for delivery.
Please tick box if you do not wish to receive any additional information. ☐